Ice Cold Murder

A Charlie Kingsley Mystery

Other books by Michele Pariza Wacek
MPWnovels.com/books

Secrets of Redemption series:
It Began With a Lie (Book 1)
This Happened to Jessica (Book 2)
The Evil That Was Done (Book 3)
The Summoning (Book 4)
The Reckoning (Book 5)
The Girl Who Wasn't There (Book 6)
The Room at the Top of the Stairs (Book 7)
The Secret Diary of Helen Blackstone (free novella)

Charlie Kingsley Mystery series:
A Grave Error (free prequel novella)
The Murder Before Christmas (Book 1)
Ice Cold Murder (Book 2)
Murder Next Door (Book 3)
Murder Among Friends (Book 4)
The Murder of Sleepy Hollow (Book 5)
Red Hot Murder (Book 6)
A Wedding to Murder For (novella)
Loch Ness Murder (novella)

Stand-a-lone books:
Today I'll See Her (novella)
The Taking
The Third Nanny
Mirror Image
The Stolen Twin

Ice Cold Murder

A Charlie Kingsley Mystery

by Michele Pariza Wacek

ISBN 978-1-945363-33-7

Library of Congress Control number: 2022931279

For my family, for always believing in me.

Chapter 1

"Are you out of your mind?" Pat's hand paused mid-air, chocolate chip cookie halfway to her mouth as she stared at me, eyes wide.

Forsaking her cookie like that, I knew she was serious.

"She asked," I said matter-of-factly. "I'm being a good friend."

"You're being insane," Pat muttered as her hand finally completed its journey. "Do you have any idea what you've agreed to?"

"Why yes," I said. "I agreed to accompany Claire to her grandmother's reading of the will."

"In a *haunted* house," Pat added.

I gave her a look. "Well, first off, as you know, *I* live in a haunted house. Why on Earth would spending the weekend at someone else's bother me?"

"And that leads me to the second issue," Pat said, waving the hand holding the cookie. Crumbs scattered everywhere, making me momentarily wish I had a dog instead of a cat. A dog would be on it already, cleaning up the mess. Midnight, my black cat, could care less. "Why would a reading of a will take an entire weekend?"

"Well, I grant you, that IS weird," I admitted.

"Did Claire have any explanation for it?"

"Not exactly."

Pat raised her eyebrows, clearly waiting for more.

I sighed. "I guess there are some … issues, in the family."

Pat yelped. "Issues? You're willingly going to spend an entire weekend in a haunted house with a family working through their *issues*?"

I winced. When she put it like that, she definitely had a point. "So, to be fair, I didn't know about the haunted part until right now," I said. "Claire didn't mention that."

"But she mentioned the *issues*," Pat said. "And that didn't stop you from agreeing to this insanity?"

"It's hardly like that makes her family some sort of weird anomaly," I said, thinking of my own strained relationship with my sisters. "All families have issues. Which is part of why I decided to go. It's not *my* family, so I won't be triggered. It might be a little uncomfortable, but so what? I'm sure I'll survive. And Claire is worth it. If she needs a neutral, supportive person to help her through this, I'm happy to be that for her."

Pat gave me a look but kept her mouth shut. I was sure the same thoughts were running through her head that had gone through mine.

Ever since she had gotten pregnant with Daphne two-and-a-half years ago, Claire hadn't looked well. While I knew some of it was the result of grief—a couple of her good childhood friends had disappeared without a trace around the time she got pregnant—I had a feeling there was more to the story.

Something else was wrong with Claire. I wasn't entirely sure what, but my hope was that by accompanying her to this rather strange family obligation, she might trust me enough to share the truth of what was really going on with her.

"I don't know, Charlie," Pat said. "There's something about this that doesn't feel right."

Claire was the first person I met when I first arrived in Redemption, Wisconsin, completely by accident. The truth of the matter is that I was on the run from an abusive fiancé and only stopped in Redemption because I was lost. I never meant to stay, but as I've since learned, Redemption has its own ideas about who stays and who goes. Before I knew what was happening, I had bought a house (and not just any house, but what the locals considered the "most" haunted house in an already haunted town) and had opened a tea business out of it.

Pat was one of my first customers, and she also became one of my best friends … despite being well over a decade older than me. She was my "partner in crime," so to speak, as I found myself inadvertently roped into helping solve crimes related to my tea customers. Like everything else in Redemption, this was not anything I'd planned. I would have been quite happy to spend my days quietly puttering around in my garden and creating blends and tinctures. I very much disliked calling attention to myself, which unfortunately, solving crimes had a tendency to do.

But, alas, what I wanted had little to do with what I got.

At least this weekend trip, as uncomfortable as it might turn out, would provide me a reprieve from mystery-solving.

"I agree that it doesn't feel right," I said. "The fact that I'm going instead of Doug doesn't exactly help." Doug was Claire's husband and the father of her daughter.

"Speaking of which, why isn't Doug going?" Pat asked, selecting another cookie, even though I knew she'd end up complaining about the added calories ruining whatever current diet she was on. The best way to describe Pat was "round"— round face, round body, round black-rimmed glasses, and short, no-nonsense brown hair that was turning grey.

"Claire said because of Daphne. They don't have anyone who can take her with such short notice for three full days, and they think she's too young to come with them. Not to mention the house isn't exactly baby-proofed."

Pat rolled her eyes. "That's an understatement."

"It made sense when she explained it," I said. "The house is old, and I guess it hasn't been used a lot. Although Claire was rather vague about why."

"I'll tell you why," Pat said. "Because it's haunted. That's why."

I sighed. "All right. I'll bite. Tell me more."

"Well, I don't remember all the details," Pat said as I shook my head in exasperation. "Hey, it's Redemption," she said defensively. "I can't keep track of all the weird things that happen here. That'd be a full-time job."

"So, you don't have *all* the details, but I assume you have *some*?"

Pat glared at me. "You're *so* funny. Okay, this is what I know. About twenty or thirty years ago, or …" she squished up her face. "Maybe it's longer. I can't remember anymore. Anyway, Florence, that's Claire's grandmother, decided to have some work done on the house. Was she redoing the kitchen? Maybe it was the basement. Anyway, whichever it was, something happened, and the contractor was killed."

My eyes widened. "Killed?"

Pat nodded. "Yeah, it was some freak accident. He fell off a ladder or something. Well, when they were investigating, it came out that there had been all sorts of weird stuff happening. Things kept getting moved around, even though everyone at the site swore they hadn't touched anything. Tools stopped working, and batteries would die, even if they were fresh. His assistant flat out refused to go back after his boss was killed. Said it was too creepy, and he didn't want anything to do with it."

"Wow," I said. "Was the work ever finished?"

Pat frowned. "I'm not sure. I do know it wasn't easy. A lot of contractors refused the project, and the few who took it ended up walking off the job."

"What did Florence say? She was living there when all this was happening, right?"

Pat shook her head. "No, it was always a second home. I'm not sure how Flo ended up with the house. If I recall, her husband's family bought it, and somehow, she ended up with it. But she always lived in town. She loved spending long weekends out there, though, even in the winter. She was big into cross-country skiing and ice skating. She just thought it was too remote to live there full time."

"Did she still go out there even after everything happened?"

"For a while, yes," Pat said. "Flo used to laugh about it. The ghosts, I mean. Said it was nothing compared to Helen's … well, your house, now."

"So she didn't believe."

Pat hesitated. "Nooo. Not then, anyway. Although I think it did cause a rift in the family, as Claire's mom, Daisy, did believe in ghosts. I don't remember all the details now. It wasn't until Billy disappeared that everything changed."

"Who's Billy?"

"Flo's only son. Claire's uncle. I think it was, well, it has to be twenty years or so by now, which is why I think the contracting work was done earlier. Anyway, he disappeared, and Flo was so devastated, she quit nearly everything. Stopped going to church, stopped seeing friends, quit going up to the 'cottage,' as she called it, even though it's apparently huge. Bigger than most houses, anyway. So now do you see why this is all very peculiar? Her having the will reading in a house she probably hadn't even been to in twenty years?"

Now that Pat had explained the whole story, I was starting to understand her reaction to my going with Claire. "Did you know Flo?"

Pat nodded, her eyes sad. "I knew her through church. She was one of my Sunday School teachers, and later on, we served on some of the same volunteer committees. It wasn't like we were best friends or anything, but I liked her. Every time she was involved in something, it was always more fun." Pat picked up a napkin to dab her eyes. "I'm sorry she's gone, and I'm especially sorry that she never recovered from Billy's disappearance."

"What happened with Billy?"

Pat frowned. "It's been so long now. I seem to recall there was some sort of family fight. Billy was upset with someone else … Daisy, maybe?"

I gave her a surprised look. "Claire's mom?"

"Yeah, there was some conflict between Daisy and the rest of the family. Claire, too. I'm not sure about the details."

"What do you mean, 'Claire, too'?"

Pat sighed. "Again, Flo was always vague on specifics. The only thing that was clear was both Daisy and Claire are, well, I guess 'estranged' from the rest of the family. Although that's not quite the right word either, as I think they occasionally attend the big family get-togethers."

"Claire doesn't get along with the rest of her family?" This was news to me.

Pat gave me a look that clearly said, "Now do you get it?"

"It started with Daisy. Flo never really talked about it, but it was obvious Daisy was the black sheep. Then, when Claire and Amelia came along, Claire took on the same black-sheep role as her mom."

"Amelia?"

"Claire's sister."

"Claire has a sister?" More news.

Pat sat back in her chair with an "I told you so" smile, shaking her head. "Still think it's a good idea to go?"

"I think it's a little late to back out now."

When I first arrived in Redemption, lost and confused, I had decided to take a break and have a cup of coffee and bite to eat at Aunt May's Diner. I hoped it would clear my head and help me figure out how to get back to the main highway. Claire was my waitress. One thing led to another, and eventually, she became one of my best friends.

Which is why I found her not telling me about her sister peculiar. While I had never assumed she had shared *all* her secrets with me, having a sibling seemed like a pretty big life detail to have never mentioned.

Pat shrugged. "Your funeral. Hopefully, not literally."

I rolled my eyes. "Hopefully. Although I will say, this does shed a new light on the 'family issues.' A sister she doesn't talk about and the fact she and her mother are the black sheep of the family ... I wonder why she doesn't just go with her mother, then, instead of asking me."

Pat shifted in her seat as she reached for her tea. "I take it you also don't know that Daisy has dementia."

I pressed my hand against my lips. "Oh no."

Pat nodded sadly. "Yes, the whole situation is tragic. She's in a nursing home."

Again, I wondered how well I knew my friend. "When did this happen?"

"Oh, it's been years," Pat said. "A decade at least. Maybe longer. Long before you arrived. It was early onset, very early. I remember when it happened. Flo was beside herself with grief.

First Billy disappeared, and then Daisy's health … Flo was starting to feel like the family was cursed. Anyway, Claire never did like talking about it, so I'm not that surprised she never told you."

"Wow," I said, trying to take in everything Pat had shared. All that tragedy in one family. A haunted house. And a will reading on top of it all. No wonder Pat thought I was crazy.

For a moment, I toyed with the idea of backing out, but even as the thought entered my mind, I dismissed it. Claire needed me. The tone of desperation when she asked me to go made that clear. I didn't understand it at the time … thought maybe I'd mistaken grief for desperation. But now, I knew that wasn't the case.

She needed me to be with her. Not Doug, her husband, but me.

And I couldn't let her down.

"Still going?" Pat asked me, raising an eyebrow.

"I think it would be really crappy of me to back out now," I said. "Plus, it's only a weekend. I can survive a weekend."

Pat let out a guffaw.

"You'll still keep an eye on Midnight, right?"

Upon hearing his name, Midnight opened one green eye and looked at me. He was curled up on the seat of one of the kitchen chairs, which of course was pushed close to the window, so he could bask in the sunlight.

Pat shifted her gaze over to the cat. "Of course. A poor, innocent animal shouldn't have to suffer for his human's mistakes."

Midnight closed his eye and presumably went back to sleep.

"Clearly, he appreciates you feeling his pain," I said.

Chapter 2

"So, you want to tell me a little bit more about this will reading?"

Claire barely glanced at me as she carefully maneuvered her car through town on the surprisingly busy streets. Snow was falling—not heavily enough to impact visibility, but the road was getting slippery. "What do you want to know?" Under her cheery, red, knitted cap, her face was pale, and there were tension lines at the corners of her hazel eyes.

"Well, it's kind of strange, isn't it? A will reading taking place over a weekend in a remote cottage? It feels more like a family holiday than something that typically only takes an hour in a lawyer's office."

A small smile touched Claire's lips. "That's my Grandma Flo for you. She always had to be different." The smile faded, and she let out a sigh. "I know there are things I should have told you sooner. It's not that I don't want you to know. It's just difficult to talk about. But isn't family stuff always that way?" She threw me a sideways glance. "What did Pat tell you?"

"How do you know Pat told me anything?"

She gave me a look. "Oh, come now. You really think I don't know you told Pat?"

"Well, I did ask her to watch Midnight."

"Of course you did."

"I wasn't trying to gossip behind your back or anything," I started to say, but she waved a hand at me.

"I know. That's not what I meant to imply. I know you would never intentionally hurt me. Why do you think I asked you to come? All that said, I also know Pat."

"She wasn't trying to hurt you, either," I said, feeling a need to defend my friend.

Claire looked at me, bemused. "I'm sure she wasn't. I just know how much she likes, ah, 'sharing' stories about her fellow friends and neighbors."

"Well." I couldn't think of anything to say, as Claire was right. Pat did love to gossip. "She did warn me ... said I was going to be staying in a haunted house."

I half-expected Claire to laugh, but instead, her nose wrinkled in concentration. "I don't know if the house is 'haunted,' per se. Not like your house. But there *is* something there." She shivered, and then paused to carefully turn down one of the main roads that headed out of town.

I gave her a questioning look. "What do you mean, 'something's there'?"

"It's hard to explain. Initially, it seemed fine. Growing up, I visited the house regularly, and when I think back to my childhood, most of my memories are happy." She hesitated and narrowed her eyes as she gripped the steering wheel harder.

"'Most'?"

She pursed her lips. "You know those days that start out sunny and beautiful, but then suddenly in the afternoon, a rainstorm appears out of nowhere? All of the sudden, it's dark and cloudy and cold, and maybe there's even thunder and lightning. And, then, the storm blows through, the clouds part, and it's sunny again. That house is like that. There are these moments when everything just seems ... dark. Like a shadow falls over the whole place. It's dark and heavy, and hard to move ... it's even hard to breathe. In fact, I remember when a friend of mine went up with me one year. She had asthma, and when that shadow fell over everything, it caused a terrible asthma attack. It was so bad, we ended up taking her to the hospital. Needless to say, that was the end of our friendship. But, anyway, back to these ... well, 'dark spells,' I guess ... just as quickly as they appear, they disappear. Just like that, everything clears up, and it's all back to the way it was. It leaves you wondering if you imagined the darkness altogether. But you know in your heart, you didn't."

I could feel my chest tightening up just listening to her. Maybe Pat was right, and this was a mistake. "Was it during one of these 'dark spells' that the contractor died?"

Claire pressed her lips together. "Probably. I wasn't there, of course, so I can't be sure. But if I had to guess, yes."

"So, what's the story with that?"

The snow was starting to come down more heavily. Claire squinted at the windshield and eased her foot off the gas. "Over the years, Grandma had been hiring workers and whatnot to do small remodeling projects. She always scheduled them for while she was there, so she could keep an eye on things, she said. But I think it was because of the dark spells. She wanted to be there so in case one of them happened, she could smooth things out."

"So your family knew about the dark spells?"

Claire's mouth twisted in a sideways smile. "That's a loaded question."

"What do you mean?"

"Of course they did. How could they not? But what they choose to acknowledge now is something else altogether."

"I don't understand."

Claire glanced at me, her eyes haunted. "You will. But to answer your question about Grandma, yes, she knew about the dark spells. Yet if you asked her about them, she would say it was all nonsense. Just like the house being haunted was nonsense. She didn't believe in ghosts, and felt there was nothing wrong with the house.

"Be that as it may, she always made sure she was there when the house was being worked on, and she kept the projects small enough so she could work them around her schedule. But then she decided she wanted to completely remodel the basement—turn it into a massive den with a game room and bar. It was to give us kids more indoor activity options when the weather was bad outside. Especially in the winter, there were days it was too cold to be outside for long.

"This project was too big for her to be there all the time. And, of course, when the contractor died, she wasn't there."

"Do you know how he died?"

She shook her head. "Some freak accident. I can't quite remember. But I do know that the other contractor who was with him completely flipped out. He was convinced the house *was* haunted, and by something dangerous. Not surprisingly, he refused to finish the job. Also not surprisingly, other contractors heard about it and didn't want anything to do with the house, either. The few who were brave, or desperate, enough for the work didn't last long. I don't think anything necessarily happened to them; the house was just completely tainted. Needless to say, the basement was never finished."

"What about you? Did you still spend time in the house after the contractor died?"

"At first, yes. My grandmother didn't want to admit that anything was wrong. She was trying to prove a point. So she made us all go up like everything was just fine. But," Claire paused, biting her lip. "There WAS something wrong. Something changed after the contractor died. It's hard to explain, but everything just felt … different. Maybe it was because we were all uneasy, knowing someone had died there just a few months earlier. Or, maybe the house was haunted. Either way, no one seemed to be having all that much fun there anymore. Even my grandmother was uncomfortable. So, over time, our visits just started petering out.

"My mother especially never wanted to go. She was always anxious there. But before the contractor died, she seemed more willing to deal with it. I think she wanted to keep the peace with the family, so she basically closed her mouth and did what she had to. But after the contractor died, I think it was all too much. She just couldn't handle being there anymore. I was glad we stopped the visits. I didn't like it, either. When I was young, it was fine, but the older I got, the more uneasy I felt there, too. Still, my grandmother never wanted to hear anything against it. She used to claim we were all just trying to cause trouble." Even though her expression didn't change, there was a tension in Claire's body that hadn't been there earlier.

"Why would your grandmother have such a reaction?"

Claire shook her head. "I'm not sure. Something happened when my mother was a child, but she would never talk about it. Said it wasn't anything a child needed to deal with. But once I got old enough to have that conversation, she was diagnosed with dementia. So, that was kind of that."

"I'm sorry to hear about your mother," I said.

Claire nodded tightly. "I should have told you sooner," she said again. "Just like I should have told you about my sister. Did Pat say anything?"

"She did. But all I know is that you *have* a sister. Nothing else."

"Did she tell you about my mother?"

"Yes. But, again, no specifics. Just that she's in a nursing home."

"Well, that's pretty much the whole story," Claire said. "She went downhill quickly. Physically, she's in good shape, but mentally, she's pretty far gone. Occasionally, she still has moments of lucidity, but they've been getting fewer and further between over the years."

I reached over to put a hand on her knee. "I really am sorry."

Claire glanced at me and smiled slightly, a sheen to her eyes. "Thanks. So, what else did Pat say?"

I took my hand off her knee and leaned back in my seat. "That there was a rift between you and your mother and the rest of the family. But again, she didn't know why."

Claire went back to focusing on her driving. "That's a nice way of saying it."

"Is that why you didn't tell me about your sister? Or anything about your family?"

Claire frowned as she thought about it. "I guess 'yes' would be the easy answer, but it's more complicated than that," she said finally. "It's more because I don't want to think about it. I don't like talking about it, because then I have to think about it, and it's not something I want to think about. I can't do anything about it now." She glanced sideways at me again. "I don't want you to take this the wrong way, because we would have been friends regardless, but I really loved the fact that you didn't know my history. Everyone else here does, so I could never escape it. But you were always so relaxing to be around, because I knew I never had to talk about it."

"I get it," I said, thinking about my own history I had escaped from. Coming to Redemption meant I didn't have to talk about what I had left in New York. "It's not like I want to talk about my past, either."

She smiled slightly. "That's for sure. You're the worst." Her smile faded. "But seriously, it's been painful. My mother was my best friend and biggest champion. When she was diagnosed with dementia, it was like the bottom dropped out of my world. I didn't feel like I had a family anymore."

"I get it," I said, and I did. No one in my family understood why I had just upped and left New York and moved out to a small town in Wisconsin. None of them had believed my fiancé was abusive—they all thought I was exaggerating. Worse, they still hadn't completely forgiven me.

"I know you do." The look in her eyes reflected the pain that was probably mirrored in mine.

"So, what happened? Why the family rift?"

She blew the air out her cheeks with a loud noise. "You know how I sometimes just know things?" She paused, eyeing me nervously, as if I might suddenly jump out of the car rather than listen to what she had to say. "Or how I get feelings about things, even though they haven't happened yet?"

I nodded.

"Well, my mother did, as well. Hers were stronger than mine, though. Anyway, we're the only two. The rest of the family doesn't have anything like that, according to them."

I waited as Claire slowed down to turn on an even narrower country road. The snow was starting to accumulate faster, leaving small mounds on the side of the road. "And …" I prompted when she didn't say anything.

"And, what?"

"What else? There has to be more."

Claire sighed. "There probably is, but I don't know it. All I know is my grandmother hated any talk about either my mother or I feeling or knowing anything. That's one of the reasons she never wanted to hear anything about anything being off with the cottage. I don't know the history or what happened when my mom was a child, but whatever it was, neither my grandmother nor my Aunt Iris wanted to hear a word about any kind of 'knowing' or 'feeling' my mother or I had. It actually wasn't until I was older that it started happening to me. But when it did, it drove a wedge between me and the rest of family. Especially Amelia."

"Your sister?"

She nodded. "We were close when we were kids. But as we grew older and I started having the same experiences as my mother, Amelia stopped wanting to have anything to do with me. She started hanging around my Aunt Iris and our cousins more than me." She let go of the steering wheel to swipe at her eyes, but not before I saw the pain reflected there.

"That's rough," I said.

"Yeah. It was. It was right around the time my Uncle Billy disappeared, too, which made things even more difficult." She shot me a look. "I'm sure Pat told you about that?"

"Yeah, she did mention you had an uncle who disappeared."

Claire nodded. "When that happened, it was the final straw. No one went to the cabin after that. Not even my grandma. Well, other than a handful of visits a year just to check on things. One of the neighbors used to stop by regularly, as well. If I remember correctly, he also used to do small repairs and other handyman-type work up there. But that was it."

"If no one was using the cabin anymore, why didn't she sell it?"

Claire snorted. "Think selling a haunted cabin is easy? Try selling your house, and see what happens."

She had a point. "She could have sold it to someone outside the area, though. To someone who hadn't heard the stories about it being haunted."

"Yes, but when that person saw the basement half-finished and asked what happened, the realtor would have to disclose the contractor's death, and that they were never able to find someone to finish. As you can imagine, that pretty much ends the discussion."

"So your grandma has just hung onto it for all these years?"

"Pretty much."

"Wow." It was so peculiar to me. "I'm surprised she didn't try to do something about it. Did she ever think about asking the neighbor-handyman to finish the basement?"

"I'm not sure. But quite honestly, I don't know if she would have sold it, anyway."

"Why not?"

Claire frowned. "She had an … attachment, to the cottage. I guess that's the easiest way to explain it. She just loved it so, and even after everything that happened, she couldn't let go of it. And to be fair, there were a lot of good memories associated with the cabin, as well. So, she may have been holding onto hope that we could all eventually get back there again. Especially if Uncle Billy ever turned up."

"I guess that makes sense." I watched as Claire made another careful turn and began climbing deeper into the woods. "Boy, the snow is really coming down now." It was in fact blanketing the trees, weighing down their branches with mounds of white.

"Yeah, this time of year was always the most fun at the cabin." She smiled briefly. "I don't know that we'll be doing a lot of snow fort making and snowball fighting this time, though."

"What *do* you think we're going to be doing? I mean, this is a little crazy, having to spend a weekend up here, considering everything you've said. Don't you think?"

"It is, but it isn't. Like I said, grandma loved it so. I'm wondering if she was trying to get us to recapture the fun we used to have there. One last time, before it gets sold."

"You think it's going to sell now?"

"I don't see anyone in the family hanging on to it."

"But if a haunted house didn't sell years before, why would it now?"

"Because I think whoever inherits it will be motivated to sell," she said, "and willing to do whatever it takes to make that happen. If we have to finish the basement, the basement will get finished, one way or another. If we have to drop the price, we'll drop the price. At this point, I don't see anyone simply hanging on to it for old time's sake."

I studied Claire's determined face, the set of her mouth. "Do you think you'll inherit it?"

"I have no idea, but that's why I'm going," she said.

I gave her a surprised look. I never thought Claire to be so mercenary.

She saw my expression. "Not for me," she said. "For Daphne."

"You think your daughter might inherit it?"

"Daphne is her only great-granddaughter," she said. "Or great anything. Neither my sister nor cousins have any children yet. So, yeah, I think it's possible. And for my daughter's sake, I'll deal with whatever happens. But ..." she paused, and her face grew pensive. "I do want to say goodbye, as well. Grandma was thrilled when Daphne was born. She was so excited to be a great-grandma. Having Daphne gave me the opportunity to heal my relationship with her, which was just, well, wonderful." She gave me a faint smile. "It made me realize how much I missed having a relationship with my family. After my mom went into the nursing home, I pushed a lot of those feelings down. They were just too painful. But these past couple of years with grandma ... well, it was really nice."

"I'm glad you had that time with her," I said.

She nodded. "Thank you. I am, too. Oh, look, we're here." She made another tight turn onto a very narrow road. Actually, it was more like a path than a road. The tire tracks lining it made it clear we weren't the first to arrive. We continued on, the tires crunching over the packed snow as tree branches scratched the windshield.

"There's a larger parking area past the house," Claire said, driving very slowly. "Hopefully, it's been maintained. Grandma put it there so we would have room for all the cars during our getaways, and I suspect we'll need it today."

"How many people do you think will be here?"

Claire frowned. "Hard to say. Maybe a dozen?"

"*A dozen*?" Now that the reality of what I had agreed to was sinking in, the idea of spending a weekend in a small, remote cabin with a dozen people I didn't know was making me feel overwhelmed. "How big is the cabin? Where are we all going to sleep?" Outside, the snow fell harder, obscuring the view of the stark trees naked of leaves. Pat had warned me it was secluded, but I hadn't realized exactly how much so until that moment. I couldn't even remember the last time I had seen another house.

Claire grinned at me, the first true smile I had seen on her face in a long time. "Trust me, it won't be a problem. The cabin is huge. Five bedrooms plus a living room and den. The den also has a pullout couch. We'll bunk together in one of the rooms."

"They know I'm coming?"

"Well, they know I'm bringing a guest, yes. I didn't specify who."

I shot Claire a look. Great. Perfect start to this perfectly weird weekend. I wasn't even expected.

"There's the cabin," she said, pointing to her side of window as we continued to slowly drive by. I didn't get much sense of what it looked like other than the logs and sloping roof covered in mounds of snow.

"Looks like we will be able to park in the parking area. I can see cars."

I peered out of the windshield and spotted a black truck, blue SUV, and a couple mid-size cars already too covered in snow to make out the colors. Claire carefully pulled into a spot and turned off the engine.

"We made it."

Chapter 3

Claire was right. The "cabin" easily accommodated a dozen adults.

After a bit of production dragging our two suitcases and two grocery bags through the increasing snowdrifts (I was taken aback when I realized Claire had brought food with her, and let her know I had no idea I was supposed to bring anything more than my tea, but she insisted it was enough … I was there supporting her, and besides, she wouldn't ever hear the end of it if she hadn't brought her share of food for the weekend), we finally managed to wade our way up to the porch and inside the house.

It was a huge A-frame, log-cabin-style home with hardwood floors, fireplaces, and a rather regretful 70s-style design. The living room (or maybe I should say 'great room,' as it was massive) featured a huge stone fireplace complete with a wooden mantle above that held candles and framed photos. Directly across from us was an open staircase, zig zagging upward to the floor above. An orange shaggy rug stretched out across the living room, and the couches and chairs were olive-green and held mustard-yellow pillows. Next to the fireplace was a maroon beanbag.

"I can't even remember the last time I saw a beanbag," I said to Claire.

"That's nothing," she said, nodding toward one of the corners. "Check out our lava lamp."

I followed her gaze, and sure enough, there really was a lava lamp tucked away on one of the side tables.

"Think it works?" I asked.

"I'm sure someone will turn it on to check," Claire said.

The house smelled a little odd. On the surface, there was the sharp scent of disinfectant from cleaning supplies and lemon polish. Yet as strong as they were, they couldn't cover up the the underlying waft of dust and neglect that lingered beneath.

"I see Amelia must have been cleaning again," Claire said, her voice resigned.

Before I could ask what she meant, a woman appeared from around the corner. "I thought I heard voices," she said, her voice reproachful. "Nice of you to finally get here."

"Hi Amelia," Claire said. "Nice to see you, too."

Even if Claire hadn't said her name, I would have known they were related. Amelia's hair was more of a darker auburn than Claire's strawberry blonde, but her eyes were more brown than hazel, just like Claire's. Amelia's hair was cut short in a pixie style, and her makeup was flawless. Even though her outfit was casual—tan turtleneck sweater paired with jeans and gold jewelry—she somehow looked quite elegant and put-together.

Amelia sniffed. "Well, at least you made it before the storm got much worse. How bad was the drive?"

"Not great," Claire said, unwinding her scarf and pulling off her hat, the process creating static electricity that caused her long locks to fly around her face. Unlike her sister, Claire wore no makeup, and her red sweater had a stain across the front. "But not too bad, either. Definitely getting slippery and harder to navigate."

Amelia stepped to the side to peer out the front window. "Looks like the weatherman was right … we are in for a big storm. That's why I wanted everyone to get here early—to avoid driving in the worst of it. Not to mention we definitely could have used help getting the house ready for visitors."

Claire flinched slightly. "I didn't want to leave Daphne for any longer than I had to."

Amelia snapped her head around. "You could have brought her. Doug, too. I don't know why you didn't."

"A toddler has no business running around this house," Claire said. "Plus, she would have been a distraction. This is my friend Charlie, by the way."

Amelia turned her head to study me, her eyes cool and appraising. I felt the heat rise in my chest at her scrutiny, causing me to reassure myself that there shouldn't be anything wrong with my oversized dark-green sweater and jeans. My brownish-blonde hair was having one of its wild days, so I just left it loose and curly. Maybe that had been a mistake. Like Claire, I had very little makeup on—just a little mascara to help emphasize the green in my hazel eyes and lip gloss.

"This isn't a party, Claire," Amelia said, her tone dripping with disapproval. "This is supposed to be family only. Although," her eyes narrowed. "I guess it could be worse. You could have brought a date, like your cousin."

Claire's eyes went wide. "Jeremy brought a date?"

Amelia rolled her eyes. "*Jeremy* isn't even here yet, but knowing him, he'll probably bring a date and maybe a few others. No, I'm talking about Lucy."

"Lucy brought a date? I didn't even know she was dating anyone," Claire said.

"It helps to attend family get-togethers," Amelia said, as Claire's face flushed. "However," Amelia continued, wrinkling her nose. "In this case, it wouldn't have mattered. No one knew she was dating anyone."

"Are you talking about me?" A bright, perky voice sang out, the owner of which appeared a few seconds later. She was petite and curvy, which her tight pink sweater accented, and had a mound of blonde hair that had to have come out of a bottle, as it didn't quite match her brown eyes and skin tone. She paused when she saw me, her pink lipsticked mouth forming an O. "See Amelia? I'm not the only one who brought a guest," she said.

"That doesn't mean it was the right thing to do," Amelia snapped. "We're here to honor Grandma, not to party."

Lucy gave her head a quick shake, tossing her mane of curls over her shoulder. "A party is exactly what we're here for. If Grandma wanted a traditional funeral, she would have had the lawyer read the will in his conference room, like everyone else does it. The fact that she wanted us to spend the weekend together as part of the will reading means she wanted us to honor her life by doing something she always enjoyed. Namely, spend time in this drafty old house. And, if you recall, it wasn't un-heard of to bring our friends with us." She turned to me and smiled. "I'm Lucy, by the way."

I was opening my mouth to respond when another voice answered.

"Charlie?"

It was deep, and instantly familiar. It also instantly turned my stomach into a giant knot.

"Wyle?"

Lucy's date—a tall, lean man with dark hair and dark eyes—stepped into the living room. Officer Brandon Wyle. Ugh.

He wore a navy-blue sweater that stretched across his broad chest along with jeans and Timberland boots. I had never seen him without his uniform on, and I did a double take as I almost didn't recognize him. Unfortunately, he was even better looking in street clothes than in uniform. Double ugh.

At least he looked as shocked to see me as I was him.

"Oh, you two know each other?" Lucy asked.

"We've had a few … dealings," Wyle said. He was still star-ing at me.

"Dealings" was certainly one way of referring to the en-counters we'd had when I found myself trying to help my clients out of murder accusations. Wyle was less than thrilled, shall we say, with my involvement.

Lucy let out a little tinkering laugh. "I hope that doesn't mean we have a criminal in our midst," she said.

"Not as far as I know," Wyle said, eyeing me. I flashed an innocent-looking smile in response.

"Wait," Amelia said, squinting at me. "Are you that crazy tea lady who lives in Helen's old house?"

"That would be me," I said, glancing out the front window to see exactly how bad the snow was coming down. Was it too late to leave? I could always return in a couple of days and pick Claire up, assuming I wouldn't get lost in the process. Although with my horrendous sense of direction, that was probably a bad assumption.

But alas, if anything, the snow appeared to be coming down even harder. So much for my escape.

"She's not crazy," Claire said. Wyle cleared his throat, holding his hand over his mouth like he was trying to hide a smile.

"She's living in a haunted house," Amelia said. "Who in her right mind chooses to live in a haunted house?"

"Allegedly haunted," I corrected.

Back in the early 1900s, Martha Blackstone, the wife of the man who built the house, had reportedly gone mad, killing her maid Nellie and then herself. "Mad Martha," as the locals referred to her, supposedly continued to haunt the house to this day.

I had bought the house from her daughter Helen. And while I did have some, well, let's just say "funky" experiences in the house, I had yet to run into Mad Martha's ghost.

"Is it true you sell potions and spells?" Lucy asked.

"I absolutely do NOT sell potions or spells," I said. "I sell teas and tinctures, which may have health benefits but are, of course, not guaranteed."

"Oh, I get it," Lucy said, giving me a wink.

"No, really," I started to say when Amelia interrupted. "That's exactly what I heard. And that you're a witch."

My eyes widened. "A witch? Are you serious?" Wyle started coughing again, pressing his hand against his mouth.

"Amelia, what are you talking about?" Claire demanded. "Charlie isn't a witch. She makes herbal teas, and they're lovely. Plus, they've been helping me sleep again, which I've sorely needed after having Daphne and my hormones going berserk."

"I brought some, if you want to give them a try," I said.

"Absolutely," Lucy said as Amelia shot Claire a horrified look.

"Claire, I can't believe you would bring this … this woman here. This is a serious family weekend …"

"What is going on?" An older woman stepped into the living room. She looked to be around sixty, with the same auburn hair and brown eyes as Amelia, although the color appeared to be from a bad dye job, probably to cover up the grey. She wore a red apron over a sky-blue sweater set and pearls. "Oh, Claire.

Good, you made it." Her voice didn't necessarily sound like it was a good thing. It was actually more like she was a bit disappointed. "Has anyone heard from Jeremy?"

"Not yet," Amelia said.

"The weather is really getting bad. I wish he'd get here," she fretted, adjusting her gold-rimmed glasses.

"Aunt Iris, I'd like you to meet my friend Charlie," Claire said.

"You brought a friend, too," Iris said as she quickly glanced at me before returning her eyes to the window.

"Charlie is the one who bought Helen's old house," Amelia said.

"Oh?" Iris turned back to me, a lot more interest in her expression. "Are you the one who makes teas?"

"That would be me."

"Oh! I've been wanting to talk to you. Ellen, my friend, has been raving about your tea helping her sleep."

Amelia rolled her eyes. "Not you too, Aunt Iris," she groaned.

"What? There's nothing wrong with a nice herbal tea," Iris said.

"Amelia thinks she's a witch," Lucy said.

"Who's a witch?" an older man asked, joining us in the living room. He was balding, a few long strands combed over his bald spot, and he wore a thick pair of horn-rimmed glasses. His grey argyle sweater vest stretched over his significant paunch. His cheeks were ruddy, and his chin sported a few whiskers.

"Charlie, Claire's friend," Lucy pointed.

"Hi, Uncle Martin," Claire greeted him.

Martin adjusted his glasses and peered at me. "*Are* you a witch?"

"Not to my knowledge," I said.

"Well, then, that's settled," he replied without hesitation.

"To be clear," Amelia said, "I never said I thought she was witch. Simply that I'd *heard* she was a witch."

"Why do people think that?" Iris asked.

Amelia flapped her hands. "Because of the potions and spells."

"What potions and spells?" I asked. "That's not what I do. I told you, I grow herbs and flowers and turn them into teas and tinctures. That's it."

"And they're wonderful," Claire said, throwing her sister a hard look. "You should try them."

"Hmph," Amelia said.

"So, is this it?" Wyle asked, clearly changing the subject. "Are we waiting for anyone else? The weather is looking pretty bad out there."

"I know," Iris said, pressing a hand against her chest. "I wish Jeremy would hurry up and get here."

"He's fine, mom," Lucy said. "You know how Jeremy likes to make an entrance."

"So, just one more?" Wyle asked, looking at Lucy. "Your brother, Jeremy?"

"And George," Amelia said.

"Who's George?" Wyle asked.

"The lawyer."

The lawyer? I glanced at Claire, who looked as confused as I was. "Why is the lawyer coming today?" Claire asked.

"Why do you think? Someone needs to do the reading."

"Yes, but why today?" Claire asked. "I mean, we're not doing the will reading tonight, right? So why isn't he coming right before the reading?"

"As I'm sure you know," Amelia said stiffly. "George is an old friend of the family. He and Grandma go way back. I thought it would be nice for him to be able to say goodbye, as well."

Claire stared at her, astonished. "You just gave me a hard time for bringing Charlie only to find out you also invited someone who isn't a member of the family?"

"The difference is, George knew Grandma," Amelia said. "He's not a boyfriend or the crazy tea lady who never even met Grandma."

"Brandon met Grandma," Lucy chimed in.

Amelia rolled her eyes. "Bringing your boyfriend to a family gathering once hardly counts."

"No, that wasn't it. Brandon gave her a speeding ticket," Lucy continued. She turned to Wyle. "Isn't that right?"

Wyle looked exceedingly uncomfortable.

"Oh for heaven's sake," Amelia grumbled. "The point of this weekend is to celebrate Grandma's life in a place she always loved. Therefore, only people who knew and loved Grandma should be here. End of story."

"Where's Elliot?" Claire asked suddenly, looking around. "You did invite him, right?"

"Oh course he's here," Amelia said. "He's my husband. Elliot?" She shrieked his name.

"I'm here, I'm here," Elliot said, stepping forward between Iris and Martin. "You don't have to shout."

Elliot was one of those men who was so average-looking, he always blended right into a crowd. Average height, average build, light-brown hair thinning at the top, and glasses. A pleasant face, but nothing that stood out, although his cheeks seemed redder than normal. He sniffed loudly and fished a tissue out of the pocket of his brown slacks.

"Where have you been?" Amelia asked.

"Outside," he said. "I was looking for the woodpile. Like you asked."

"Did you find it?"

He shook his head. "Not yet."

"What woodpile?" Martin asked.

"The woodpile I asked Hal to leave for us," Amelia said. "I thought we could make a fire." She turned back to Elliot. "Did you check the woodshed?"

Elliot looked at her blankly. "Woodshed?"

Amelia opened her mouth to answer, but a loud bang outside interrupted her, and the front door burst open, sending a shower of snow and cold air into the room.

A figure bundled up in a heavy winter coat and carrying a duffle bag appeared as if blown in by the wind. There was a brief tussle with the door before whoever it was finally slammed it closed.

"Jeremy? Is that you?" Iris asked.

"In the flesh," came the muffled reply.

Jeremy turned, shaking the snow out of his hair and stamping his feet on the mat. "Boy, is it coming down. I was afraid I wasn't going to make it."

Iris came forward to greet him. "That was why we wanted you to leave earlier," she said, her voice slightly reproachful as she displayed her cheek for him to kiss.

He did so, then removed his jacket and surveyed the room. Even with his damp hair sticking to his head, it was clear how good-looking he was. It was difficult to tell what color his hair was, as it was wet, but I had a feeling it was close to the same strawberry-blonde as Claire's. His eyes were a dark green, and his face had an elegant quality to it, almost like royalty.

He raised an eyebrow. "What's going on? Why are you all standing there like you're in a receiving line of a wedding?" His voice was rich, like carmel melting in the pot, but there was an edge to it I couldn't quite decipher.

"Claire just got here a few minutes ago. We were greeting her," Amelia said.

Jeremy's eyes slid along the crowd, finding Claire and nodding at her before landing on me. "Who is this?"

"This is my friend Charlie," Claire said.

Both of Jeremy's eyebrows went up. "A friend?" He turned to Iris. "You didn't tell me I could bring a … friend?"

"She isn't the only one," Iris said, hanging his jacket in the closet. "Your sister brought a date."

"A *date*? Why wasn't I told?"

"No one was supposed to bring anyone else," Amelia said. "I don't know why Claire and Lucy weren't able to figure that out on their own."

"Probably because this is supposed to be a celebration," Lucy said. "We're celebrating Grandma's life."

Jeremy clapped his hands together. "That sounds like a party. Where are the drinks? Let's get this thing started."

Amelia turned to head to the kitchen. "Actually, we do need to focus on dinner, especially with the added guests."

"Do you want help?" Claire asked.

"You and Jeremy should get settled in your room first," she said. "The rest of us have already done that. I'll get into the kitchen and see what's available."

Claire picked up the grocery bags. "I brought food," she said.

Amelia pressed her lips together but didn't answer as she stalked toward the kitchen. Claire stood still for a moment, biting her lip, her arms holding both bags of groceries. I reached over to take one from her when Elliot materialized in front of us.

"I can take care of these, Claire," he said with a smile. "Why don't you go up, put your bags in the room, and give your friend a quick tour of the house?"

Claire didn't respond, just stood there still holding the bags.

"She'll get over it," Elliott said. "You know your sister. She just hates surprises. Give her a few minutes to adjust."

"I think it's deeper than that," Claire said.

"She'll be fine," Elliott said again. "It was really thoughtful of you to bring food. But go on, and get yourself settled. There will be plenty of time to talk to Amelia this weekend."

Claire hesitated for a moment longer, but then, as if realizing Elliot's words made sense, she handed the two bags over. "Do you know which room is mine?"

"The two that are left are the ones at the end."

"Oh, the ones with twin beds," Jeremy said, coming up behind us. "Great."

Elliott grimaced. "Would you rather share a bed with George?"

Jeremy stared at him. "George? The lawyer? I'm supposed to share a room with him?"

"If he shows up." Elliott squinted at the window. "With how it's coming down, I suspect he won't be arriving until later this weekend."

"I can't believe you would stick me with the lawyer."

"Come on, Charlie," Claire said, picking up her suitcase. "I'll give you the grand tour."

I picked up my own bag and proceeded to follow Claire across the living room and up the stairs. The room was emptying out as the rest of the family also wandered into other areas of the house. Well, everyone except Jeremy, who was still arguing his case to Elliott. "Who invited the lawyer to spend the weekend with us, anyway?" Jeremy asked, his voice floating up after us.

Claire sighed and shook her head.

I trailed after her, clutching the handle of my suitcase tightly, wondering again what I had gotten myself into.

Chapter 4

The stairs creaked as we ascended. "It certainly sounds like a haunted house," I muttered to Claire.

She stifled a laugh.

"So, we'll just take the room at the end of the hall," she said, leading me down a long hallway with doors on either side. It would have been striking with the hardwood floors and matching oak beam walls, but the ugly carpet runner ruined the effect. Red with yellow and orange paisleys was bad enough, but it was also stained and dirty.

"The bathroom is here," she said, indicating a door about halfway down. She knocked once, then pushed it open for me to peek inside. It was actually very nice, with a huge clawfoot tub, separate shower, and large vanity.

"Only one bathroom?"

"Two. The second one is part of the master bedroom." She pointed to the other end of the hall. "Plus, there's a third half-bath on the main floor. I'll show it to you when we go back down."

"Still, three bathrooms doesn't seem like enough for a five-bedroom house."

"Yeah, that was another reason Grandma wanted the basement redone. She was going to add a full bathroom down there, as well. But, alas, we're stuck with three." She continued down the hall until she reached the last door. "Here we go," she said, pushing it open.

Just like the bathroom, the room was larger than I expected. There were two twin beds, two dressers, two nightstands, and one closet. Claire dropped her bag and stood in the middle of the room, holding her arms out and twirling in a circle. "Home sweet home. Do you have a side preference?"

I shook my head as I followed her in. The olive-green/orange/yellow decor had unfortunately slithered its way into the bedroom, as well. A gold shaggy carpet lay in the center of the room, and the bedspreads were olive-green and accented with orange throw pillows.

"Who did the decorating?" I asked as Claire picked up her suitcase and tossed it on one of the beds.

She snickered. "Awful, isn't it? But it was all the rage back in the day. When Grandma was remodeling the house, she also decided to 'modernize' the decoration." Claire placed air quotes around the word "modernize." "Anyway, needless to say, it hasn't been touched since that last update."

I gingerly sat down on the opposite bed, not sure what to expect. After all, the mattress had been sitting here, neglected, for over twenty years. What sort of shape could it be in? But to my surprise, it was more comfortable than I'd imagined.

"Beds seem to be okay," I said.

Claire nodded. "Yeah, and I'm sure the sheets are clean, as well. Thanks to Amelia."

The room smelled just like the living room—that peculiar mixture of cleaning products and mustiness. Still, all that really mattered was that it was clean.

"Sorry for all of that," Claire said.

I looked at her in surprise. "For what?"

"I guess for everything. Inviting you here, making you listen to all that unpleasant family stuff, getting called a 'crazy tea lady' …"

"And a 'witch,' don't forget."

Claire rolled her eyes. "I'm truly sorry for and embarrassed about how my family behaved."

"Well, you have nothing to be sorry about," I said. "When you told me there were issues with your family, I figured there would be unpleasant stuff. As for being the 'crazy tea lady,'" I shrugged. "Maybe I am."

She laughed again. It suddenly occurred to me that it was the first time I had heard her laugh in months. It made me feel better—like I had done the right thing in coming, even if there would be uncomfortable moments.

"But what about you?" I asked.

"What about me?"

"How are you doing? I mean, because of what you were talking about before. Those dark spells. Have you felt any since we've been here?"

She shook her head. "Although it's not surprising. I don't think they've ever happened right upon my arrival. Takes at least a couple of days."

Well, that was good to know. We were only going to be there for three days, so we'd hopefully be gone before anything happened at all.

Claire hopped off the bed and stretched. "I want to freshen up a bit. Maybe even put on some makeup."

I widened my eyes. "Makeup? Are you sure you're feeling okay?"

She grinned. "Knowing my sister, I had a feeling I would feel the urge to get a little more … dressed up. Anyway, are you fine here?"

"Is there a reason I wouldn't be?"

Claire bent down to dig her toiletry bag out of her suitcase. "I guess not. Feel free to use whatever dresser you want or the closet, if you want to unpack." She turned to head out of the room.

I listened to the floor creak as she made her way to the bathroom and winced. Hopefully, there weren't any nocturnal ramblers in the group who would inadvertently keep us all up.

Despite my customary overpacking, it didn't take me long to empty my suitcase. Just as I was shutting the drawer, I heard the creaking again.

"Claire, is that you?" I turned around, but the room was empty.

Strange. I was sure I heard her come in. Was someone else up here? Feeling vaguely uneasy despite not being able to put a finger on why, I went to the door and poked my head out.

The hallway was empty.

What was going on? I had clearly heard footsteps. Could it have been the house creaking and groaning in age? Or maybe Claire left the bathroom and went downstairs for some reason, even though that didn't seem right to me, either. The footsteps had been coming toward my room, not away.

"Claire?" I carefully walked toward the bathroom, testing the floor for creak-free spots, but not finding many. "Claire?"

I reached the bathroom and leaned closer to the door, intending to knock. I paused, hearing the sound of water running.

So, Claire was still in the bathroom. Then what had I heard in the hallway?

"Charlie?"

I startled, nearly jumping out of my skin as I whirled around. Wyle was standing behind me.

"You almost gave me a heart attack," I said, pressing my hand against my chest. "Why are you skulking around up here?"

"I'm hardly 'skulking around.' I was in my room." He gestured toward the door behind him.

"Didn't you just come up here?"

"No."

I glanced around the hallway, that now-familiar uneasy feeling creeping up my spine again. "Did you hear someone walking around out here?"

"Yes. You. That's why I came out. To talk to you."

I shook my head. "No, before me."

He looked puzzled. "You mean Claire going to the bathroom?"

"No, before me and after … oh never mind. What did you want to talk about?"

Wyle folded his arms across his chest, studying me. His expression was carefully neutral, giving me no hint as to what was going on beneath the surface. "Why are you here?"

"Why am I here?" I stared at him in disbelief. "Why are you here? You're not family, either. Or is there a suprise announcement coming?"

Wyle ignored my question. "I was told this was a family reunion celebrating Lucy's grandmother's life," he said. "It's not unheard of for people to bring dates to a family event like that. But," his eyes narrowed. "I haven't heard of married mothers bringing a friend with them before."

"And based on how Claire was greeted, this somehow surprises you?" I asked, lowering my voice. "Why would she ever bring her toddler into such a dysfunctional situation?"

"Where is her husband?"

"Watching their toddler," I said impatiently.

Wyle raised an eyebrow. "They couldn't find someone else to watch her?"

"I guess not, with such short notice," I said. Although now that we'd arrived, I suspected it was less about Daphne and more about Claire wanting someone else with her for support. Claire's marriage wasn't the happiest. Doug was a doting father and decent provider, but he had never been good at providing emotional support to Claire, and clearly, that was what she needed. "But why do you care so much about who Claire brought with her?"

Wyle frowned. "I guess … mostly, I was wondering what Claire told you to get you here. Did you know there was going to be a will reading?"

"Yes. And I agree it's an odd request to make for a will reading, but according to Claire, this was her grandmother's favorite place when they were kids, so maybe Lucy isn't completely wrong that her grandmother wanted the family to spend the weekend together, celebrating her life."

"Maybe." He turned his face away, gazing down the hallway. I fought the urge to tell him that his girlfriend not telling him the full truth had nothing to do with Claire and me, but I kept my mouth shut. His relationship didn't have anything to do with me, either, even if I did find it annoying. "There is something that just feels … off, about this whole situation." He looked back at me, gazing intently into my eyes. "Do you feel it?"

His eyes were so intense, I felt my breath catch in my throat, and for a moment, I forgot what I was going to say. But then I gave myself a quick shake. Wyle had a girlfriend, who was somewhere in that very house. Even more than that, I had no interest in dating anyone—especially a cop. "You know the house is haunted, right?"

His eyes flickered, and I knew I had surprised him. "Haunted? Are you serious?"

"I am. In fact, a contractor even died here."

"Seriously?"

"Yeah, he was doing some work on the basement when some freak accident happened. The guy with him insisted the house was haunted. Claire's grandma was never able to finish the remodel after that."

"So, you're saying the reason the house feels off is because it's haunted?" Wyle looked skeptical.

I shrugged. "I'm just saying. If the shoe fits …"

Wyle gave me a look, but before he could say anything, the door to the bathroom opened behind me.

"Oh," Claire said. "You surprised me. Did you need the bathroom?"

I turned to face her. Although she was still wearing the stained sweater, she looked much better. Her hair was brushed and tied back in a neat ponytail, and her makeup covered the bags under her eyes. "I was just telling Wyle that the house is haunted."

"Oh, are you feeling anything?" she asked, peering at Wyle.

Wyle looked uncomfortable. "I don't believe in ghosts."

Claire looked thoughtful. "Yeah, I'm not entirely sure if it's a ghost haunting this place. There's definitely something off about it." Even though I wasn't looking at Wyle, I could feel him start next to me. He had used that exact same phrase to describe the house. "Anyway, I should go change my sweater and get down to the kitchen. Amelia always says she doesn't want help, but she really does." Claire pressed her lips together and gave her head a little shake. "And then we'll have to listen to her passive-aggressive barbs all night. Plus, I'm sure they've already opened the wine by now, and I for one could use a drink. Meet you down there?"

"Sure, I was about to go down anyway," Wyle said, backing away from us. "Talk to you later, Charlie." The tone of his voice was perfectly clear.

Our conversation wasn't done yet.

Chapter 5

"Care for a refill?" Jeremy stood in front of me holding a bottle of wine, a teasing grin on his face.

"I'm good for now," I said. I was still nursing the second glass I had poured with dinner, which was more than I normally drank.

But these were extraordinary circumstances.

After spending more time than I cared to alone with Amelia in the kitchen (Claire ended up disappearing for a bit, claiming she wanted to call home and speak with Daphne before her bedtime—I suspected her real motive was to get out of the kitchen before she threw a knife at Amelia) and consuming the huge dinner of roast chicken, pot roast, mashed potatoes, gravy, biscuits, and buttered carrots and green beans, I was more than ready for some wine. The first glass went down a little too quickly; hence, my nursing the second.

But even if I hadn't drank that first glass so fast, I would still need to go slow. Jeremy's flirting glances were trouble enough, let alone all the family drama. Not to mention Wyle, who was looking less and less happy the longer the night wore on. I was going to need all my wits about me to get me through it … at least as many as I could wrangle after two glasses of wine.

With dinner over, we had all migrated to the living room with our drinks. Well, except for Amelia, who was finishing the clean-up. Nearly everyone chipped in, so it had gone pretty quickly, but it was also more chaotic. In the end, Amelia had chased everyone out, insisting she needed to "fix" it. She claimed she wanted to make sure everything was put in the proper place, as there was already a butcher knife missing, and she didn't want anything else lost.

Jeremy waved the bottle, his eyebrows wagging up and down. "You sure?"

"Positive."

"I'd love a refill," Lucy called out, holding out her glass. She was sprawled out on the beanbag.

Jeremy took one last look at me before sauntering over to his sister. "Just wanted to make sure there was enough for everyone else," he said as he poured.

"Oh, like you should talk." Lucy's face was flushed, and her arm wasn't quite steady. "I saw how much you had at dinner."

"Just trying to keep up with you, dear sis," Jeremy said. He glanced up at Wyle, who was sitting nearby on a chair. "How about you?"

"I'm good, for now," Wyle said. His tone was pleasant, but his expression was carefully neutral.

Jeremy shrugged. "Suit yourself." He turned toward Iris, who held her glass out expectantly.

"The snow is really coming down," Iris said. "I hope George is okay."

"I'm sure George is fine," Jeremy reassured her as he filled her glass. "He probably took one look outside and decided not to even try."

"If that's the case, why didn't he call?"

"Maybe he couldn't find the number to the cabin," Jeremy said. "Or he had an emergency. Chances are, there is a perfectly logical explanation."

"You're probably right," Iris said, taking a sip of her now topped-off wine. "I still wish he'd call. That weather looks truly dreadful."

"Yes, that's why we need a fire," Amelia announced, walking into the room with a glass of wine in one hand and a tray of chocolate chip cookies in the other. "Elliott, did you bring in the wood?"

Elliott was standing in the corner talking to Martin, but at the sound of his name, he jerked his head up, blinking in confusion. "Wood?"

"Yes," Amelia said impatiently. "Hal was supposed to leave us wood so we could have a fire. Just like when we were kids. Remember?"

Elliott blinked a few more times. "Uhh, we didn't know each other as kids."

"I didn't mean you. I was talking to the others." Amelia gestured with the hand holding the treats. "Remember how we used to sit around the fireplace drinking hot cocoa and eating cookies?"

"Yes," Claire said. "We'd all get so high on sugar, we wouldn't want to go to bed. We'd be up for hours."

"And we'd tell ghost stories to see how badly we could scare each other," Lucy said.

"Yes!" Amelia said, depositing the cookies on the table. "Exactly what I thought we'd do now. Sit by the fire, eat cookies, and share our favorite stories about Grandma."

"What about the hot cocoa?" Jeremy asked.

"I didn't bring any. I figured everyone would prefer wine now," Amelia said.

"You never heard of hot cocoa and Baileys?" Jeremy asked.

Amelia put one hand on her hip. "You know what, Jeremy? Next time, YOU can be in charge of the food and alcohol, since I'm clearly doing such a lousy job."

"I have tea," I offered.

Everyone swiveled their head in unison to look at me. I wasn't sure why I jumped in—this wasn't even my fight. Must have been the second glass of wine.

"It's my own concoction," I added.

Amelia pressed her lips together and shook her head.

I smiled pleasantly. "I am the 'crazy tea lady,' after all. It would be remiss of me to not bring any."

"Did you bring any vodka to go with it?" Jeremy asked.

"That, I unfortunately did not," I said.

"I definitely want to try some," Lucy said. "Maybe not tonight, though."

"Enough with the tea," Amelia said, exasperated. "This is all beside the point. We're supposed to be remembering Grandma, not talking about tea, or cocoa with Baileys, or any other nonsense."

"You were the one who brought up the cocoa," Jeremy began, but just then, there was a flickering of lights, and the room suddenly plunged into darkness.

There was a shriek, followed by everyone trying to talk at once.

"Did we blow a fuse?"

"Where's the fuse box?"

"Does anyone know where Grandma kept the candles?"

"Are there flashlights anywhere?"

"What are we going to do without electricity?"

"Aren't there candles by the fireplace?" That was Claire. Next, there was some banging and loud "ows" as everyone began searching the unfamiliar room in the dark.

"It's a wonder that orange carpet doesn't light the place up," drawled a voice instantly recognizable as Jeremy's.

"Jeremy, that's not helpful." Clearly Amelia, though I noticed she didn't say he was wrong.

"Yes," Claire's voice again. "Right here. Candles. And here, matches."

A moment later, there was a burst of flame, and three candles magically lit on the mantle.

"Are there any more?" Wyle asked. As my eyes adjusted, I realized he was standing next to Claire.

"I think in the kitchen," she said. "The bottom cabinets."

Wyle crossed the room in a few strides, heading toward the kitchen. Everyone else was having a lively discussion about where the fuse box was located.

"Wouldn't it be in the garage?" Eliott asked.

"No, I'm pretty sure it's in the basement," Martin said. "The garage is where the generator is."

"There's a generator?" Elliott asked.

"Yes, but I don't know how well-maintained it is," Martin said.

"So, this happens a lot?" Elliott asked. "Losing power?"

"Often enough," Martin said. "Especially during storms."

"Maybe we should get the generator running and not worry about the fuse box," Elliott said.

"Like I said, I don't know how well it's been maintained," Martin said. "We need to check it out first before we do anything. It would be better if the power came back on."

"You should check the fuse box first," Iris said. "If it's just a blown fuse, you don't need to mess around with the generator. I'm almost positive it's in the basement."

Wyle reappeared. "I found more candles, matches, and a couple of flashlights. Why don't we start by getting some more light in here?" He went over to the coffee table and lined up the candles to light them. "I don't suppose your grandma had a kerosene lamp or anything like that here."

"You know," Iris said. "Now that you say that, I think she did have one. I'm not sure where it is, though. It might be in the basement."

Wyle straightened up. With multiple candles lit, I could pretty much make out everyone in the room again. Plus, my eyes were adjusting to the dimness. The candles created a soft, warm, almost romantic glow along with the non-romantic smell of burning dust. "Okay, we need to go in the basement anyway to check on the fuse box, so we can look for a kerosene lamp then. But my guess is it's something more serious, likely related to the storm."

"If that's the case, should we just get the generator going?" Elliott asked again.

"I would feel better waiting until morning," Martin said. "It would be lighter in the garage then and easier to check it out. It won't kill us to go without electricity tonight."

"Hopefully, it's just a fuse," Lucy said.

"Hopefully," Wyle repeated. "It's an old house, so it's possible. Although I wouldn't count on it."

"See," Amelia said. "We should have had a fire. It would be so much easier to see in here if we had a fire going."

"A fire might not be a bad idea, especially if it turns out not to be a fuse," Wyle said. "Is there wood?"

"There's supposed to be."

"Do you know where?"

"In the woodshed," Amelia said. "Elliott was supposed to get it."

"I couldn't find any," Elliott said.

"Did you look in the woodshed?" Amelia asked, getting more and more exasperated.

Elliott raised his hands in disgust. "I don't know what a woodshed is. I looked in a shed out there, yes, but it was filled with fishing tackle and life preservers."

"That's the boat house," Amelia said.

"Boat house?" Elliott stared at Amelia in disbelief. "How many sheds are out there?"

"Three," Jeremy said. "Not including the garage."

"What's the other shed called?" I asked, fascinated by the conversation despite myself.

"The toolshed," Jeremy said with a grin.

Oh, of course. I should have known.

"So, where is this woodshed?" Elliott asked.

"It's at the end," Claire said. "The farthest from the house."

Elliott looked even more bewildered. "Why is the woodshed the farthest from the house? Wouldn't you want the wood to be closer, when it's winter and snowing out there?"

"Because it's closest to the parking area," Claire answered. "Grandma would always order wood, and it was easier for the truck to pull in there and unload and stack it for her."

"This is why I asked you to get it earlier," Amelia said, "when it first started to snow. We could already have the wood in here and not have to worry about fighting the elements in the dark."

"Ohhhh, now I see," Elliott said, glancing out the window. "I agree a fire would be nice, but the weather is pretty bad out there. Maybe we just skip it for today and plan better for tomorrow ..."

"Fine," Amelia said, snatching one of the flashlights off the table. "I'll go."

"Amelia, I don't think you should ..." Elliott started.

"No, if you don't want to do it, I'll do it myself."

"Elliott is right," Martin said, coming over to her and putting a hand on her arm. "You shouldn't be out there in this weather. Let me go."

"No, it's fine." Amelia said, shaking his hand off. "I'll be fine."

"Amelia, listen to your Uncle Martin," Iris said. "Let him and Elliott go get the wood. You stay here."

"Yes," Martin said. "I'll go get my boots on right now and …"

"No!" Amelia practically shouted, whirling around to face everyone. Her cheeks glistened in the candlelight like a couple of angry tears had sprung forth. "I'll do it myself. No one is taking any of this seriously. Grandma is dead. Dead! We're sup-posed to be celebrating her life as a *family* this weekend, and instead, we have boyfriends and other friends here, and no one is talking about Grandma, and no one is doing anything in hon-or of her. It's like we're just here having a big party, but we're not! We're supposed to be celebrating her life, and instead, I'm the ONLY one who is trying to do anything to honor her, and all I'm getting is pushback. Grandma loved having a fire, so there-fore, I'm going to make sure we have a fire." With that, Amelia turned and stomped off toward the back of the house.

There was an uncomfortable silence.

"Martin, you need to do something," Iris said, but Martin was already turning. "Amelia," he called.

"I'll go with her," Claire said, getting up and walking to the front closet where she'd left her boots and jacket.

Martin looked even more unhappy. "No, that's crazy. You shouldn't be out there dragging wood back any more than Amelia."

"No," Claire said quietly but firmly, her arms full of her win-ter clothes. "This is between Amelia and me. Clearly, we have some things to talk about. We'll be fine."

Martin looked like he wanted to protest, but Claire patted his arm as she passed him, heading toward the backdoor.

"So, while they deal with the wood, we'll take a look at the fuse box," Wyle said. "Elliott, Martin, do you want to come help?"

Neither man looked like he wanted to have anything to do with helping Wyle, but it was also clear they didn't think they could refuse. "I really think I should go help the girls," Martin said.

Wyle handed him a flashlight. "I don't think they want your help. But what if we compromise? They're not back in fifteen minutes, we'll go looking for them. Deal?"

Martin sighed and accepted the flashlight. "Deal," he said, sounding resigned.

Elliott hadn't budged. "I don't know if I'm going to be of much help," he said. "I've never been in the basement."

"Neither have I," Wyle said shortly. "Which is why the more people we have searching, the faster we'll find the fuse box. Now, which way to the basement stairs?"

"This way," Martin said, leading them out of the room.

"That was intense," Jeremy said. He flashed another grin. "Bet you're wishing you hadn't agreed to this madness, huh?"

"Jeremy, you know that basement pretty well," Lucy said from her seat on the bean bag, thankfully preventing me from answering. Why didn't you volunteer to go down and help them find the fuse box?"

"I think your boyfriend has it under control," he said. "Besides, as a general rule, I like to associate as little as possible with cops."

"What a shock," Lucy said.

I noticed that Iris hadn't said anything in a while and glanced over at her. She was hunched over, like she had collapsed in on herself.

It suddenly hit me that Grandma Flo was Iris's mother. I couldn't believe I had allowed that to slip my mind. Again, I blamed that second glass.

I got off the chair and went to sit next to Iris, also conscious that her two children were still bickering. "Are you okay?"

She nodded. "Yeah. It's not like mom's death was a huge shock. Her health had been poor for a while. It was clear she was in a downward slide. But, Amelia is right. We should be focused more on her this weekend. And I should have taken a more proactive role with this whole thing instead of just letting her do it all."

"It seems to me Amelia likes taking charge," I said. "I suspect she didn't mind."

Iris sniffed. "Amelia does like being in charge, that's true. And in so many ways, she's such a Godsend. Sometimes I almost feel like ..." Iris paused, her eyes flickering toward her kids. "She's a good niece," she said.

I wondered what Iris was going to say. Did she wish Amelia was her child rather than her other kids? Did she feel like Amelia was more her daughter than her actual child?

She drew in her breath, as if she was going to say something else, but I didn't get to hear it. At that moment, there was a loud bang followed by a slam, as if a door had blown open, hit a wall, and then slammed shut. It was followed by the sound of loud footsteps and panicked breathing.

Iris pressed her hand to her chest. "What is going on?" she whispered as she struggled to stand.

I was already on my feet. Something wasn't right. I glanced over and saw Jeremy standing, as well. He met my eyes, and I could see he had the same feeling I had.

"Crap," Lucy said, staring down at her pink sweater. "I just spilled my wine."

No one had a chance to respond, because Claire and Amelia appeared in the doorway still wearing their boots and jackets, snow falling off in clumps and landing on the beautiful hardwood floor. From what I could tell in the dim light, their eyes were wild.

"Oh thank goodness. Charlie?" Amelia asked, her voice high and breathy, on the edge of hysterics. "Charlie, you need to come right away."

"Why?"

"I told you, Charlie can't help," Claire said, but Amelia shook her head wildly.

"No, no, Charlie, you need to come now. You need to help him."

"Help who?" Did something happen to one of the men downstairs? But how would Amelia know if she had been outside in the woodshed?

"Amelia …"

"You have to help him!" Amelia yelled. "You can heal people, right? That's what you do with your … those teas, right? You heal people."

"She's not a doctor," Claire said.

"But she's the closest thing we have to someone who can help," Amelia snapped. "You said you brought teas, right? You must have something that could help."

"Claire's right, I'm not a doctor," I said. "And my teas may have health benefits, but it's not like they're medicine. What is going on? Who needs help?"

"We're wasting time," Amelia said, stepping forward to grab my arm. "You have to come."

"Amelia, even if Charlie were a doctor, that's not what we need. We need Wyle. Where is he?"

"You mean Brandon?" Lucy asked. "He's in the basement, trying to find the fuse box. Why do you need him?"

I could only stare at Claire and Amelia. I felt like I had frozen in place as a cold chill snaked up my spine. Wanting a cop sounded ominous.

Claire eyes were wide. Her cheeks and nose were bright red, but underneath, her skin was white. "We found George."

"The lawyer?" I asked. The cold chill circled around my body to my chest, making it hard to breathe.

"Oh, thank goodness," Iris said. "He got here safely. Where is he?"

"He's not okay," Amelia said. "He needs a doctor."

"What?" Iris gasped.

"He doesn't need a doctor," Claire corrected. "He's dead."

Chapter 6

"Dead?" Iris shrieked. "No, he can't be!"

"We don't know if he's dead or not," Amelia insisted, glaring at her sister. "We didn't examine him. And even if we did, we're not doctors."

"He's lying outside in the cold under a tarp," Claire said. "Trust me, he's dead."

"He's under a tarp?" I asked.

Claire nodded.

"Like outside in the snow?"

"No, in the woodshed," Claire said.

"He's in the woodshed?" Iris repeated, her hands fluttering near her face. "Why would George be in the woodshed? What was he doing there?"

"It sounds like someone put him there," Jeremy said.

Iris staggered backward a step. "What? No. Who would do such a thing?"

"I'm just spitballing here, but maybe the person who killed him?" Jeremy said.

"We don't know if he's dead or not," Amelia said again.

"If he's not dead, it's mighty strange he chose to cover himself with a tarp rather than come inside the nice warm house," Jeremy said.

"Maybe he couldn't, because he was too hurt," Iris said. "Amelia is right. We need to bring him inside before it's too late."

"Did someone scream?" Wyle appeared in the room, Martin and Elliott close behind.

"George is in the woodshed," Iris said.

Wyle blinked. "George? Who is George?"

"The attorney," Amelia said. "We need to get him inside and have Charlie look at him."

Wyle looked even more confused. "Charlie? Why is Charlie going to look at him?"

"Because he's hurt," Iris said.

"But Charlie isn't a doctor," Wyle said, before giving me a look. "Are you telling them you're a doctor?"

"No, I am not," I said, exasperated. "Why do you always think the worst of me?"

"You have to hurry," Iris said.

"There's no need to hurry," Claire said flatly. "He's not hurt. He's dead."

"Dead?" Wyle stared at her. "Are you serious?"

"He's not dead," Amelia insisted. "He's hurt."

"He's on the floor in the woodshed with a tarp over him," Claire said. "Does that sound like someone who is still alive?"

Wyle was already in motion, moving toward the closet where his jacket and boots were kept. I headed over and started collecting my own.

"What are you doing?" he hissed at me, keeping his voice low.

"Going with you. What does it look like?"

"No, you're not. If this is a crime scene, it's already been compromised enough."

"I'm not going to compromise anything," I said. "But we have two people with two very different stories about the state of George's health, and if he IS hurt, you're going to need help bringing him back to the house."

He eyed me. "You're going to help me carry a grown man through the snow?"

I pulled my boots on. "I'm stronger than I look. And if we need more help, Claire or Amelia can come back for one of the men, but if George IS still alive out there, we're not going to want to waste any time getting him inside."

Wyle pressed his lips together, but he didn't argue. "I'm going to need at least one of you to show me where George is," he said, grabbing his jacket and striding toward Claire and Amelia. I snatched mine off the rack, knocking another one down in the process, and hurried to keep up.

"See?" Amelia was saying to Claire. "I told you Charlie could help."

Claire shook her head. "I'll go," she said, heading through the house with Wyle close at her heels. I closed the gap between us as I struggled with my coat.

Claire wove her way to the mud room near the back of the house. It was lined with coat racks and low shelves and filled with an odd assortment of shoes. I could see flip flops mixed with hiking boots and galoshes. She put her hand on the doorknob. "Brace yourselves," she said. "It's pretty bad out there. We'll want to stick close together, as it's difficult to see."

"You ready?" Wyle asked me grimly. I finished winding my scarf around my neck and put my gloves on.

"Let's go."

Claire pushed the door open, and immediately, a snowy gust of air blasted us. She bent her head down and stepped outside. Wyle and I followed.

My foot immediately sunk into snow that was deeper than my ankle-high boot, and I could feel the wet, cold chunks sliding inside. My socks were going to be soaked. Luckily, my overpacking would pay off, as I had brought several additional pairs of socks for no good reason. I definitely saw the wisdom in that decision now. The wind whipped about us, pelting me with snowflakes that were as hard as pebbles. It was dark out, but the snow made its own light. I could see how easy it would be to get turned around. I stayed as close as I could to Wyle's broad back as I floundered through the snow, my feet getting wetter and colder by the step.

This was ridiculous. I couldn't imagine George could possibly be alive, even in some sort of structure. But, I had committed, and turning back wasn't an option. I would have to get both Wyle and Claire's attention to tell them I was returning to the house, and with my luck, they would insist on walking me back, which would just be embarrassing.

It felt like it took hours to reach the woodshed, but in reality, it was probably more like five minutes. It was behind another shed, which I presumed was the boathouse. I didn't see the third shed anywhere.

Claire wrestled with the door for a moment before forcing it open, and the three of us tumbled inside. Then, a second fight ensued to slam the door shut behind us.

For a moment, the three of just stood there, trying to catch our breath. The wind howled on the outside, but it felt almost warm where we stood. It smelled nice, too, of fresh-cut wood.

Wyle was the first to recover, clicking his flashlight on and shining it around the space. Directly in front of us was a neatly stacked pile of cut logs, and several were scattered across the floor. "So where is he?"

"Over there," Claire said, clicking her flashlight to the side. A blue tarp was stretched out across the floor, part of it flung back to display George's head.

Wyle muttered something under his breath. "I'm assuming it was one of you who moved the tarp like that?"

"Yes, it was me," Claire said.

Wyle started toward George. "You two stay here," he ordered. He gingerly stepped around the wood, then crouched down near George's head. I couldn't quite see what he was doing, but he stayed there for a few minutes, bending his head to hover his ear near George's mouth and taking a glove off to touch his neck, presumably to look for a pulse. Finally, he straightened and came back toward us. "Definitely dead," he said.

Claire let out a big sigh. "Of course I hoped I was wrong, but ..." she shook her head.

"Did you touch the body?"

"Other than moving the tarp, no," she said. "Shining my flashlight on his face was enough to convince me." Her skin had a slightly greenish tint.

Wyle nodded, then used his flashlight to examine the shed. "It looks like this was the murder weapon," he said, shining his flashlight on a piece of wood that was lying near the body. "Although we'll know more once the medical examiner gets here. Is this shed ever locked?"

Claire shook her head. "None of them are. Not even the toolshed, although that one really ought to have a padlock, as there are … well, at least there were some expensive tools in there. But as far as I know, we've never had an issue with break-ins or anything."

"Any signs that someone was here?"

"Other than George and the wood?" She waved her hand toward the stacked wood. "We didn't stack that wood there. That must have been Hal."

"Who is Hal?"

"Our neighbor. He's lived here full-time for, well, as long as I can remember."

"Where does he live exactly?"

"Just down the road."

"How far down the road?"

"Hmm," Claire paused. "Not far. Maybe a mile? A little more?"

"And he brings you wood?"

"Along with other things. I guess you'd call him a caretaker, of sorts. Grandma paid him to keep an eye on the house, check in regularly, do odd jobs … that sort of thing."

"Would he have any reason to want to kill George?"

"I can't even imagine he even knew George."

Wyle nodded. "Okay, so tell me what happened."

"There isn't much to tell. After Amelia and I came in, we turned on our flashlights like you did and looked around. I saw the blue tarp stretched out and was wondering why Hal did that, especially as I could see it was bunched up in the middle. I thought maybe he was using the shed to store things in."

"'Things'?" Wyle interrupted. "You mean, his own things?"

"Yeah. He's done it before. He's not supposed to. Grandma would always tell him not to, but his house is a lot smaller than ours. Anyway, I wanted to see what he was storing here, so I went to investigate. Amelia told me to leave it alone. It didn't matter, she said. It's not like we were going to call him in the middle of a blizzard to come get it, and we should focus on collecting wood and starting the fire. But ..." she gave her head a quick shake. "Something didn't feel right to me. I wanted to check it out. So I pulled back the tarp and ... well, you saw it. I jumped back. Amelia screamed, dropped the wood she was carrying, and backed up against the door. She started babbling about getting some help for him and bringing Charlie out here. I told her George was dead, but she didn't want to listen. Instead, she opened the door and went running back to the house. Well, maybe not 'running,' as that's not really possible in the snow, but you get the idea. Needless to say, I wasn't about to stay here alone, so I went after her."

"Do you know what tipped you off that something wasn't right?"

Claire shook her head. "Not really. Sometimes, I just get a feeling. That's kind of what this was." She shivered.

Wyle noticed and flickered his light toward the wood. "It doesn't make sense to stand here in the cold. It would be great to get a fire going. Claire, is there anywhere else we could find wood?"

Claire pursed her lips as she thought. "We could check the garage," she said at last. "It's possible Hal may have stacked some in there for us, too. I seem to recall there being some sort of box in there that holds wood, so we wouldn't have to constantly go outside in the cold to keep the fire going. Although I would assume someone would have thought to look in the garage before we trekked out here. On the other hand, it's been so long since any of us have been here in the winter, it's possible no one else remembered."

Wyle nodded, his mouth a thin line. "It's going to be a long night. I think getting a fire going is important to help calm nerves and keep us warm while the electric is out, but I'd rather not use this wood until the rest of the crime scene investigators have examined it. Unless we have no choice, of course." I saw him grimace. "I doubt anyone is going to get much sleep tonight."

Chapter 7

"Who would possibly want to kill George?" Iris asked again to no one in particular.

We were all back in the living room again, our glasses re-filled, except I had swapped my wine for tea. Thank goodness for a gas stove—even with the electricity out, we would still have hot food and water for tea. With the fire blazing in the fireplace and candles lit, on the surface, everything appeared warm and cheery.

But appearances can be deceiving.

"Should we try the phones again?" Amelia asked, cupping her mug of tea. Initially, she had made a face when I brought the tea down, but she ended up accepting a cup, along with Claire. Even though the room was very warm, the chill from the outside felt like it had sunk into my bones. I had a feeling Claire and Amelia felt the same.

"I doubt anything has changed," Wyle said. He was drinking coffee. The coffeemaker wasn't working, of course, but deep in the cupboards, he had located a jar of instant. It was anyone's guess how old it was, but as he put it, it was hot and contained caffeine, which was good enough for him.

The first thing Wyle had done when we returned to the house was locate a phone to report the murder. Unfortunately, along with the electricity being out, the phone lines were also dead.

Needless to say, none of this news was welcome.

"Where's George?" Amelia asked as soon as Wyle appeared in the living room, arms full of wood from the garage. Luckily, Hal had indeed thoughtfully piled more wood in the box, which had been tucked away in a corner of the garage. No wonder no one remembered it being there. "Weren't you able to carry him? You could have waited to bring the wood in."

Wyle didn't immediately answer, instead walking over to the fireplace and dumping the logs on the floor. "George is dead," he said, after straightening up and brushing his jeans off.

"What?" Amelia gasped as Iris wailed. "That can't be. I was sure I saw his chest move."

"You didn't see anything of the sort," Claire said, but it was under her breath, so only I heard her as we deposited our wood next to Wyle's.

"I think we should get a fire going," Wyle announced. "Is there any kindling and paper?"

"Yeah, I put some here," Elliott said, moving toward an antique cabinet.

"What's going on?" Jeremy asked. "What aren't you telling us?"

"I just think we need to get a fire going," Wyle repeated as Elliott brought over a couple of rolled-up newspapers and an armful of smaller logs.

"Why?" Jeremy asked, his eyes narrowing suspiciously. "What's going on?"

"We need to call someone," Iris said. "We need to tell them about George. Martin, go use the phone in the kitchen."

"Phone is dead," Wyle said.

Everyone stared at Wyle, including Elliott, who was in the middle of arranging the kindling and paper.

"Dead?" Amelia asked. In the candlelight, her skin had taken on a greenish, waxy tone, and her eyes were like dark pools.

"It's not a big deal," Wyle assured her. "With the storm as bad as it is, it isn't any wonder that the electricity and phones are out."

"So, it's not a fuse," Amelia said.

Wyle shook his head. "Unfortunately not."

"But …" Iris looked perplexed. "What are we going to do about George? We can't leave him in the woodshed. That's just … unseemly."

"I'm afraid that's exactly what we're going to do," Wyle said firmly.

"But that's just not right," Iris countered.

"Well, it's what we have to do," Wyle said. "We can't disturb the crime scene."

Silence. The only sound was the tiny flame cracking as it spread from paper to wood.

"So that old, stodgy attorney was murdered after all," Jeremy said, attempting to sound like his normal, sardonic self. Instead, his tone came across more like a hollow echo of it.

"Certainly appears to be the case," Wyle said.

"But ... but who would murder George?" Iris asked.

"We won't know that until we investigate," Wyle said.

"Why do you think he was murdered?" Martin asked. "Maybe he just had a heart attack or stroke or something."

"Yeah, that's exactly what happened," Jeremy said drily. "George decided to take a few minutes and explore the woodshed and just happened to have a heart attack while he was in there."

"Maybe it was because he wasn't feeling well that he went into the woodshed," Martin said. "Or maybe he was confused. That can happen when you have a stroke. He thought he was going into the house, but he went into the shed, instead."

"Well, someone else covered him with a tarp," Claire said. "He didn't do that himself."

"What if he was cold?" Iris asked.

"How did his face get covered then?" Claire asked.

"Look, the medical examiner will be able to tell us more, but it appears he was hit in the back of the head, so we're treating this as a murder," Wyle said.

More silence. Then, Amelia stood up. "I don't believe you," she said. "I didn't see anything of the sort. How could you see the back of his head, anyway?"

"If you look closely, you can see the evidence," Wyle said briefly. "I'll spare you the details, but if you want to follow me back out, I can show you."

Amelia turned even paler than before and sat back down.

"Look, there's no reason to panic," Wyle said. "Once the storm blows over, I'm sure the phones and electricity will come back on in no time. It might even be as soon as tomorrow morning. So, let's just sit tight and relax. I'm sure by tomorrow, we'll have this all taken care of."

No one seemed terribly comforted by his words. Jeremy disappeared into the kitchen and brought back the wine while I borrowed a flashlight to fetch my tea.

"Claire, why don't you go with Charlie?" Wyle suggested.

I gave him a sharp glance. "I'm okay. I think I can find my way to the bedroom."

"That's not it," Wyle said with a sigh before straightening his shoulders. "I don't want to alarm anyone, but until we know what happened to George, I think we need to make a point of always going with a buddy."

"Wait, a 'buddy'?" Lucy asked. She had changed out of her stained pink sweater and into an oversized sweatshirt, most likely something of Wyle's. "Why would we need a buddy? Are you trying to say one of us killed George?"

Wyle raised his hands in the air. "I'm not saying anything of the sort. I have no idea who killed George, but for safety's sake, it would be a good idea to never be alone."

Iris pressed her hand to her chest. "You surely can't think any of us had anything to do with this horrible tragedy."

"I'm just saying for safety's sake," Wyle said.

"But that's absurd," Iris interjected. "It couldn't possibly be one of us. It must have been an accident. Or ... or ... maybe George had a heart attack and hit his head when he fell."

"I'm not saying it's anyone in this room," Wyle said. "I'm just saying we should be careful."

"So you're saying it could have been a stranger?" Amelia asked. "You think someone else is here with us?"

Iris gave a little scream, and everyone started talking at once.

"Maybe that's why the phone and electricity don't work," Jeremy said. "Someone cut the lines."

"Oh my heavens," Iris said, clutching Martin's arm. "We're all going to die! We're going to be slaughtered, aren't we? Just like poor George."

"Hold on," Wyle said. "Again, let's stay calm. We don't know when George was killed, so there's no reason to think whoever killed him is still here."

That seemed to quiet everyone down.

"I'm just saying, simply for safety's sake, that we don't go anywhere alone. Just until the phones and electricity are working. There's no need to panic or assume the worst. Okay?"

I looked at Claire. "I guess you're coming with me."

Claire smiled, but it seemed a little forced. "I guess so."

She trotted behind me as I moved up the stairs and down the hall, listening to every creak and groan. I wouldn't have admitted it, but I was glad she was there.

"So, what do you think happened to George?" I asked her, keeping my voice low despite being fairly sure it wouldn't carry to the living room.

"I don't know," she replied, her voice equally quiet. "Who would kill George? Other than the fact he was a lawyer, he was really as bland and inoffensive as toast. I never quite understood Grandma's friendship with him, as she was always so vibrant. But, opposites attract, I guess. I suppose he could have had some sort of secret life we didn't know about, but honestly, he really didn't seem the type."

I reached the end of the hall, opened the door to our room, and snapped on the light. Of course it didn't work. Claire and I both shone our flashlights around the room before we entered.

"Well," I said, closing the door after us and moving over to the bureau to find my tea. "You'd think if he was killed for something he did in his personal or professional life, it would have happened in Redemption."

Claire blanched as she perched on the edge of her bed. "What are you saying? That one of us killed him?"

"Doesn't that make the most sense? You really think someone followed George out here to kill him?"

"Maybe they were trying to throw suspicion off themselves."

I plucked my tea out of the drawer and sat across from her on my bed. "That seems like a big risk. How would they know where George was going? And don't you think he would have noticed a car following him up here? It's pretty remote. Not to mention, how would they know about all the sheds?"

"I suppose," Claire said doubtfully. "But why would any of us kill George?"

"Well, I can think of one big reason," I said. "The will."

"What about the will?"

"Someone didn't want it read."

"But that's silly," Claire said. "Even if they took the original from George, surely there's a copy floating around?"

"If they have the original, they could alter it. Or they could create another version that was signed after the original," I said. "So, even if there did happen to be a copy somewhere, it wouldn't matter, because the last will signed is the one that sticks."

"But that seems really risky," Claire said. "If we ever found the copy and compared it to this new original, it would be clear who killed him."

"IF you ever found a copy," I said. "But, let's set that aside. Do you have any idea as to who was inheriting what?"

Claire shook her head. "I haven't a clue. There's not a lot of money. Some assets … this house, for one. Her house in town. She probably had insurance, along with her investments. Stocks and whatnot. There used to be a lot more money, years ago. My grandpa's family, the original buyers of this house, was wealthy. But most of that is gone."

"So you can't think of any reason why someone wouldn't want the original will read?"

"I honestly can't. Now, it's true Grandma and I weren't that close. Our relationship was on the mend these past couple of years, thanks to Daphne, so while she never said anything to me about the will, it's possible she told other people in the family. So, I don't know anything, but that may not be true for the others."

"Well, maybe it didn't have anything to do with the will," I said. "Maybe the timing is just a coincidence. But I don't know. It doesn't feel right to me."

"It doesn't feel right to me, either," Claire said, her voice strained. "But this is my family we're talking about. I know I've been estranged from them for a long time, and there's plenty of hurt feelings and issues and personal crap between us. Still, I just don't see any of them as killers. Maybe this WAS a horrible accident."

I lifted an eyebrow. "Which is why you found the body in the woodshed?"

"Well, what if whoever did it panicked? Wyle did say it looked like he was hit in the back of the head. Maybe something just went horribly wrong, and whoever did it wasn't thinking straight, so they dragged George into the woodshed and covered him with a tarp. And later, when they had a chance to calm down, they realized what an awful mistake they'd made, but they had already covered it up … and then, they didn't know what to do."

"It's possible," I said, though I didn't think it was likely. If that were true, I would have thought whoever was responsible would have confessed after Claire and Amelia came running into the house. But Claire was clearly still trying to sort everything out in her head and come to terms with the idea that a member of her family was a killer. I didn't think I needed to push her just then. She would likely come to the same conclusions I did on her own.

"We probably should get back down," I said, holding up the tea. "I think we could all use a cup."

"I definitely need something," Claire said.

Now, sitting in the living room, cupping the hot tea in my hands, I listened as the rest of the family went through the same denial Claire had.

"It had to be an accident," Iris fretted.

"We'll be looking into that," Wyle said.

"Or someone followed him up here," Martin said.

Wyle nodded. "Yes, once we're able to open an investigation, we'll look into all of that. What about your neighbors? Can you tell me anything about them?"

"What neighbors?" Jeremy asked. "Did you pass any houses on the way up here?"

"That doesn't mean there aren't people living here," Wyle said.

"Jeremy is right," Amelia said. "We're pretty isolated. Even Hal lives a mile away. But even if we weren't, none of us have been up here in years. I certainly wouldn't know who is or isn't here now."

"Tell me more about Hal," Wyle said.

"Why? You think he had something to do with George's death?" Martin asked.

"You think Hal is trying to kill us?" Lucy asked.

"I'm just asking questions," Wyle said, giving Lucy a look. "I'm certainly not trying to imply that Hal wants to kill anyone."

"But you just said you don't want us to go anywhere alone," Lucy said. "So you must think someone is out to get us. And now, you're asking questions about Hal."

"I'm just being cautious," Wyle said. "We don't know what's going on, so until we do, it's better to be safe than sorry."

"Hal wouldn't hurt a fly," Iris said.

"But he *was* the one who filled the woodshed with wood," Jeremy said. "Right?"

"That doesn't mean he did anything to George," Iris said.

"Jeremy is right," Wyle said. "It would help to talk to Hal and find out when he left the wood and if he saw anything suspicious. He's the caretaker here, right?"

"Yes," Amelia said. "He's been taking care of the house for, well, as long as I can remember."

"And your grandmother was happy with him?"

"Very," Iris said firmly.

"How well do you know him?"

"Well enough to know he's not a killer," Iris said. "Plus, I'm not sure he even knew who George was."

"Did Hal know why you all were coming up here?" Wyle asked.

"Of course," Amelia said. "He was heartbroken to hear about Grandma. I invited him to come by this weekend to celebrate her life, but he declined. Said the family should be spending this time alone."

"Do you know if your grandmother promised him anything?"

There was an uncomfortable silence. "What do you mean, 'promised'?" Amelia asked suspiciously.

"In the will," Wyle said. "Do you think she left him anything, or promised to leave him anything?"

Another uncomfortable silence, except this one lasted longer.

"Is that why you think Hal killed George?" Lucy asked. "Because of the will?"

"I don't know enough to have an opinion on who killed George," Wyle said.

"But it makes sense," Lucy said. "Hal did always like this house. And his house is, well, kind of a dump."

"Lucy! That's enough," Iris snapped.

"Why? It's true," she said.

"Hal did not kill George because he was trying to inherit this house," Iris said. "That's absurd."

"But someone did," Jeremy said. "That's what Brandon is saying, right? That someone murdered George because of the will."

"He's not saying that," Iris interjected, but she didn't sound very certain. "Right, Brandon? I mean, you don't really think George was murdered over the will. It must have been some sort of mistake, or accident. Or maybe George had a heart attack or something."

"I'm not saying anything," Wyle said. "As I said, we're very early in the investigation. It's too soon to draw any sort of conclusions."

"The will should be relatively straightforward," Iris offered.

"How so?" Claire asked.

"Well, you know." Iris shifted in her seat, looking uncomfortable.

"I don't," Claire said. "Does everyone else?"

"Not me," Lucy said.

"Did Grandma say something to you?" Amelia asked her aunt.

Iris looked even more uncomfortable. "Well, clearly, as her daughter, you all know I'm the main beneficiary," she said.

"So we didn't get anything?" Lucy asked.

"Well, I'm sure she gave you kids a little something," Iris answered. "Otherwise, why would she have requested you be here this weekend?"

"But Grandma had two daughters," Claire said.

Iris shifted in her seat. "Of course she did," Iris said. "No one's trying to say otherwise."

"But you *are* implying that my mom ... *our* mom," Claire gestured toward Amelia, who was staring into her tea, "was disinherited."

"For heaven's sake, Claire," Iris said irritably. "Don't be so dramatic. It's not like Daisy is even aware that mom is dead."

"Don't talk about my mother that way," Claire shot back defensively.

Iris flushed. "I'm sorry. That was uncalled for. But honey, you must see the reality of the situation."

"All I know is how much Grandma loved being a great-grandma," Claire said. "I don't believe for a second that she wouldn't have remembered Daphne in her will."

"Well, I'm sure she did," Iris said. "But leaving Daphne a little something has nothing to do with me being the main beneficiary."

"How do you know that?" Claire asked. "Did Grandma tell you?"

Iris looked a little flustered. "If you're asking whether she told me specifically what she was leaving Daphne, no, she didn't. But why would she? As you pointed out, Daphne is her first great-grandchild. Of course she'd leave her something."

"Did Grandma tell you that you are her main beneficiary?" Lucy asked pointedly.

"Not in so many words," Iris said.

Lucy gave her mother a hard look. "In any words?"

"Why are you asking me all these questions?" Iris cried out, her voice plaintive. "I'm not the enemy here."

"No, but if someone killed George over the will, we really ought to find out what was in it," Lucy said.

"Are you accusing me of something?" Iris asked, her voice dangerously quiet.

"No one is accusing anyone of anything," Wyle jumped in, holding his hands up and fixing Lucy with another hard look. She glanced away as she took another sip of wine. "As I said, it's very early in the investigation."

Iris muttered something into her drink. I thought I made out the words "ungrateful" and "brat." Watching the friction between Iris and Lucy, I wondered about their relationship. When Claire had first told me about her family, I assumed it was going to be Claire against everyone else. But it was becoming clear that there were more rifts than Claire's.

"There's another explanation for what happened to George," Jeremy said. "One that doesn't involve Hal or anyone currently in this room."

"You mean a stranger?" Amelia asked.

"Yes, a stranger just happened to be strolling by our very remote house in the middle of a snowstorm, saw George floundering about in the snow, and decided to pop him on the head and drag him into woodshed," Jeremy said.

"Well. You don't have to be such a jerk about it," Amelia said with a huff.

"What about a dissatisfied client?" Lucy guessed. "George was a lawyer, after all. He had to have made some enemies."

"He was a general family attorney," Iris said. "Not a criminal attorney. What sort of enemies does a general family attorney make? No, I'm sure this was an accident or a stranger. Those are the only options that make any sense."

"I suppose a dissatisfied client *is* another explanation, but no, that's not what I was thinking," Jeremy said.

"Then what?" Lucy asked.

Jeremy smiled a sideways smile. "Why, the ghost, of course."

"Oh heaven's, Jeremy," Iris said tiredly, but I noticed a lack of the irritation she'd had with Lucy. "There's no need to dredge up all that unpleasantness."

"Are you talking about the contractor who was killed?" Wyle asked.

"The one and same," Jeremy said.

"Oh, don't tell me you believe in that nonsense," Iris said. "There's no such thing as ghosts."

"Indulge me," Wyle said, turning to Jeremy. "Was the contractor's death similar to what happened to George?"

"I'm pretty sure it was an accident," Jeremy said. "Or I'd think his assistant would have been charged with something."

"He fell off a ladder, didn't he?" Lucy chimed in.

"Yeah, now that you say it, I think that's exactly what happened," Jeremy said. "It was a bad fall. Cracked open his head."

"So he died of a head injury?" Wyle asked.

Lucy's eyes went wide. "Oh! George died of a head injury, too," she whispered. "Maybe it *was* the ghost."

"Nonsense," Iris said again, but her skin looked pale, like it had been leeched of blood.

At that moment, there came sounds of creaking and groaning from above, almost as if someone were walking down the hallway. Lucy let out a little scream as everyone's eyes went toward the ceiling.

"It's just the house settling," Martin said. "That's what this old house does. You kids must remember that."

"I don't remember anything that ever sounded like that," Lucy said nervously.

I glanced over at Claire, and her face was as white as chalk. "Something's not right," she said. "I can feel it."

"Oh, don't you start," Iris said, but her voice trembled. "We don't need any of that talk right now. Everyone's nerves are already on edge."

"Not like this," Claire said. Even her lips had turned pale. "It was never like this."

"Like what?" Wyle asked, his voice gentle.

Claire pressed her lips together and shook her head for a moment. "Anger," she whispered. "Whatever it is, it's consumed with rage."

Chapter 8

"Stop it," Amelia snapped. "Just stop it. You always do this. Suck the air right out of the room."

"I'm just saying …"

"You're not saying anything," Amelia said. "You and I both know whatever *this* is," she waved her hands frantically, "isn't real. You're just looking for attention. Just like mom."

"That's a lie, and you know it," Claire said.

"No, Claire, it isn't." Amelia stood up. "It's about time someone told the truth around here. Mom couldn't sense anything, and neither can you."

"Don't say that," Claire gasped, her eyes wild. "Mom is in that home because of this curse."

Elliott stood up and moved toward his wife, taking her arm. "Amelia, maybe this isn't the time."

Amelia shook him off. "Not now, Elliott. It needs to be said." She turned back to Claire. "Mom is in that home because of bad genetics. Yes, she is cursed, but it's by terrible luck, not some supernatural/psychic thing. She won the dementia lottery. That's it."

"You were always so jealous of my relationship with her," Claire said quietly. "But this is a low blow, even for you."

"I wasn't …" Amelia started to say, but Elliott tried to take her arm again and Martin interrupted. "Kids, enough. Talk about this later. It isn't helping."

Amelia closed her mouth, glaring at both Claire and Elliott, and sat back down.

Wyle turned back to Jeremy. "Has the ghost killed anyone else as far as you know?"

"Oh for heaven's sake," Iris said. "You don't really believe this nonsense."

"No ma'am," Wyle said solemnly. "But I find it best to keep an open mind this early in the investigation, as you just can't know what's going to end up being relevant."

Iris's mouth puckered, like she'd eaten a sour lemon. Clearly, she wanted to say something else, but she kept her mouth shut.

"As far as I know, no one else died because of the ghost," Jeremy said. "But that's probably because no one wanted to spend any time up here after that."

"That's not true," Iris started to say, but Wyle held his hand up, and she closed her mouth again.

"What do you mean?" Wyle asked.

"Grandma never was able to finish the work," Jeremy said. "She couldn't get any other contractor to stay out here to finish. But it wasn't just the contractors. We stopped spending time here, as well."

"Not because of the so-called ghost, though," Iris interjected.

Wyle glanced at her. "So it's true? You didn't come up here as much?"

"It's true, but it had nothing to do with any ghost."

"Then why?"

"Well, because of life," Iris said. "You kids were getting older, and you had things like sports and extracurricular activities, so it just wasn't as feasible as it was when you were younger."

"Hmm," Jeremy said. "I seem to recall we were in plenty of extracurricular activities before and still found time to come up here. It only started tapering off after the contractor incident."

"Well, you were a child. You have no idea how difficult balancing all of it was," Iris said.

"Yeah, I'm with Jeremy," Lucy said, her tone sharper than necessary. "Except it wasn't the contractor's death that stopped the visits. It was Billy."

Silence. Iris stared at her hands, and Martin put an arm around her.

Wyle glanced around, his expression confused. Apparently, no one had filled him in on who Billy was, but he was aware enough of the energy of the room to keep his mouth shut.

"Lucy, I think you've had too much to drink," Jeremy said quietly.

"I'm fine," she said. "Trust me, discovering the body of your attorney in the woodshed can really sober one up."

"Well, I don't think this is really the time ..." Jeremy started.

Lucy slammed her wine glass down on the end table next to her, so hard I thought she might have shattered the glass. "Why?" she demanded. "It's been over twenty years. And you all know I'm right. Has anyone in this room set foot in this house since Billy disappeared? Other than to check a couple of times a year that it's still standing, and Hal hasn't made off with all our belongings? No. When Uncle Billy disappeared, we stopped coming here."

"Lucy, as you pointed out, that happened twenty years ago," Amelia said. "What could it possibly have to do with George's death? Why would you even bring it up?"

"I have no idea if it has anything to do with anything," Lucy said. "But Brandon asked us to tell him everything. He also asked us the last time we were here. The fact that we used to vacation up here frequently when we were younger and now never, ever come needs explanation. And that explanation is two-fold: the contractor died and everyone blamed a ghost, and then Uncle Billy disappeared."

"She's right," Claire said quietly. "Grandma lost her desire to come up here after Uncle Billy."

"That doesn't mean we need to talk about it now," Amelia hissed, angling her head toward Iris. "She just lost her mother, and now we're going to discuss her missing brother? Have a little compassion."

"It's okay," Iris said. "Lucy is right. It has been twenty years. And if it helps Brandon figure out what happened to George, then we need to talk about it."

Wyle cleared his throat. "Billy was your brother?"

Iris nodded. "He was the baby of the family. And an accident. The doctors told my mother she wouldn't be able to conceive again. She had an extremely difficult pregnancy with Daisy—that's Claire and Amelia's mother—and the doctors said she was done. But then, a decade later, she was suddenly pregnant with Billy.

"My mother doted on Billy. I don't know if it was because he was the youngest or the only son, but he could do no wrong in her eyes. Not like Daisy and me." She bit her lip, as if remembering brought her pain. "My mother was pretty strict with us. It often seems parents are more strict with the eldest child, and by the time the youngest comes along, they're so worn down, they let him get away with murder. I don't know if that was the reason or not, but she was a completely different parent to Billy."

"So, what happened to him?"

Iris shrugged. "No one knows. He told us he needed to take a break and 'find' himself. 'Find' himself? He was almost thirty, for goodness sake. But that was Billy. He was a '60s child, often disappearing for weeks or even months at a time, hitchhiking around the country or protesting or whatever.

"Anyway, he told us he was going to join a commune and live there for a while. He wanted to clear his head and focus on 'getting to know himself,' or some nonsense like that. My mother wasn't happy about it. She tolerated his ramblings for the most part, but she really didn't want him moving to a commune, especially because he wouldn't give her any details about it other than it being in California.

"But despite her objections, in the end, he left. And that was it. We never saw him again."

"That's it?" Wyle asked. "Did your mom ever try to get in touch with him?"

"She did," Iris said. "Even hired a private investigator. But it didn't help. Do you have any idea how many communes there were in California in the 1970s? As the years went by and Billy didn't come back or get in touch, my mother became more and more convinced he was dead."

"Wow," Wyle said. "Was there any evidence of that?"

"No," Iris said after a brief hesitation. If I hadn't been watching, I would have missed it—the slight pause and sideways glance at Claire. There was something there ... I just wasn't sure what. I made a mental note to ask Claire later.

"So, what you're saying is, none of you have spent any time here in twenty years?" Wyle asked, looking around the room. Nearly everyone nodded in response.

"And that includes your grandmother?"

More nods.

"If that's the case, does anyone know why she would want you all up here for a weekend to read the will?"

"Because she loved it here," Amelia answered. "It was one of her favorite places."

"But you just said she hadn't spent any time here in twenty years," Wyle said. "How could it still have been her favorite place if she hadn't been here in that long?"

"It *was* her favorite place," Amelia insisted, but her voice faltered. "She surely wanted us to remember a happier time."

"Why now and not sometime over the past twenty years?" Wyle asked.

Amelia's face twisted as she struggled to think of an answer.

"The truth is, we don't know," Jeremy said. "You're right. It doesn't make a lot of sense. And now with George gone, we may never know."

"I'm sure that's not true," Iris said. "There's probably a copy of the will somewhere. And maybe George has it on him. We should go check …"

"No one is going anywhere near the body," Wyle interrupted. "The scene is contaminated enough already. If the will is there, it will be returned to you after we've processed it."

"But …" Iris started.

"No 'buts,'" Wyle said firmly. "Stay out of the woodshed, at least until after the investigators have had a chance to collect evidence."

Iris sat back in her chair, her expression disgruntled.

"Speaking of investigators," Wyle continued. "With any luck, the storm will stop and the roads will be clear enough for them to arrive sometime tomorrow. It's quite late. We should all probably try to get some sleep. Tomorrow will be a busy day."

"I thought you said we should stick together," Amelia said. "For safety's sake."

"We should, but we also need to get some sleep," Wyle said. "We're all sharing a room with someone else, yes? Also, make sure you lock your doors."

"All of us except Jeremy," Amelia said.

"I'll make sure my door is double-locked," Jeremy offered.

"Why don't you stay in our room?" Iris asked. "I think there's a cot in the basement. Martin, go look for it."

"I don't need a cot," Jeremy said. "I certainly don't need to be sleeping in my parents' room at this point in my life. I'll be fine."

"We don't mind," Iris said. "It's not a problem."

"I'm fine," Jeremy said again, tossing back the last of his drink and getting to his feet. "In fact, I bid you all goodnight."

"Wait," Iris said, awkwardly getting to her feet. "At the very least, you can't go upstairs alone. Martin, Elliott, go with him and check out his room."

"Mother, please," Jeremy said rolling his eyes.

"That's not necessary," Wyle said quickly. "I'll go first and check out each room. Everyone else should go up together. Either grab a candle for your room or blow them out. And if you do bring a candle up, make sure you blow it out before you go to sleep."

I stood up, trying not to roll my eyes at his instructions. On the other hand, what did I expect from a cop? I selected a candle from the fireplace mantel. There was a framed photo next to it, and I glanced at it as I removed the candle.

It was a photo of a young boy, maybe ten or eleven. He wore a short-sleeve blue shirt and shorts and was holding a fish he had presumably caught that was almost as big as he was. His grin was wide and infectious. Around his neck was a silver necklace, although I couldn't make out exactly what it was. A St. Christopher's medal, maybe? From what I could see, it appeared to be.

I wondered if it was Billy. I could see shades of Claire around his eyes and the shape of his mouth.

He looked so young and innocent in the photo. What really happened to him? Was he still alive, maybe living in California and soaking up the sun and ocean air?

Or was he dead, like his family suspected?

And why *was* his family so quick to assume that? Wouldn't at least one person still hold out hope of seeing him alive one day? Was there more to the story?

I thought about Iris's pause when she told Wyle that there was no proof of his death.

So why didn't the family believe he was still alive?

"Charlie?" Claire asked. She was standing by the edge of the living room, holding a candle as well. Her face was streaked with shadow, and for a moment, I didn't recognize her. It wasn't Claire, but someone—some*thing*—else pretending to be her, so it could lure me upstairs without my sensing anything wrong …

"Charlie?" The candle wavered, causing the shadows to dance across her face. Her voice was uncertain.

I blinked, and just like that, everything went back to normal. It was Claire, my friend, waiting for me to follow everyone upstairs. "Are you okay?" she asked.

"Yes," I said, smiling even though I wasn't sure she could see it. "Everything is fine."

Chapter 9

A cold, wintery light was just beginning to brighten the house when I eased my way out of the bedroom, careful not to wake Claire, to make my way to the kitchen. I made a point of locking the door behind me.

I was not in a good mood, having gotten very little sleep. Every creak and groan the house made had jerked me awake. I had a feeling I wasn't the only one. Claire was tossing and turning as well, only finally falling into an exhausted sleep shortly before dawn. I wasn't as lucky.

All I wanted was a cup of coffee, which in and of itself put me in a worse mood. I rarely drank coffee, and the fact that I was sneaking downstairs to the kitchen for it, of all things, left me feeling faintly disgusted with myself. I would even settle for that foul-looking, and probably foul-tasting, instant Wyle had the night before.

After Claire and I had settled in our room, door locked (although it was only one of those privacy locks) and chair dragged in front of it for good measure, I asked her about Billy, and why the family was convinced he was dead. "I mean, there's no proof," I said. "Right? So I don't understand why everyone would give up so quickly."

Claire didn't respond for a moment, instead focusing on putting her candle down on the nightstand so she could dig through the bureau for her pajamas. "It's hard to explain," she said finally. "I'm not even sure I completely understand."

"Well, with the snow, it appears we're stuck here for a while, so might as well give it a try."

She turned her back to me as she pulled her sweater off, the flame flickering at the sudden gust of wind. "I think it's because my mother told Grandma that he is."

"Your mother?"

Claire nodded as she dressed in her night clothes. I decided to follow her lead and get my own pajamas on. "I told you it was hard to explain."

"But that doesn't even make sense," I said. "How did your mother know what happened to Billy, but not your grandmother?"

"It was one of her 'feelings.' She knew Billy was dead. She wasn't going to say anything to my grandma about it, because Grandma usually didn't want to hear anything about mom's feelings, but this time, Grandma asked. And mom told her the truth." Claire paused as she finished dressing and pulled the bedspread back to get into bed. "I was there when Grandma came over. We had just gotten home from school. Amelia was in her room, probably on the phone. I was in the kitchen with mom having a snack when there was a knock on the door. Mom was really surprised to see her. Grandma rarely dropped in unexpectedly. Well, she rarely dropped in at all, at least at our house. Normally, we only saw her at family get-togethers. But there she was, and she came in and sat down at the table. Mom got them both coffee. It took her a few minutes to ask ... I think partly because she didn't want to do it in front of me and risk upsetting me. Little did she know it wouldn't have been a shock. I had already sensed the same thing as my mother. Anyway, while she was sitting there stewing about it, Mom figured it out and sent me into the family room to watch TV. But I only pretended to go. Really, I hid in the utility-room closet.

"My grandma had to convince my mom to tell her. My mom kept denying she had had any feelings, but Grandma refused to believe her. Anyway, she eventually told her that yes ... she felt Billy was dead.

"I thought Grandma would yell at my mom ... tell her she didn't want to hear about it, but she didn't. Instead, after a moment's pause during which she seemed to gather herself, she got up stiffly, thanked my mom, and left. I suspect she wanted to get out of our house so she could fall apart in her car. Anyway, after that, Grandma was convinced Billy was dead, and no one could tell her otherwise. Other family members, especially my aunt, tried to persuade her there was still a chance he was alive. Eventually, though, everyone in the family came to believe it."

"Did your grandma tell anyone? That this is why she believed Billy was dead?"

"I don't know. I always suspected she told Aunt Iris, but maybe Aunt Iris just figured it out on her own. She was always touchy about the subject. Of course, it was her brother we're talking about, but ..." Claire shook her head, pressing her lips together. "Aunt Iris had this way of getting especially irritated and annoyed when it came to my mother. Whatever happened between them when they were children, they never outgrew it. It was too bad, I guess. I think Mom was especially sad about it, but Aunt Iris made it perfectly clear she wanted as little to do with my mother as possible."

I was silent, thinking about my own strained relationship with my sisters. I too often wished things could be different, but there was too much water under that bridge. There were some things in life you could never undo, no matter how much you might want to.

"Did your mother ever say anything more about what happened to Billy?"

She shook her head. "I'm not sure she ever knew anything more. I always hoped a cop would show up on our doorstep with news about what really happened to Uncle Billy, but alas, that never happened. I suspect he ran into the wrong people while he was on the road. Or maybe that commune wasn't all it was cracked up to be."

"You really think it happened on the road? I mean, this IS Redemption, after all. You know how people tend to disappear."

Redemption, Wisconsin, had a very troubling past. Back in the late 1880s, all the adults disappeared. It had been a particularly hard winter, so some deaths were expected, but when spring rolled around and people started visiting the town again, they found only children.

The children claimed they didn't know what happened to their parents and the other adults. One morning, they woke up, and they were gone. To this day, no one knows what happened to them.

Since then, there had been many strange occurrences linked to Redemption—disappearances, hauntings, murders, madness. There was no question that the percentage of unexplained events was much higher in Redemption than in other areas, and that was probably the reason the townspeople were convinced that the town itself decided who would live there. This of course doesn't make any sense. A town can't do anything like make decisions and carry them out.

Yet sometimes, it seemed the only explanation.

"At first, I did wonder about that," Claire said. "You can't live here and not think Redemption may have had something to do with a disappearance. But the longer it goes on, the more I think that, if it was Redemption, it would have revealed itself by now."

"You don't know that, though," I said. "Maybe the timing wasn't right."

"Maybe. Regardless, I don't see the connection between Billy disappearing and what happened to George. I get that Wyle wants to know everything, because it's his job to, but I personally don't see what the two have to do with each other." Despite the confidence in her words, her tone didn't match, and her expression was pensive.

"Did George and Billy know each other?" I asked.

"Of course. George has been a friend of my grandmother for as long as I can remember. But I don't remember George and Billy having any sort of relationship. They really just exchanged a few pleasantries when they ran into each other."

"So you don't think George would have anything to do with Billy's disappearance, then."

"What?" Claire looked shocked. "No. Of course not. Billy left on his own accord. I doubt George was even aware of what was happening until after Billy had been gone for a while."

Listening to Claire, it seemed to me she was right—there was no connection between Billy and George.

But that didn't stop something from niggling at me.

Needless to say, I should have known there was no way I was going to calm my mind down enough to fall asleep, but I also didn't particularly want to wander around the house in the dark by myself, either. As soon as it was light enough so I didn't think I would be stumbling around (or have someone sneak up on me), I pulled on a pair of jeans and a dark-blue heavy turtleneck sweater and headed for the kitchen.

I crept down the hall, trying to be as quiet as possible. I was sure no one had slept all that well, but if anyone had happened to finally fall asleep, like Claire, I didn't want to wake them. I made it down the stairs, hitting only a few creaking steps along the way, and padded my way into the kitchen.

And nearly screamed when I saw Wyle standing there.

"You scared me," I said, pressing my hand against my chest.

Wyle gave me a bemused look. He was holding a mug, presumably of that awful instant coffee. "Good morning to you, too," he said. "Also, I feel like I should point out, you're the one sneaking up on me."

I moved into the kitchen, heading for the stove and kettle. "I didn't think anyone would be up this early."

"Neither did I."

I eyed Wyle as I filled the kettle. He had dark circles under his eyes and needed a shave, both of which gave him a haggard look. "How well did you sleep?"

He took a sip of coffee, wincing slightly at the taste. "Apparently as well as you."

I smiled despite myself. "I guess I deserve that. Anymore of that powdered drudge?"

He reached behind him to produce the jar, waving it at me. "I didn't think you drank coffee."

"Under normal circumstances, I don't. These are not normal." I reached into the cupboard for a mug before rummaging around for a spoon.

"Well, as soon as Martin is up, I'm hopeful we'll get the generator started. Then, we can have a real cup of coffee."

"That would be nice." I said as I measured the mixture. "What would be even nicer is getting out of here today."

"Yeah, that would. Unfortunately, I don't think it's happening."

"Why? The cops will need to ask us questions, right? Can't they do that at the station?"

"They could," Wyle said. "If it would clear up enough for us to leave."

I stared at him, then hurried to the front window.

Snow was *everywhere*. There must have been five feet piled in drifts. Everything—the trees, the bushes, the roads—was covered in a blanket of white. There was a certain soft, untouched beauty about it … so white that, even without the sun, it created brightness.

But the utter stillness, the isolation, made me shiver.

Not to mention it was still coming down.

"Unless there's a snowplow in the toolshed, I just don't see us being able to go anywhere today," Wyle said. He had come up behind me as I continued staring out at the beautiful-yet-bleak scene. "It's not like anyone is going to prioritize plowing these roads when I'm sure Redemption needs to be dug out first."

"Well, if they're able to repair the phones, you could tell them there's a body here," I said. "That might move us up on the list of priorities."

"It probably would," Wyle agreed. "Do you see that happening anytime soon?"

I squinted at the falling snow. "Probably not. At least not until the snow stops."

"Exactly. I think we're on our own. At least for another day."

I turned to stare at Wyle. His face was impassive as he sipped his coffee, his thoughts carefully hidden. "Do you think we're in danger?"

"Why do you ask that?"

I gave him a hard look. "I saw the body. George didn't cover himself up. Someone here knows what happened to him."

"Probably. But that person isn't necessarily in this house."

"Oh? You think 'Hal-the-Helpful' is to blame?"

"Or a different neighbor." It was his turn to give me a hard look. "What makes you think someone in this house is guilty?"

I rolled my eyes. "If you're going to interrogate me, I'm going to need some coffee." I brushed past him to head back to the kitchen. While it was true I wanted coffee, I also didn't want to be overheard. Standing in the living room with its open staircase was giving me the willies, like I was being watched. The kitchen was at least tucked away in a corner, making it less likely someone could sneak up on us without the creaking and groaning of the floorboards giving him or her away.

I ignored Wyle strolling in after me as I made my way to the stove to prepare my coffee-sludge. "Well?" he asked.

I turned and saw him leaning against the counter, one eyebrow raised, waiting for me to answer. I focused on stirring my drink. "Wyle, you're being ridiculous."

"Why?"

"Because the answer is obvious," I said impatiently. Man, what I would do for some cream. Even though I knew opening the fridge was a no-no when the electricity was out, I wondered if it would really matter. Martin should be getting the generator working soon, I reasoned. Would it be that big of a deal if I opened the fridge for thirty seconds to retrieve some cream?

"How is it obvious?"

"Wyle, for heaven's sake, you know why."

"Brandon."

I blinked at him. "What?"

"My name is Brandon."

"What does that have to do with who killed George?"

"Probably nothing."

"Then why are you bringing it up?" I asked crossly.

"Well, as we're both guests and neither of us are here in a professional capacity, don't you think it makes sense to call each other by our first names?"

Wyle tilted his head as he studied me, his expression innocent, but I was suddenly aware of how alone we were. The only two downstairs while everyone else was tucked away in their rooms, behind locked doors. My stomach did a strange flip.

"But you have a girlfriend," I said. "Who is currently upstairs."

"And what does *that* have to do with you calling me by my first name?" he asked.

"But ... it's ...." I realized I had no idea how to answer him. All I knew was it didn't feel right to call him by his first name— like it would signal some sort of shift in our relationship. A dangerous shift. Calling him "Wyle" felt safer. For both of us.

I also realized I didn't want to think about it anymore. And I especially didn't want to think about why I was so against calling him "Brandon."

Argh. Enough. I yanked open the fridge, deciding I didn't care anymore. I desperately needed the coffee, and I didn't think I could bear it without cream. If all of the food inside the fridge rotted away over the weekend, so be it.

"You shouldn't open the fridge when the electricity is out," Wyle said.

"There are a lot of things that shouldn't be happening," I countered as I rummaged around the shelves. The fridge was definitely well-stocked, which was good to see. Food wouldn't be an issue, and if the generator was to become one, it might make sense to just cook it all that afternoon. "Which is why I require cream in my coffee to deal with it all." I located the half-and-half near the back with a triumphant "ah-ha."

"Okay, so what were talking about?" I asked as I straightened up, cream in hand.

"You agreed to call me 'Brandon,'" he joked.

I rolled my eyes as I poured the cream into my 'coffee.' That most definitely wasn't going to happen. "Besides that. You haven't told me if you think we're safe or not."

"You haven't told me why you think we might not be."

"Because anyone else doing it doesn't make sense," I said. "I know you know this. Unless that supposed ghost can manipulate the physical environment, it has to be a current member of this household."

"You don't think it could be someone else?"

I took a sip of my doctored coffee, trying not to make a face. The cream made it tolerable. Barely. I wondered if I had enough ingredients to do some baking. That would take my mind off of everything. "I don't see how anyone else could have timed it right," I said. "As far as I can tell, George never made it to the house. So, someone must have intercepted him on his way here, hit him on the head, and dragged him into the woodshed. What are the odds it could have been someone who wasn't already here?"

"Hal is here," Wyle pointed out.

"You and I have different definitions of 'here,'" I said. "Hal is at least a mile away, according to Amelia. Or maybe it was Iris."

"Also according to them, Hal comes here a lot," Wyle said. "A mile isn't that far away. He could have gotten here earlier in the day and hidden in the woods. For that matter, anyone else who lived in this area also could have arrived early and waited in the woods for George."

I raised my eyebrows. "You think someone was hiding in the woods in a snowstorm?"

"Stranger things have happened."

"Yes, but a snowstorm?"

"Maybe the person waited in the car. Or maybe there's a structure out there we don't know about."

I thought Wyle was reaching. "Snowstorm aside, you're also assuming other people knew George would be arriving yesterday," I said. "As far as I know, Amelia was the only one who knew. How would anyone else have found out?"

"George could have said something."

My eyes widened. "You think George told his killer where he was going to be?"

Wyle shrugged. "Why not? Again, we'll know more once the M.E. is able to examine the body, but he was clearly hit on the back of the head. That means he turned his back on his killer, which likely means he trusted him or her on some level."

"Well, if that's the case, then maybe this is less about the will and more about George," I mused.

"Or, it could still be about the will, and whoever killed George used their friendship against him."

I gave Wyle a hard look as I took another sip of coffee. At least it was getting easier to drink. "You're really convinced the will is the motive, huh?"

"It's what makes the most sense," he said, echoing my own thoughts during my conversation with Claire. "If it was something unrelated, why didn't it happen while he was in town? This seems to me a really long way to go to kill someone. Plus, how would they know how the property is laid out, or about the woodshed?"

"Maybe it's a distraction," I said. "They wanted to throw the investigators off the real trail."

"Maybe, but again, my money is on simplicity."

"Okay, but if the will is the motive, why are you arguing that the killer might not be in this house? Supposedly, everyone who is going to benefit from it is under this roof right now."

"Until the will is read, we don't actually know that," Wyle said. "Flo could have set it up so only certain members of the family had to be here to inherit. Also, we don't know if there's someone out there who thinks they should have inherited, and didn't … hence, their motive for getting George and the will out of the way. Either way, it all seems to lead back to the will, to me."

What Wyle said made sense on the surface. Killing George so as not to reveal the contents of the will did seem the most obvious motivation. It was also certainly possible that the will was the motive, and the killer wasn't under the roof.

And yet …

"Okay, let's play your game," I said as Wyle raised an eyebrow. "Who do you think did it?"

A ghost of a smile touched his lips. "Who do you think did it?"

"No fair. I asked you first."

Now, he did smile. "Well, for starters, I know it wasn't me."

I rolled my eyes. "Seriously? Well, I know it wasn't me or Claire."

"How do you know it wasn't Claire?"

"Because I was with her, remember? We drove here together."

"Were you with her every single minute since you got here?"

"Were you with Lucy every single minute?" I retorted.

"Actually, no." His expression was thoughtful. "I left her in the room for a bit to unpack and freshen up."

I stared at him. "Seriously? You suspect your girlfriend?"

"I didn't say that," he corrected. "I said I wasn't with her the whole time."

"So, what? You think she's capable of sneaking out when you weren't looking? Or that Claire is?"

"Probably not," he said. "But I will tell you in a murder investigation, you need to look at everyone."

"Well, then, what about you?" I asked. "What were you doing while Lucy was freshening up?"

"I was on the phone."

I didn't expect that answer. "On the phone? With who?"

"I had some work business I needed to sort out," he said.

"Were you in the kitchen?" I was trying to picture Wyle standing in the kitchen while Amelia exasperatedly banged pots and pans.

"Actually, the den. There's a phone back there." In the back of the house, there was another large room not quite as big as the living room, but still a decent size. Along with a fireplace and the obligatory 70s decoration, it also housed a large console television. "I wanted some privacy."

"So basically, you don't have a clue who might have snuck out and offed George."

"Alas, no," he said. "Although nailing down the time of death will make things easier."

"Who was here when you and Lucy arrived?"

"Amelia, Elliott, Iris, and Martin."

"Those four? They seem like the least likely suspects," I said. I was having a hard time imagining any of them clobbering George on the head.

He eyed me. "You're forgetting about Jeremy."

"No, I'm not. He came after us, remember?"

"Which might have given him the perfect opportunity," Wyle said. "He could have been waiting in his car for George to arrive, and once George did, he could have walked with him to the house … except George never made it to the house. Once he got rid of the body, he circled around and pretended to just get here."

I had to admit, that made a certain amount of sense. "But Jeremy seemed surprised to hear that George was coming."

"It's called 'acting,'" Wyle said.

There was a creak on the stairs, and we both jumped back. Even though I knew we weren't doing anything wrong, I was also feeling something close to guilt. Maybe because discussing the possibility of one of your hosts being a killer didn't feel very polite.

A few minutes later, Martin appeared in the doorway. "Oh," he said in surprise. "I didn't think anyone was up yet."

"I'm not sure if I ever went to sleep," I said.

A smile touched his weathered face. "I can understand that." He glanced around the room. "Is the electricity back?"

"Nope," Wyle said. "And it doesn't look like it's going to be any time soon, if the snow doesn't let up."

Martin's eyes widened. "Still snowing, eh? I guess I better go check out the generator. Cross our fingers there isn't anything wrong with it."

I held up my hand with my fingers crossed. "Good luck." I smiled, trying to hide my disconcertion. The idea of being stuck there for who know's how long with no electricity made me want to run screaming into the snow.

Wyle must have sensed my unease, because he flashed a quick smile at me, which only managed to ratchet my edginess … but in a different way.

And then, it hit me.

Wyle never did answer my question about whether or not we were safe.

Chapter 10

Seeking a few minutes of privacy to get myself together, I headed to the downstairs bathroom. Martin had left to tinker with the generator, and Wyle had disappeared upstairs, but not before reminding me about his thoughts on amateur detectives.

"You know, you don't have to worry about solving this," he said. "In fact, it might be better if you don't get involved. You might inadvertently taint the investigation."

I stared at him in amazement. "What was that conversation about then? You were asking me for my thoughts on the case. Why would you do that if you want me to stay out of it?"

"Well, I was curious," he said, his expression a little embarrassed. "Plus, it helps to talk things through, especially with someone objective. It's not like I have a lot of options."

He had a point. Even though it wasn't likely that either Lucy or Claire had anything to do with George's death, neither were objective, as it was their family making up the suspect list.

But still ...

"Admit it," I said. "You like my help, don't you?"

"I most certainly do not," he said firmly. "The more people involved in an investigation, the more likely something gets messed up. It would definitely be better if you kept a low profile."

I guffawed. "I'll take that under advisement."

"I mean it," Wyle said, but his tone was resigned. He probably knew everyone in the entire house was bound to play amateur detective.

At least I had a proven record of solving cases.

As soon as Wyle headed upstairs, I hurried to the bathroom and locked myself inside. I needed a moment to get my racing thoughts under control.

I sank onto the toilet, rubbing my temples with my fingers, trying to ward off a monster headache that was just waiting to pounce. With no lights, the bathroom was dim, but not too dark. A high, small window let in enough light from outside to at least make out what everything was, but honestly, I welcomed the dark. It felt soothing to my dry, burning eyes.

Could it be possible? Could someone in the house have killed George? Even though I of all people knew how far people will go under the right circumstances to protect something (or someone), I was having trouble wrapping my brain around killing an attorney over the contents of a will.

Was someone so greedy that they couldn't bear the idea of anyone else inheriting a piece of Flo's estate? Even if it was as small as Claire believed it to be?

Or … was it that they were financially desperate? That made more sense to me. Someone got in over their head, and it was all about to crash down around them, so they had no choice but to try and eek out whatever money they could get out of Flo's estate.

I would have to put that bug in Wyle's ear, although knowing him, he was probably already thinking along the same lines.

In fact, the more I thought about it, the more the word "desperate" applied to George's murder. Whoever killed him took an awfully big risk. And hiding him in the woodshed covered only by a tarp? Especially knowing the rest of us would be in there fetching wood? Why didn't the killer drag George's body off to a different shed—the toolshed, for instance—that no one apparently used? Of course, the snow probably complicated things, and leaving a body outside, even if covered by the elements, probably felt like too big a risk.

Despite Wyle talking about a neighbor lying in wait, the whole thing felt sloppy and unplanned to me. Like the killer felt like he (or she) had no choice.

Which also probably meant the rest of us were more or less safe. I couldn't believe whoever killed George would have the stomach to kill a half-a-dozen (or more) relatives. They would likely try to brazen this out, hoping the police never figure out what really happened. Isn't it something like over 80 percent of murder cases remain unsolved? Maybe the killer was hedging their bets.

Maybe.

I massaged my fingers against my temples. I could just tell the headache, most likely caused from lack of sleep, was going to be bad. Maybe more coffee was the answer. Hopefully, Martin would get the generator going quickly, which would mean the coffee maker would work, and I could have a real cup. In the meantime, splashing some cold water on my face would help.

I stood up and moved to the sink, which is when I saw the dark lump in it. Sure it was some sort of animal, like a rat or a squirrel that had somehow fallen in the sink and died, my initial reaction was to jump back in disgust. But then I remembered how Amelia had spent the past few days cleaning the house from top to bottom. It was highly doubtful she would have missed a dead animal in the middle of the bathroom.

I stepped closer, wishing I had a flashlight or even a candle, peering through the darkness to make out what it was. It didn't move, so I reached down and poked it.

It felt like wet yarn.

What on Earth …

Creak.

I jumped and let out a little shriek. It took a second to catch my breath and realize someone likely wanted to use the restroom. Man, the whole weekend had put me really on edge. "Just a minute," I called out.

Silence. Then, another creak.

"I'm just finishing up," I yelled. I thought I was loud enough, but apparently not.

More creaks. It sounded like someone was pacing on the other side of the door.

"There are other bathrooms, if you're in a hurry," I yelled. What was going on out there? Why would someone walk back and forth outside a bathroom and not answer back? Surely, I had been loud enough to hear. Or …

What if it's the ghost? I thought.

It popped into my head so suddenly, I let out a gasp and took a step back from the door. Images of the dead contractor filled my mind.

How did a ghost kill a contractor, anyway? No one had explained that.

No. That was ridiculous. A ghost couldn't have killed George. And even if it were possible—like it somehow scared George to death—there was no way it could have then also covered him with a tarp.

Right?

Creak.

I gasped despite myself, taking another step back from the door. Trying to calm myself, I reasoned that even if a ghost had killed George for some inexplicable reason, that didn't mean it was after me. And it certainly didn't mean it was outside the bathroom right then, causing the floor to creak.

At that moment, the lights burst on way too brightly, causing me to let out yet another shriek and jump back again. I really needed to get a decent night's sleep. I was way too on edge.

I shielded my eyes, allowing them to adjust to the brightness. Clearly, Martin succeeded with the generator, or the electric company was able to fix whatever caused the outage. Regardless, the good news was that we finally had electricity.

With the lights on, I started to feel a little silly about my reaction to the creaking floorboards. If it wasn't a person, then it was probably just the house settling. Definitely not a ghost.

I could also finally make out what was in the sink. Whatever it was, it was pink. I poked at it again, trying to figure out what it could possibly be. It sort of reminded me of a sweater ... but why would a sweater be in the bathroom sink?

Then I remembered. Lucy had spilled red wine down the front of her pink sweater after Amelia and Claire burst in with the news about George. Of course. There was no electricity then, so she couldn't have tossed it in the laundry. Thus, she soaked it in the sink.

Now that the electricity was on, though, I figured it was time to get it into the washing machine.

I moved the sweater aside so I could finally splash that cold water on my face before heading off in search of Lucy. Yet as I pressed the towel to my face, I found myself strangely reluctant to open the door.

I told myself I was being silly. I hadn't heard any creaks in the last few minutes, so clearly, there was nothing there. Just the sounds of an old house.

That was it.

Still, I remained rooted in place, staring at the doorknob.

Enough. I was being ridiculous. I'd lived in my own haunted house for long enough to know that house hauntings were overrated. Sure, there was the occasional unexplained occurrence of an unsettling dream, but all in all, it wasn't that bad.

Although I never had to deal with an unsolved murder in my house. I knew exactly who was responsible for all of the deaths.

I gave myself a quick shake. Unless I planned to spend the rest of the day in the bathroom, it was time for me to leave.

I marched to the door, unlocked it, and before I could lose my nerve again, threw it open.

The hallway was empty.

Of course it would be. Did I really think there would be some apparition hovering outside, waiting to pounce the moment I emerged?

Feeling more than a little embarrassed, I continued my march to the kitchen.

Lucy and Wyle were already there when I arrived, standing very close. Feeling like I was interrupting a private moment, I nearly tripped over myself to keep from entering the room.

Of course, my flailing got Wyle's attention, and he glanced over at me.

"Sorry," I said. "I didn't mean to interrupt."

"You didn't," Wyle answered as Lucy reluctantly stepped away. She shot me a look that made it very clear I most definitely was. She wore a baby-blue sweater set and was perfectly made up, which I found impressive, considering the lack of light. Her blonde hair was pulled back in a loose ponytail, and a couple of strands framed her face.

"Lucy, I'm glad I found you," I said, deciding to ignore her obvious displeasure at my being in the kitchen. In reality, there were a lot of folks staying in the house—if she thought she was going to get some private alone time with Wyle this weekend, she was in for a world of disappointment.

Lucy raised a perfectly shaped eyebrow. "Oh?"

"I found your sweater."

She gave me a confused look. "My sweater?"

"From yesterday? It's soaking in the downstairs bathroom."

Her expression cleared. "Oh, that's right. I forgot I left it there."

"Good to see everything is working," Martin said behind me as he brushed past and headed to the sink to wash his hands.

"No problem with the generator?" Wyle asked.

"Nope. Hal did a good job of keeping it maintained," Martin said as he busied himself at the sink.

"Great! Now we can have a real cup of coffee," Lucy said. But instead of moving to make it, she gave Wyle an expectant look.

"Lucy, is there a washing machine here?" I asked.

Lucy eyed me. "Washing machine? Yeah, there should be one in the basement."

"Perfect. We can get your sweater washed, then."

Finally, she turned to me, hand on her hip, eyes narrowed. "Why are you so interested in my sweater?"

What I wanted to say was that there were nine adults in the house and three bathrooms, so it would be nice if one of them didn't have a sweater in the sink. But I held my tongue. I didn't need to start an argument, especially since I was pretty sure I wasn't the only one feeling on edge. Instead, I forced a smile on my face. "It's such a pretty sweater. I would hate to see it ruined by a spill. We don't want to stain the set."

"That's why I soaked it overnight. So it wouldn't stain." She frowned, and then let out a sigh. "You're right. I probably should put it in the washer. Brandon, do you want to come with me?"

Wyle's eyes flickered toward me. "I thought you wanted the coffee started," he said smoothly. "Charlie could probably go with you."

Me? The last thing I wanted to do was go down into the basement with his girlfriend. And by the way Lucy's expression flattened, she felt the same.

"Oh, but I would feel safer being in the basement with you," she said.

"I don't mind making the coffee," I offered.

Wyle waved his arm at both of us. "You'll be fine," he said. "I was down there yesterday, remember? Let me focus on getting the coffee started while you and Charlie take care of your sweater."

Wonderful. Since it was my idea, I could find no good reason to refuse.

Lucy gave me a tight smile, then disappeared to fetch her sweater. Wyle grinned at me before turning his attention to the coffee maker.

"That better be the best coffee ever," I said.

His grinned widened. "I'm here to serve."

Lucy appeared at my elbow before I could think of a suitable answer. "Ready?"

"Sure." I gave Wyle one last glance before following her to the basement.

Even with the electricity on, it wasn't very bright. The stairs felt rickety beneath my feet, and I could smell mildew. Lucy muttered under her breath as she picked her way down, and I clutched the handrail, which also felt a little wobbly.

Lucy pulled a chain, illuminating another dusty, naked lightbulb, and I found myself blinking at the scene. The place was a mess … everything from tattered boxes to broken appliances. Half-finished wooden beams crisscrossed the walls in one area, and there was a half-built wall in another.

"This place really is a disaster," I said, following Lucy as she wove her way around the mess. "I'm surprised the guys made it to the fuse box without tripping over something."

"I suspect there was plenty of tripping," she said as she maneuvered around the piles. "Although if you think this is bad, you should see Grandma's main house. It makes this look like a *Better Homes and Garden* shoot. Grandma was always a bit of a hoarder, but that tendency increased as she aged. Here we are."

She pulled the string of another naked bulb. The ancient washer and dryer were pushed up against the wall. Next to the washer was an old utility sink, and above it, a plain set of cupboards. A few feet away was a makeshift wooden structure complete with a door in the front.

Lucy stared at the machine. "I forgot how old it is," she fretted. She studied the wet sweater in her hands, which had dripped all the way through the house and down the stairs.

"Think there's a delicate cycle?"

She snorted. "I doubt it. On the other hand, if it ends up stained, it's ruined anyway." The harsh light of the bulb revealed her thick makeup, and how it still didn't cover the bags under her eyes or the tension around her mouth. Now that I was closer, I could also see how bloodshot her eyes were. Remembering how much she had drank the night before, I was amazed she wasn't acting more hung over.

She started fiddling with the washer while I went to the sink to look for laundry detergent. Nothing other than cobwebs and mouse droppings there, but in the cupboard above, I found a box of a very old off-brand laundry detergent I had never heard of before.

She peered at it, clearly disappointed. "Is there anything in there for delicates?" she asked. "Like Woolight?"

"I think this is it." I rattled the box. "Unless there's something in there." I angled my head to point to the structure with the door.

Lucy furrowed her brow. "Where?"

"There. Where that door is. It looks like a pantry of sorts."

She glanced over, and her forehead smoothed out. "Oh, that. That's the cistern."

"Cistern?"

"Yeah. If you hadn't figured it out yet, this house is old. Like almost a hundred years old. That's how they got water back then."

"I don't understand."

She sighed loudly. "I don't know all the details. You'd have to ask my dad to explain it, but basically, it was a way to store rainwater from the roof. Clearly, we don't need it now, as we have indoor plumbing. So, Grandma walled it off."

I stared at the door. There was something about it that felt … off, to me. But what?

"What does it look like?"

"Just like a big cement tub. Nothing all that exciting. I think Grandma wanted to pull the whole thing out with the remodel, but we know how that worked out. Now what are you doing?"

I had moved over to the door and was trying to open it. "It's stuck."

"The wood probably just swelled up," she said. "That happens a lot here."

I jerked harder. "I don't know. It feels different than that."

Lucy gave me an exasperated look. "I'm sure that's all it is. What, you think we lock it or something? Why do you want to go in there, anyway?"

"I just … I've never seen a cistern before. I was just curious." While that was true, there was also more to it. I couldn't put my finger on it, though. All I knew for sure was that I wanted to get a look at the cistern.

"It's really not that exciting. Trust me. Can I have the laundry detergent, so I can start the washer?"

I looked down, realizing I was still holding the ancient box. I gave the door a final, frustrated jerk (it still didn't budge) before returning to Lucy.

She sighed as she took the detergent, pouring it into the machine. Chunks of rock-hard powder dropped out.

"I guess you're right about the moisture level," I said. "Maybe the door did just swell."

She looked sadly into the machine.

"Your sweater should be fine," I offered. "It's just one wash."

She still didn't move, just continued staring at the sad, wet little bundle. Then, she gave herself a quick shake, muttered something that sounded like "screw it," and slammed the lid of the washer down.

I expected her to turn it on and immediately turn to leave, but instead, she paused and started digging around in the front pocket of her jeans. A moment later, she produced a thin tube. Lip gloss. She twisted off the cap and started to apply.

"How did you meet Brandon?" she asked, giving me the side-eye. I was a little mesmerized by how well she applied the shimmering, pale-pink gloss without a mirror.

"During one of his investigations."

"He was investigating you?"

"Not exactly." I wondered where she was going. "More like my friends and clients."

"So your friends and clients have problems with the law?"

"Initially, sometimes. But we get it sorted out in the end," I said.

She put the cap back on her lip gloss and rubbed her lips together. "You know, I think Brandon's mentioned you a few times."

"He did?" I wasn't sure how I felt about that.

She nodded. "Yeah. He talked about a 'Charlie' interfering with his cases."

I relaxed slightly. That sounded like something Wyle would say. "I don't know if I was 'interfering.' I like to think of it as helping."

She leaned against the washer. "I think he would prefer to do without your help."

"That may be, but we don't always get what we want."

Her eyes narrowed briefly. It hit me that she was acting like some sort of jealous girlfriend. Did she really think I was after Wyle? I wanted to tell her she had nothing to worry about—that I didn't have the least bit of interest in Wyle—but before I could figure out exactly how to say it, there came a scream from upstairs.

Chapter 11

"What happened?" Lucy yelled as we burst out of the basement. "Brandon, are you all right?"

"Someone tried to kill me!" It sounded like Amelia.

"What?" Lucy demanded as we both ran toward her voice, which was coming from the kitchen.

Quite a scene greeted us. Amelia was huddled on one side, and Wyle was near the counter, examining a smoking toaster oven. A bitter, burnt odor was filling the room.

"What happened?" Lucy demanded as Claire and Jeremy appeared in the kitchen. Claire looked disheveled, a robe tossed over her pajamas and her hair a mess. "And what is that horrid smell?" Lucy continued, wrinkling her nose.

"Someone tried to kill me," Amelia said again.

"I don't know about that," Wyle said.

"How else do you explain it?" Amelia demanded. "I was almost killed!"

"It was probably an accident," Wyle said.

Amelia's eyes widened. "An accident? George is dead outside, and you're calling this an 'accident'?"

"Amelia, what happened?" Claire asked, keeping her voice calm. Her face was puffy, and she raised a hand to rub one side of her head, as if she had a headache. I could definitely relate.

She pointed. "That."

I followed the direction of her finger. It was impossible to tell if she meant the smoking toaster oven or Wyle.

"Did Wyle do something to you?" Claire asked.

"Wait, you're saying Brandon tried to kill you?" Lucy asked, aghast.

Wyle put his hands up as Amelia said, "Not Brandon, unless he's the one who rigged the toaster oven."

"The toaster oven?" Jeremy questioned, his voice holding a note of disbelief. "You think someone used *the toaster oven* to try and kill you?"

"It's the perfect crime," Amelia said, her voice haughty. "Everyone would think it was an accident." She glared pointedly at Wyle.

"I'm still confused," Claire said. "How did the toaster oven almost kill you?"

"I was going to make breakfast," Amelia said, "since no one else got anything started yet. And I knew everyone would be up soon and feeling hungry, so someone had to."

Claire was making a Herculean effort to not roll her eyes. "Okay, you're starting breakfast. How does the toaster oven fit in?"

Amelia sniffed. "Well, I was going to make eggs and toast." She nodded to the stove, where a large frying pan sat along with eggs, butter, and milk. "Maybe some bacon, too. I hadn't decided."

"Can we hurry along to the part where the toaster oven makes an appearance?" Jeremy asked as Claire hid a smile.

Amelia glared at him. "You know, you're perfectly welcome to jump in and cook healthy meals for NINE adults. It's not easy …"

"Amelia," Claire interrupted, raising her voice. "We all appreciate everything you do. And we also want to keep you safe and healthy, but we can't do that if we don't know how the toaster oven almost killed you."

"The toaster oven tried to kill Amelia?" Iris gasped. She was standing in the doorway, dressed in a blue-and-white striped dressing gown. Her face was greasy, as though she had put one some sort of night cream and hadn't taken a moment to wipe the residue off her skin yet. "You poor dear. How did it happen?"

"That's what we're trying to find out, Mom," Jeremy said. "Amelia hasn't gotten to that part of the story yet."

Amelia looked like she was ready to throw the toaster oven at Jeremy, but after a quick glance at her aunt, thought better of it.

"As I said before, I hadn't decided on the bacon yet, but I knew I wanted to make toast, so I was getting it started. After I dug out the toaster oven and wiped it off, I went to plug it in, and there was a bang. Then, smoke started coming out of it."

"Oh, heavens," Iris said, pressing a hand against her mouth. "You poor child. Are you all right? Charlie, did you examine her yet?"

"Charlie isn't a doctor," Claire said yet again.

"But someone should make sure she is all right."

"I'm fine," Amelia said. "*For now.*"

"What do you mean 'for now'?" Iris asked, perplexed. "Amelia, maybe you should sit down. Someone get her a glass of water."

"I mean, I'm fine until someone tries to kill me again."

Iris's eyes went wide. "Someone is trying to kill you?"

"I just told you that. The toaster oven," Amelia said impatiently. "Clearly, someone sabotaged it."

"Well, hold on," Wyle said. "We don't know if the toaster oven was sabotaged. It looks pretty old."

"Yeah, maybe rats chewed the wiring or something," Elliott added.

Amelia recoiled. "Rats? You think there are rats running around the kitchen?"

"Well, honey, no one has lived in this house for a while," Elliott said. "Who knows what happened to the toaster oven."

"Martin," Iris said. "Go look at it. See if there are signs of rats."

"I don't see any signs of anything being chewed," Wyle said, "which doesn't mean it wasn't. And while yes, I agree we should examine the toaster oven and see what made it spark, I really don't think this was intentional."

"Of course it was," Amelia said.

Wyle looked like he was trying to keep his patience. "Why do you think someone intentionally tried to kill you?"

"Well, isn't it obvious?" Amelia asked, astonished. "I found the body."

"*We* found the body," Claire corrected. "And no one attacked me."

"Not yet," Amelia said.

Wyle closed his eyes briefly. "Even if you're correct, and someone is targeting you, sabotaging the toaster oven seems like a stretch. The killer would have no way of knowing you would be the one to plug it in."

"Well, of course it would be me," Amelia said. "I'm the only one doing the cooking."

I stepped forward. "How would everyone like some fresh-baked zucchini bread for breakfast?" I smiled at their flabbergasted expressions.

"You're going to make zucchini bread?" Amelia asked suspiciously.

My smile widened as I started rolling up my sleeves. "Why, yes. I saw some fresh zucchini in the fridge, and if you're okay with me using them, I'll get started. Does everyone like it?"

"That should at least get rid of the awful burnt smell," Lucy said.

"Zucchini bread is great," Jeremy said. "There are some bananas over there, too."

I turned to look. "Oh, why so there is."

"I would prefer banana bread if we have a choice," Elliott said.

"Seriously," Amelia snapped. "Someone tries to kill me, and you want banana bread?"

"I'll make both," I said, heading to the sink to wash my hands. "How does that sound?"

"And I'll make the eggs," Claire jumped in, pulling her hair into a ponytail. Despite the exhaustion around her lips and eyes, her face was determined. "Maybe some bacon, too. We have cheese, right? Let's do a few omelets." She winked at me as she moved to the fridge.

Amelia opened her mouth and closed it. "I can make the eggs," she said, her voice small.

"Nonsense," I said with a smile. "Your aunt is right. You should rest after what happened. I'm sure after a nice breakfast, all will feel better."

"Then it's settled," Iris said, clapping her hands. "While they take care of breakfast, Martin, you go look at the toaster oven."

"I'll have to go get some tools," Martin said.

"I can go," Elliott volunteered. "Where are they?"

"Martin, go with him," Iris said, turning to leave the kitchen. "Elliott doesn't know where anything is."

"Well," Wyle said, pushing the toaster oven to the side. "I'll get out of your way and let you bake. How much time do you need?"

I was already lining the ingredients up on the counter. "Give me twenty to thirty minutes."

Wyle flashed me a quick smile as he backed out of the room, followed by Lucy.

Amelia was still standing in the same place as before.

"Seriously, Amelia, we've got this," Claire said. "Grab yourself a cup of coffee and go relax. You've earned it."

Amelia didn't immediately answer, but she looked like she wanted to argue. She was dressed more casually this morning, in jeans and a blue sweatshirt sporting a glass of red wine and the words "It's five o'clock somewhere" on the front.

"Go on," Claire said again, and that finally spurred Amelia to move.

As I watched her pour herself some coffee, I wondered why she was being so hesitant to leave Claire and I alone in the kitchen. Did she actually think one of us was going to poison her food?

Or was there something she was hiding that she didn't want us to discover?

* * *

Martin and Elliott arrived with a toolbox about the same time I was taking bread out of the oven. "Perfect timing," I told them as Martin set it next to the toaster oven. "Breakfast is on the table. After you eat, you can figure out what happened with the toaster."

Jeremy was already helping himself to a piece of zucchini bread as the rest of the group filed in and found seats at the table.

"This looks wonderful," Iris said as Claire placed the pile of bacon in front of her.

"A few days like this, and I might not fit into my clothes anymore," Jeremy said, winking at me.

"Oh, I don't think that will be a problem," I said. "There's plenty of shoveling to do … that'll burn off all sorts of calories."

Jeremy winced.

"Speaking of shoveling," Amelia said. "Are we going to be able to leave here soon?"

"It looks pretty bad out," Wyle said.

"Yeah, it's still snowing," Elliott said, reaching for the banana bread. "I doubt the plows will get up here for a while. Maybe another day or two."

"A day or two?" Amelia and Lucy said it in unison.

Elliott paused to look at them. "Well, yeah. We're pretty far out. They're going to focus on making sure the streets in town are clear first, and then they'll make it up here. But since it's still snowing, it's going to take a bit to finish the town first."

"But George," Iris said. "We can't leave him in the woodshed for days on end. It's … unseemly."

"Would you rather bring him in here?" Jeremy asked.

Iris blanched. "It just doesn't seem right, is all," she said. She was much more presentable now, having changed into a cream sweatshirt that had an embroidery of a pair of cardinals. She had also brushed her hair and washed her face.

"It's actually better to keep him out there," Wyle said. "The shed will protect him from the elements, and the cold will help preserve his body. It's really not much different from the the freezers in the morgue."

Iris blanched again. Clearly, that was more information than she wanted to know about George's future once the police arrived.

"What about the phones?" Amelia asked.

Wyle shook his head. "My guess is, the weather needs to calm down before the lines work again."

"This is awful," Amelia said. "We're sitting ducks out here. What are we going to do if whoever killed George tries to kill one of us?"

"There's no evidence that anyone is in danger," Wyle said. "We don't know what happened to George."

"But the toaster oven …" Amelia began.

"Could have been a simple accident," Wyle finished smoothly. "Again, let's not jump to conclusions yet."

Iris reached over to pat Amelia's hand. "Martin will get to the bottom of whatever is wrong with the toaster," she said. Amelia gave her an unconvincing smile.

"So, this is what I suggest," Wyle said. "We accept that we're likely going to be here for another day, maybe two. We remain calm. We have heat, food, and now electricity, so we're going to be fine. And while I do think we keep our eyes open and be aware of our surroundings, there's really no evidence that anyone else is in danger. So let's not assume the worst."

"But if you don't think we're in danger, why did you tell us last night not to go anywhere alone?" Amelia asked.

"Because it was dark, and tempers were high," Wyle said. "It was safer for everyone to stay together. Plus, we had just found George, and there was a lot we didn't know. But now that some time has passed, and nothing else has happened other than the toaster oven blowing up," he gave Amelie a hard look as she opened her mouth to protest, "it seems safe to say we're likely going to be fine until the roads open again."

"That seems reasonable," Elliott said, even as Amelia gave him the side-eye. "What?" he asked. "Not panicking is always a good idea."

"Even when your own wife is in danger?" she asked bitterly.

"Honey, we don't know that yet," Elliott said, giving the rest of us an embarrassed look. "Let's let your Uncle Martin look at the toaster before we jump to any conclusions, okay?"

Amelia muttered something under her breath, but thankfully chose not to continue the argument. There was an awkward moment of silence, until Claire rose to start clearing the plates. I stood to help her.

"You two made breakfast. You shouldn't be cleaning up as well," Iris protested before addressing her daughter. "Lucy, why don't you help?"

"Me?" Lucy asked. "What about Jeremy?"

"It's fine," Claire said quickly. "Someone else can handle lunch and dinner. We can rotate the cooking and cleaning."

"I better get started on that toaster oven," Martin said, standing up. "Great breakfast, girls." Elliott jumped up, thanking us for the food as he followed Martin into the kitchen.

I scraped the leftovers off the plates and into the trash, then moved to the sink to fill it with hot, soapy water.

"Well," Martin said. "This is a little weird."

"What is?" Elliott asked.

Martin held out the toaster oven. "See these scratches?" I craned my neck to get a look.

"Oh, what do you think it means?" I asked.

Martin glanced over at me. "It may be nothing, but it does look like someone tried to take these screws off at some point."

"So, what … are you saying it was sabotaged?"

"Well, we don't know for sure," Martin said before asking Elliott to find him a screwdriver. "Who knows when this happened. Maybe one of the kids was messing with it years ago and scratched it up."

"Wow," I eyed Amelia, who was still sitting at the table, trying to determine if she was hearing us. She didn't appear to be listening. Between the hot water running and Elliott digging in the toolkit, it might have simply been too loud.

"Hey! Ouch," Elliott said, jerking his hand back.

Martin glanced at him, his eyebrows furrowing. "What?"

Elliott stared at his hand. "I'm bleeding."

"You're what?" Martin adjusted his glasses and put the toaster down while Elliott showed him his hand. "How did you do that?"

"I have no idea."

"Elliott, come wash off your hand," I said, turning on the water and gesturing. "Claire, is there a First-Aid kit here somewhere?"

Claire was back at the table. "A First-Aid kit?"

"Yeah." Elliott had moved to the sink, and I dunked his hand into the sudsy water. He hissed under his breath. "Elliott cut himself."

"He what?" Claire came closer, and Amelia rose from her chair to see what was going on, as well.

"Something in the toolkit got him," I said, examining the cut. "Man, this is deep. Martin, can you find what did it?" I was worried Elliott might need a tetanus shot, and soon, it it were a rusty nail. If it was really gnarly, he might even need a course of antibiotics.

Martin was already rummaging through the toolbox. Wyle had wandered back in by then as well, and was looking over his shoulder. "I think I found it."

"What is it?" Elliott asked.

"A knife. But ..." he paused, confusion in his voice. His eyebrows were knitted together as he stared into the toolbox.

"But what?" Elliott asked.

Wyle peered over Martin's shoulder. "Wait," he barked out. Martin glanced at him surprise. "Don't touch it."

"Why?" Martin asked as Wyle hastily looked around the kitchen before yanking off a sheet of paper towel. He nudged Martin aside and reached in with the paper towel to remove the knife.

"Elliott, are you okay?" Amelia asked. "What's going on?" There was a shrillness to her voice.

Wyle held up the paper-towel-wrapped bundle and carefully peeled back the paper.

It was a chef's knife.

Amelia gasped.

"Is that what I think it is?" Claire asked.

"What would that be doing in the toolbox?" Lucy asked.

"Let me see the handle," Amelia demanded. Wyle carefully moved the paper aside to show the dark, wooden handle.

"It can't be," Amelia muttered and swiftly turned to march across the kitchen and snatch a knife out of the wooden block. "Look at the handle," she said, waving it around and causing Elliott to duck. "That's the exact knife that went missing."

Silence. We all stared at the knife in Wyle's hand.

"But … I don't understand," Claire said. She was pressing her fingers to her temples again. "You said George was hit in the head, right? So, why hide this knife?"

"George was definitely hit in the back of the head, but I didn't examine him," Wyle said. "Remember, I didn't move the tarp. So it's possible he was also stabbed."

"Wait, you think that's the murder weapon?" Amelia asked, pointing at the knife.

"At this point, I don't know what to think, but I have to keep all possibilities open," Wyle said. "This knife may not have anything to do with what happened to George. But it's sure suspicious, it ending up in a toolbox."

"I agree, it's strange. But it's also possible that Hal needed the knife for something, and when he was done, he stuck it in the toolbox and forgot about it," Martin said.

Every eye swiveled toward Martin. "This is Hal's toolbox?" Wyle asked.

Martin looked nonplussed. "Sure is."

"I knew it," Amelia said, slamming her hand down against the counter. "I told you Hal was behind all of this."

"But why would Hal kill George?" Iris asked. "There must be some other explanation."

"There's a chef's knife in his toolbox," Amelia said. "And he probably sabotaged the toaster oven, as well."

"And we will certainly ask Hal all our questions," Wyle said. "In the meantime, is there a bag somewhere I could use?" He bobbed the knife he still held.

Amelia blinked at him for a moment and started digging in one of the cupboards for a plastic bag. I went back to washing Elliott's hand.

"Could we get a First-Aid kit, or at least some bandaids? And maybe some antiseptic cream?" I asked again.

Iris seemed to rouse herself. "Oh. Of course, dear. Back in a jiff." She hurried off.

I turned to Elliott to give him a comforting smile and let him know we'd get his hand taken care of in no time, but my smile died on my lips.

Elliott was as white as a sheet.

Chapter 12

"Well, that was a quite a morning," I said, handing Claire a cup of tea. She was sitting on the long sofa in the living room that faced the large window overlooking the snow-covered yard. I sat down next to her, releasing a long sigh as I lay my head back against the cushion.

The day wasn't even half over, and it already felt like it had lasted a week.

While Elliott's cut was deep, I didn't think it so deep as to cause him to nearly faint, but that was precisely what happened. Or, perhaps it was the combination of all the stress we had been under over those couple days and the lack of sleep from the night before. Either way, it was quite the production—we had to get him into a chair so he could put his head between his knees, all while I kept the pressure on his hand to keep the bleeding down and Iris fluttered around getting in the way. Then, Amelia suddenly decided she needed to help, too, and started getting in the way. I felt like I was spending most of my energy keeping those two calm rather than on helping the person who was actually bleeding.

Eventually, Elliott's breathing went back to normal, and he started regaining a little color in his face. I finished cleaning and bandaging the cut before instructing Amelia to help him to the bedroom to lie down. Once all that was done, I still had a kitchen to clean.

"How is Elliott?" Claire asked, taking a sip of tea. She still didn't look well, her face pinched as she continued fighting a headache.

"He'll live. Although I told him he should get it looked at by an actual doctor as soon as we get back to town. Who knows what was on that knife."

Claire shook her head. "A knife in the toolbox. Who would have thought?"

"I know. But what is especially strange to me is that, if George *was* stabbed with that knife, at some point, the killer snuck into this house and stole it, and no one even noticed. So, when did he do that? After he hit George on the head? Or did he already know he was going to kill George and took the knife a few hours or maybe even a few days before?"

Claire shivered. "That's an unsettling thought."

"And why that knife?" I continued. "I mean, why not just use one of the tools to kill George, instead of sneaking around the house and grabbing a knife?"

"When you put it like that, it doesn't make much sense," Claire admitted. "Unless ..." she paused, tilting her head as she thought. "Do you think the killer is trying to confuse us? Throw us off the scent?"

"Possible," I said. "Although it still seems convoluted. I was actually wondering if maybe someone is trying to set up Hal."

Claire's eyes widened. "Oh. Now there's a thought."

"Yeah, because it's so obvious. A chef's knife doesn't belong in a toolbox. So to use it on George and then hide it there seems fairly intentional."

"Right. If someone was trying to set up Hal, he'd want to make sure the knife was found in his toolbox," Claire said, immediately picking up my train of thought. "So of course, you'd then need to create a reason to get the toolbox out."

"Like a toaster oven practically blowing up."

We both stared at each other as it all started to slowly sink in. "That would mean ..." she said. But then she paused, her face growing paler.

"That it might be one of your family members," I finished quietly.

She pressed her lips together and shook her head. "No. I can't believe it."

I didn't say anything, just sipped my tea as Claire wrestled with her thoughts. "It can't be true," she finally said. "But ..." She let out a long sigh and rubbed her temples.

"Can I ask you a few questions about your family?" I asked. "It might help get to the bottom of this mess and prove they *didn't* do it."

I could see the struggle on Claire's face. On one hand, she would love to prove they didn't have anything to do with George's murder. On the other, what if it proved they did?

She sat there for a moment before giving herself a quick shake. "Okay, let's do this. What's your theory?"

"Well, I have two," I said. "The first one is Jeremy."

Claire looked surprised. "Jeremy? But he got here so late."

"We *think* he got here so late," I corrected. "It's possible he was here much earlier and just hiding out somewhere. But what I don't know is whether he's handy enough to have sabotaged the toaster oven."

She thought for a moment. "Probably. I mean, I don't know for sure. But growing up, he spent time fixing cars with Uncle Martin. I'm sure he would know enough to be able to do something like that. But I can't imagine him a killer."

"Well, can you see any of your family members as killers?"

She half-smiled. "I suppose not. But why would Jeremy kill George?"

"My guess is that it has something to do with the will, but we won't know for certain until we can figure out the how."

Claire wrinkled her forehead in confusion. "But Jeremy is pretty successful," she said. "He wouldn't need Grandma's money."

"What does he do?"

"He sells insurance. He's really good at it."

I could totally see that. "Well, even if someone is making good money, it doesn't mean they don't want more," I said. "You also don't know if he got himself into some sort of financial trouble. Maybe he's got some vice, like gambling or something."

"I suppose," Claire said doubtfully.

"Okay, so I was also wondering about Elliott."

"Elliott?" Claire looked surprised. "I can't see Elliott hurting a fly, much less killing George. And again, he wouldn't need Grandma's money."

"So he's successful too?"

"Well, he's not unsuccessful," she said slowly. "He's a manager somewhere ... I think at the Piggly Wiggly. But Amelia does pretty well. She runs the lab at the hospital."

"She makes more than him?"

"I would imagine, although I've never asked," Claire said.

I thought about how Amelia treated Elliott almost like a servant rather than her husband. "Do you think they're happily married?"

Claire gave me a look. "I have no idea. Remember, I haven't talked to my sister in years."

"But you see the same thing I do. Do they look like a happy couple?"

"Amelia doesn't treat anyone well," Claire said. "She's always been that way. Frankly, I was shocked when I heard about her promotion at the hospital. I always thought she should be the last person to manage others. As for Elliott, I figured he must not mind the way she is, or he wouldn't have married her."

"Well, maybe he does mind," I said. "Maybe her constant nagging has worn him down."

"Possible, but then why wouldn't he just leave her? Why kill George?"

"Well, again, money," I said.

"But Elliott wouldn't inherit," Claire said. "He's not related to Grandma."

"But Amelia would," I said. "And once the inheritance is finalized, he would get half in the divorce."

Claire squeezed her tea cup. "That's really cold."

"Well, whoever murdered George likely did it for money, so it would be cold," I said. "Do you think he could have fiddled with the toaster oven?"

"I really don't know Elliott very well, so I have no idea," she said. "Although ... he did offer to get the toolkit for Martin."

"And he was also wandering around outside when we got here," I said. "He could have easily grabbed the knife, killed George, and then hid it in the toolkit."

"But then why didn't he get the wood?" Claire asked. "He should have brought the wood in. Because he didn't, we found the body."

"Someone would have found the body anyway," I said. "And if he had brought the wood in, he would have been suspected immediately. Pretending he couldn't find the woodshed makes sense."

"Hmmm," Claire said, taking another sip of tea. "Elliott."

"Also, he could have put a bug in Amelia's ear about using the toaster oven," I said. "I mean, if Amelia wanted to make toast for nine adults, why didn't she use the big oven?"

"And why was she making toast, anyway?" Claire mused. "She could have chosen a different breakfast meal."

"Yeah, and if you're already unhappy with your wife, setting her up to get a bad shock or worse …" I shrugged. "It's like killing two birds with one stone."

Claire tapped her finger against her mug. "You make a lot of sense, but I still have a lot of trouble picturing Elliott as a killer. He's just so … "

"Vanilla?"

"I was going to say 'passive,' but 'vanilla' works, too."

"People can hit their limits," I said. "And once they do, you don't know how they'll react."

"I suppose," she said, but she still sounded skeptical.

I hesitated. Amelia being in on it crossed my mind. She and Elliott could have done it together, but I dismissed that thought almost immediately. Amelia had been so upset finding George, I didn't think it was acting. And I also didn't see her knowingly giving herself a shock with a faulty toaster oven.

But still, there was something off with her … something more than her clear dislike of Claire, but I couldn't put my finger on it. There was definitely something going on with her, although it was also possible that it didn't have anything to do with the murder at all.

"It's also possible it really is Hal after all," I said. "Do you think he's capable of doing something like this? Killing George and stealing a knife and hiding it in his toolkit?"

"You could ask him yourself." She nodded toward the window. A figure was outside snow-shoeing toward the house, a light covering of snow dusting his dark coat like powdered sugar. "There he is."

I stood up so suddenly, I spilled tea across the front of my favorite purple sweatshirt, which read "New York" and displayed the city's skyline in pink. Hal was moving faster than seemed possible through the white drifts.

"Wyle," I shouted. I wasn't sure where he was exactly—the last I'd seen him, he was accompanying Amelia and Elliott to their bedroom with Lucy hot on their heels. "Wyle!"

Almost like magic, Wyle appeared in the doorway. "What?"

I pointed. "It's Hal."

Wyle came forward to watch Hal moving toward the front door. "Well, I'll be," he muttered, slicking his hair back.

"What's going on?" Lucy asked.

"It's Hal," Claire said.

"Hal?" Lucy looked completely shocked. "Why would he be here?"

"Probably to check on us," Claire said. "Remember how he would do that when we were kids? He was always stopping by to make sure we were okay."

"Yes, but … now? In a snowstorm?"

"I imagine that's exactly why he would want to check in now." Claire gave her a strange look. "You don't think he had anything to do with this, do you?"

"Of course not," she said, but her expression didn't look convinced.

I wondered if maybe she wasn't as innocent as I had presumed in all of this.

"What happened?" Amelia's voice floated down from upstairs. "Why are you calling for Brandon?"

"Hal is here," Lucy said.

"Hal?" Amelia's voice rose a notch. "He has the gall to show up *here*?"

"Maybe we give him a chance to explain before …" Claire said, but Amelia didn't seem to hear her. She was already marching down the stairs, calling for Elliott.

There was a loud stomping on the porch as Hal presumably removed his snow shoes and knocked off the extra snow. Then, a knock at the door.

Wyle was the one to open it. "May I help you?"

"Oh!" Hal blinked in surprise. "I'm Hal. I keep an eye on the house for Flo. Well, at least I used to, God rest her soul. I was just coming by to check and see how everyone was doing after the big storm."

"Hal." Amelia stepped forward, a bright smile on her face. "So nice to see you."

Hal glanced over, a smile spreading over his own face. "Amelia. There you are. Everything good?"

"As good as can be expected. Please come in." She gestured broadly with an arm.

Wyle stepped back, allowing Hal to enter. "I'm so sorry to hear about your grandma," he said awkwardly. "She was a good, decent woman."

"Thank you," Amelia said smoothly. "Why don't you come sit down? Can I get you a cup of coffee?"

"That would be great," Hal said. His expression was bewildered as he gazed around at all of us crowded into the living room watching him, but he didn't say anything as he began removing his outer layer of clothes.

He looked quite elderly, but it was possible he appeared older than he was—if he was outside a lot, his skin would appear more wrinkly and weatherbeaten than normal. His greying hair was cut very short, military-like, and when he spoke, it was slow and deliberate. He was also in surprisingly good shape, probably thanks to all the snowshoeing.

Amelia took his coat and invited him into the kitchen, and the rest of us trailed after him. "I see you got the generator running," he remarked.

"Thanks to you," Martin said. "You did a good job keeping it maintained."

Hal ducked his head, but I could detect a faint blush on his cheeks. "Well, just doing my best," he said.

"Is the electricity out where you are, as well?" Wyle asked.

"Yep. Phones, too. But I reckon you know that," Hal said.

"Have a seat," Amelia said, placing a hot cup of coffee on the table in front of one of the chairs. "Cream or sugar?"

"Just black. Thank you." He continued to awkwardly stand, glancing uncomfortably around at each of us, no doubt wondering what was going on.

"So," Amelia began, but Wyle put a hand on her arm. "Amelia, maybe we should start with introductions. I don't think I've had the pleasure of meeting Hal." He stuck out his hand. "I'm Brandon Wyle. Lucy's boyfriend."

"Hal Tyson."

They shook hands. "Any relation to Mike?"

Hal grinned. "I wish."

"You know everyone else, right?"

"Hmm." Hal pursed his lips as he started to search the group, but I held out my hand. "I don't think we've met," I said. "I'm Charlie Kingsley, Claire's friend."

He shook my hand, his grip warm and firm, before continuing his perusal and nodding in recognition of the others. "I'm sorry again about your loss."

"Thank you," Claire said quietly.

There was a moment of silence. "Want to sit down and enjoy that cup of coffee?" Wyle invited.

Hal smiled back and seated himself.

Wyle sat down next to him. "Amelia, would you mind bringing some coffee for the rest of us?"

Amelia was getting ready to sit across from Hal, but she stopped short at Wyle's request. Her expression tightened as she glared at him. He smiled pleasantly at her. I could see her struggling with how badly she wanted to tell him off—it was written all over her face. But her eyes fell on Hal, who sat patiently waiting, and she stood back up to head to the kitchen.

"I like my coffee black," he called out to her retreating back.

She paused and turned back around, a sugary sweet smile on her face. "Anyone else want some?"

"I'll take a cup," Jeremy said.

"So will I," Martin said.

"A cup of coffee would be lovely, dear," Iris said. "And maybe some leftover banana bread?"

Amelia's sugary smile turned hard. "Of course. Claire? Charlie?"

"I'm fine with tea," I said, moving to the table and taking a seat. Even though I wouldn't mind another cup of coffee, with the murderous expression in Amelia's eyes, I didn't trust what she might do to it.

"So am I," Claire said, sitting next to me.

Lucy declined as well, and Amelia continued on to the kitchen.

"So," Wyle said. "That was some snowfall, wasn't it?"

Hal nodded, picking up his cup to take a sip. "I haven't seen a storm that bad since, well, maybe the ice storm of '76. Remember that one, Martin?"

"I do. That was one for the ages," Martin said.

"The powerlines frozen, and pure ice everywhere," Hal shook his head. "The snow hasn't stopped yet, either, though it's slowed down quite a bit."

"How long do you think it's going to be before they plow up here?" Wyle asked.

Hal squinted. "It's hard to tell. I would say at least a day or two. Maybe more. We're kind of an afterthought, way up here."

"Yeah, I was afraid of that."

Amelia brought two cups to the table, placing one carefully in front of Wyle with the same sugary smile as before. Wyle thanked her, but he didn't touch it.

"So is there any other way to get to town? Maybe a snowmobile?"

"Do you need something?" Hal asked. "Are you short on food, or ..."

"No, nothing like that," Wyle said reassuringly. "I just need to get a message to someone. It's rather urgent, I'm afraid. And with the phones not working, it would be really helpful if we could find a way to make it to town."

If Hal was curious about this urgent message, he didn't let on. Instead, he paused and took a sip of coffee before he answered. "I have a snowmobile."

Wyle perked up. "You do?"

"I do. I've been using it for parts."

Wyle's face fell. "Parts?"

"It hasn't worked right in years. I was thinking about replacing it, but I just never got around to it. Not like I ever used it all that much anyway. I prefer snowshoeing."

"Is there anyone around here who might have a running snowmobile?" Wyle asked. "Someone close enough to snowshoe to?"

Hal thought. "The Zimmerburgs have one," he said. Wyle's face lit up. But then Hal continued. "Although they're in Florida right now. Her mom is doing poorly."

"Anyone have a working snowmobile who's home?"

"Yeah, Jack should have one. I could stop by and see. He could bring it over."

"Would you? That would be great," Wyle said. "Do you think he could come today?"

Hal turned to squint out the window. "Hmm. Not sure. By the time I get over there, it might be kind of late. He may not want to run it in the dark. I know he was complaining about driving after the sun went down, so I'm not sure this would be any different."

"Tomorrow would be great, as well," Wyle said with a smile, but it was clear he was disappointed.

Hal took another slurp of coffee. "Anything else you need while I'm here? I'm happy to do what I can to make things easier for you. I know this is already a rough time for you all, and this weather certainly doesn't help."

"The toaster oven blew up," Amelia burst out. Wyle shot her a look.

Hal's eyes widened. "You don't say. What happened?"

"I plugged it in, and there was a bang and a spark. Nearly killed me," Amelia said, clearly ignoring Wyle's expressions.

"Wow." Hal knit his eyebrows together. "I wonder why that happened. Want me to look at it?"

"I've got it taken care of," Martin said.

Amelia leaned across the table. "Have you used the toaster oven?"

"Amelia," Wyle said.

Hal looked surprised. "Why would I use your toaster oven?"

"No reason," Wyle said smoothly, glaring at Amelia. "Everyone's nerves are just on edge here, Hal. Between Elliott cutting himself ..."

Hal's eyebrows went up. "Elliott cut himself? How did you do that?" he turned to Elliott then, who was resting his bandaged hand on the table.

Elliott gave Wyle the side-eye. "Uh, with a knife."

"A knife would do it."

"It was really strange though," Wyle said. "Because the knife he cut himself with was in your toolbox."

"My toolbox? Oh, was it that utility knife?"

Wyle nodded at Elliott, who looked like he wanted to disappear under the table. "Ah, no ... not the utility knife," he muttered.

"Then which one? I know I didn't leave my pocket knife in there, because I just used it the other day."

"No." Elliott cleared his throat. "It was a chef's knife."

Hal stared at him. "I'm sorry, did you say, 'chef's knife'?"

Elliott nodded.

"You found a chef's knife in my toolbox? How would that get there?"

"That's what we were wondering," Wyle said. "Did you use it and put it in your toolbox and forget about it, maybe?"

Hal looked mystified. "Why would I use a chef's knife when I have a utility knife in my toolbox?"

Wyle lifted his hands, holding them palms up. "I don't know. It's weird, how it happened."

"It is really weird," Hal agreed.

Wyle picked up his coffee but didn't drink it. "Any ideas how it could have gotten in there?"

Hal frowned as he thought. "I wonder if it was kids."

"Kids?" Amelia's voice was shrill. "You think kids got one of our knives?"

Hal looked a little embarrassed. "It's possible."

Amelia's voice went up a notch. "Possible?"

"Hal, what are you talking about?" Iris asked. "What kids?"

Hal had the grace to look embarrassed. "I didn't want to worry you ..."

Iris leaned forward. "Worry us? About what?"

Hal sighed. "We had a little break-in last summer ..."

"A break-in?" Iris and Amelia repeated at the same time.

The color rose on Hal's cheeks. "It wasn't that big a deal ..."

"Not that big a deal?" Iris and Amelia repeated in unison again, sounding almost like back-up singers.

"Let the man talk," Jeremy said. "He said it was a little break-in. So, let's hear what he means."

Hal shot Jeremy a relieved look. "So, this past summer, I'm pretty sure it was August ... yes, it was August ... when I checked on the house, I noticed the window in the back had been broken, and the back door was unlocked."

Iris gasped, her mouth forming an O. "You didn't tell us?"

Now, Hal's expression was somewhere between embarrassed and shocked. "You must know this wasn't the first time, right?"

"What are you saying? That this house is regularly broken into?" Amelia asked.

"I wouldn't say 'regularly,'" Hal said. "But kids do come up here on occasion and do goofy things. They'll sit on the porch at midnight, or even spend the night in the back, and yes, every now and then, they'll break in. I keep an especially close eye on it during summer when it's warm, and again around Halloween. And if I hear any car noises at night, I always come check on the house."

"I don't understand," Amelia asked. "Why are they doing this? Just because the house is empty?"

Hal shifted uncomfortably. "I would imagine it's because the house has a reputation for being haunted," he said.

There was a slight, uncomfortable silence. Amelia's face had puckered up like she had eaten an lemon.

"What I don't understand is why you never told us," Iris said.

Hal cleared his throat. "Actually, I did."

"What are you talking about? I didn't know anything about this," Iris said.

Hal picked up his coffee cup, moving it around in his hands. "Look, I don't want to cause trouble. But Flo knew."

Iris's eyes widened. "My mother knew? And she didn't tell me?"

"I'm guessing she didn't want to worry you," Hal said.

"Did she know about this break-in last summer?" Iris asked.

Hal looked uncomfortable. "I don't know for sure ..."

"What do you mean?" Iris demanded. "You just said you told her about these break-ins."

"I said she knew about them," Hal corrected. "But these last few years, she didn't want to deal with it herself. So she asked me to call her lawyer and let him know."

"George?" Amelia said. "You called George?"

"Yeah, that's the guy."

"You called George," Wyle repeated. His gaze had sharpened, but his tone was still friendly, like they were just a couple of buddies having an easy-going chat.

"Yeah. I had already walked through the house, and I didn't think anything was missing, but George wanted to check it out. If it hadn't been for the broken glass and the door standing ajar, I wouldn't have even known anyone had gotten in. I cleaned everything up and repaired the window, so when George got here, he didn't have to deal with it."

"Did you let George in?" Wyle asked.

"George has his own key, so I don't have to let him in per se, but yes, I met him here to walk him through what happened. He thanked me and said he wanted to check it out himself and make sure nothing was taken or destroyed. I left him and went back home."

"Did he ever contact you after that?" Wyle asked.

"No."

"Were there any more break-ins last summer?"

Hal shook his head. "No, everything was fine. And as I never heard back from George, I figured he didn't find anything, either."

"Had George come up before?"

"A couple times. Mostly, though, he would just call me to check in and see how things were going."

"Have you seen George recently?"

"Not since this summer," Hal said. I studied his face closely, but he didn't appear to be hiding anything.

"How about your toolbox?" Wyle asked. "Do you remember the last time you used it?"

Hal thought. "You know, I think it was this summer," he said. "I know I used it to fix a gutter that came loose during that big rainstorm we had. But now that you ask, I don't think I used it at all this fall. So, if a kid did stick a knife in it, I wouldn't have known."

"You really think a kid put a chef's knife in your toolbox?" Amelia asked incredulously.

Hal shrugged. "Who knows how kids think? But yeah, they might have broken in and wanted to take something from the house, and as they broke in the back door, maybe they only got as far as the kitchen. They took the knife, got spooked, ran out, and ended up sleeping in the toolshed. And at some point in the night, one of them put the knife in my toolbox, maybe for safekeeping, or maybe because they were so freaked out, they wanted something to defend themselves with."

Hal paused to take a breath, glancing around the table before continuing in a rush. "And I realize I probably should have caught that the knife was missing," he said, obviously misinterpreting the expressions he was seeing on our faces. "Both George and I went through the house, though, and I do remember looking through the kitchen. I didn't check every dish or piece of silverware, though. Anyway, that's my best guess as to how the knife ended up in the toolbox."

There was another awkward silence after Hal stopped speaking. Wyle picked up his mug. "Yeah, what you said makes sense," he said. Hal looked visibly relieved.

"Well, if there's nothing else, I probably should get going and let you all get back to your family time," Hal said, finishing his coffee and getting to his feet.

The rest of us did the same. "You're going to reach out to your friend about the snowmobile, yes?" Wyle asked.

Hal nodded vigorously. "Yes. I'll tell him you really need his help. Hopefully, he'll be able to come by tomorrow."

Wyle shook his hand, thanking him, before we all more or less walked him to the door. He shook a few more hands, repeated his condolences as he wrapped himself in his coat, hat, and scarf, and disappeared through the door. We all stood by the window watching him as he put on his snowshoes and headed across the yard.

Chapter 13

"I told you," Amelia hissed. "It was Hal."

"He does look guilty," Lucy agreed.

"I can't believe he would ever do such a thing," Iris said. "We've known him for years … invited him into our home. I don't understand how we could be so wrong about him."

Claire looked around wildly. "So just because Hal knew George, you two think he's responsible for killing him?"

"Well, how do you explain it, then?" Amelia demanded. "He comes up with a frankly ridiculous story about a break-in to explain the chef's knife in his toolbox. I don't believe for a moment it was a regular occurrence. I think Grandma would have said something. And the only other person who could verify any of this even happening is now dead. Don't you think that's suspicious?"

"But that doesn't explain why Hal would do such a thing," Claire said. "I get that it's a convenient story. But if he did indeed kill George, I'm still not hearing the why."

"We might not know the why until he tells us," Amelia said. "Maybe he and George had a disagreement about how he was taking care of the house. Or, maybe it did have to do with the will after all. Maybe Hal thought he was getting something more from Grandma, and maybe he somehow found out he wasn't, so he killed George to prevent us from seeing the will."

"That still seems like quite a stretch," Claire said.

"Well, let's hear from the expert in the room," Amelia said. "Officer Brandon, what are your thoughts on Hal?"

Wyle was still standing by the window, watching Hal's figure become smaller and smaller as he headed through the trees. "I agree it's a little … suspicious, that he knew George," he said. "It's definitely something that needs to be checked into. I'm assuming if Hal is right and someone did break a window last summer, there would be a record of it somewhere. I also assume Hal would be reimbursed for the window, so there should be a receipt, too. But yes, it is something we will check into."

"But we still don't have a motive," Claire said.

"I agree with that, too," Wyle said. "There are a lot of questions here, and unfortunately, we're prevented from getting answers."

"It could have been an accident," Iris offered.

Lucy rolled her eyes. "You think everything is an accident."

"But it could," Iris insisted. "That would explain everything, including why we never sensed anything off with Hal over the years—because he isn't a killer. Not really. Maybe it was just some sort of terrible luck."

"Of course, George's luck was even worse," Jeremy said.

The accident theory made a certain amount of sense. Maybe George was unhappy with the job Hal was doing and planning on replacing him. And maybe Hal arranged to meet George in the woodshed to make a final plea for his job, but George didn't want to listen, so in a fit of rage, Hal struck out at George, accidentally killing him.

It was possible. Although the Hal I'd just met certainly didn't seem like a man with a lot of pent-up rage.

"Well, as far as I'm concerned, the matter is solved," Amelia said, brushing her hands off. "I'm going to start dinner."

"Oh dear, you don't need to do that all on your own. Lucy, go help her," Iris directed.

Lucy glared at her mother. "Why don't you go help her?" she snapped back.

"I can help," Claire said.

"So will I," I said, thinking helping Amelia with the cooking was better than listening to The Iris and Lucy Show.

"Oh, but you two cooked breakfast," Iris began, before Claire waved her off.

"I don't mind."

"Cooking helps me relax," I said. "I'm happy to help." I smiled at Amelia, who didn't smile back. It was clear she was trying to figure out which was worse—cooking a huge meal all by herself, or accepting help from her estranged sister and the crazy tea lady.

In the end, having help won out. She turned and headed into the kitchen.

"I'll be in charge of drinks," Jeremy said. He winked at me as I walked by him. "You especially need to make up for last night."

"I'll keep that in mind," I said drily, not slowing my step. As I turned to go into the kitchen, I caught a glimpse of Wyle's face.

He didn't look very happy.

* * *

This house isn't safe.

I awoke with a start, my heart pounding so hard in my chest, I thought it might beat its way out.

I lay there, staring at the ceiling. What woke me? Had the floorboards been creaking because someone was wandering around?

This house isn't safe.

I rolled over to look at Claire. She was deeply asleep. The moonlight shone through the window, cutting across her bed. Her mouth was open, a single line of saliva snaking down her chin. As I watched, she twitched uncontrollably.

Whatever woke me hadn't come from Claire. Nor had the words that now echoed in my head …

This house isn't safe.

What did that even mean? Was it referring to the house itself, or to the people currently within it?

An image of the stuck door in the basement popped into my head. Or *was* it really stuck? Regardless, the image continued to gnaw at me. If what was behind the door was as innocuous as Lucy made it seem, why couldn't I open it?

Enough. It was far more likely that Lucy was right—the door was simply stuck from swelling, and all my uneasy thoughts were stemming from the dead lawyer in the shed … including whatever had woken me, which in reality was probably just a bad dream. If that were true, it was admittedly a bit strange that I couldn't remember anything about it. Every time I tried to recall a piece or image, it felt like I was trying to peer into a thick, black fog.

I had to get a grip. I was tired and out of of sorts. No wonder I couldn't think straight. Perhaps I should just go back to sleep. My eyes were gritty with exhaustion. There was no question I needed more rest.

The late night had caught up with everyone. Dinner had been a quiet affair, and once it was over and the dishes were washed, nearly everyone headed up to bed.

I had tried to talk to Claire about Hal. I wanted someone to help me process what Hal had revealed, but she said she was too tired and just wanted to lay down and hopefully get some sleep. She didn't look well. There were stress lines around her eyes and mouth, and I wondered if she was still suffering from a headache, even though she hadn't mentioned one.

I was worried about her. When we first started the week-end, she seemed better than she had in a long time. Now, she appeared to be regressing, looking as unwell as she had back in Redemption.

At least she was sleeping, which was more than I could say for myself.

After lying there for a while, tossing and turning to find a comfortable spot, I finally gave up. What I needed was a cup of tea. That would hopefully help relax me enough to maybe fall back asleep.

I slipped out of bed, trying hard not to wake Claire, fumbled for my robe, quietly unlocked the door, and snuck outside.

For a moment, I paused, wondering whether what I was doing was smart. While Wyle hadn't stressed our not wander-ing off alone like he had the night before, had anything really changed? Sure, Amelia seemed convinced Hal was their guy, and everyone else appeared comfortable enough in that deci-sion. I, on the other hand, wasn't so sure.

However, if the killer really was in the house, he would know everyone was blaming Hal, so the chances of him trying something were probably pretty low—doing so would certainly turn the attention away from Hal.

At least I hoped.

As softly as I could, I made my way down to the kitchen. The house was quiet and still, although it wasn't that dark. The light from the moon and the snow poured through the windows. Peering out, I was relieved to see it had stopped snowing. Hopefully, we would be able to get out soon.

There was enough ambient light in the kitchen to see, so I quickly got the water boiling and dug my tea out of the cupboard. Just the act of making it was already soothing me, settling my nerves. Maybe I would be able to get a little more sleep after all.

"You're up awfully late."

My heart slammed into my chest, disrupting my hard-won calm. The mug slipped in my grasp, and I nearly dropped it as I whirled around.

"Jeremy," I said. "You scared me."

"Sorry about that," he said, not sounding the least bit sincere. I noticed he still wore the same jeans and black sweater as before, and wondered if he had yet to go to bed. He craned his neck to see what I was doing on the stove. "Making a nightcap?"

"I'm making a cup of tea, if that's what you mean."

He wrinkled his nose. "Tea? Ugh. Wouldn't you rather have one of these?" He held up a half-filled wine glass in one hand and tilted it toward me.

"Thanks, but I'm good with tea."

"Humph." He took a sip, studying me over the rim. "You're an enigma, Charlie."

"I haven't a clue what you're talking about."

"Oh, I think you do."

The water was starting to boil. I turned back to the stove. "I think you're drunk," I said lightly.

"Maybe a little," he said. "That doesn't mean I'm wrong."

I didn't respond, focusing on my tea instead. I could feel his eyes on me.

"Why are you even here?" he asked.

I finally turned to him. "You know why. Claire asked me."

"But why would you say 'yes'? I mean, you had to know you would be walking into an unpleasant family situation, even without the dead lawyer."

"Claire needed me," I said simply. "She's my friend. And one uncomfortable weekend certainly isn't going to kill me."

"No, I guess not." He was still studying me, his eyes unreadable in the moonlight. "You have a lot of secrets, don't you?"

"What does that have to do with anything?" I was starting to get annoyed, not to mention a little unnerved. He was hitting a little too close to home, and I didn't like it.

"Because our family has a lot of secrets, as well," he said. "A lot of things that have never been talked about or dealt with on any level … simply swept under the rug. And the longer I'm here, the more I wonder if it wasn't one of those secrets that killed poor, boring George."

I was intrigued despite myself. "You don't think it was Hal?"

He laughed. "Can *you* picture Hal whacking George over the head?"

I had the same thought, but I wasn't going to share that with Jeremy. "What do you think happened?"

He paused, taking another sip of wine as he continued staring at me with those flat, unreadable eyes. "I think some long-buried secret was about to be dragged into the light. I think when my grandmother was alive, the secret was safe, but now that she's dead, whatever was keeping that secret safe is gone. And I think George just happened to be in the wrong place at the wrong time."

"You think George's death was an accident?"

He shook his head. "You misunderstand. I think what happened to George was very much on purpose. But I also think it would have happened to any attorney my grandmother hired to handle her will. George just had the bad luck to have been the one Grandma chose."

"What secret is buried in your family that would cause some-one to commit murder?"

He flashed me a sideways smile. "If I knew that, it wouldn't be a secret, would it?"

Good point. "But if you don't know what the secret is, how can you be so sure it even exists?"

He cocked his head. "Oh, come now. You know the answer to that as well as I do. When you're a kid, you always know when adults aren't telling you the whole story. Sometimes, may-be a lot of times, it's because as a child, you really wouldn't understand, but as you grow older, you eventually discover the full story. It wasn't a true secret, then. You just didn't know the whole story. However, with a true secret, no matter how old you get, you never get to the bottom of it."

I thought about what Claire had told me—that clearly, something had happened when her mother and Iris were kids—but apparently, neither had ever spoken to any of their children about it.

Was *that* the secret that ultimately killed George?

And if it was, could Iris be the one who did it?

I thought about Iris's reaction when Amelia announced George was in the woodshed. She seemed genuinely shocked.

Was she just a good actress? Or maybe, she was shocked that George had been discovered.

This house isn't safe.

Jeremy continued to study me. "You feel it, too," he said.

I lifted my mug to take a drink, mostly to hide my surprise. Jeremy's unnervingly accurate perceptions were making me very uncomfortable. I wasn't used to being read so easily. "If it is a family secret that caused all of this …" I started, deliberately changing the subject. The slight curl of Jeremy's lips indicated he knew exactly what I was doing. "Then you must also know whoever did it is likely in this house."

He shot me a look. "Did you honestly think it could be any-one else?"

"No, but I'm not related to them like you are."

He shrugged. "Not knowing the truth doesn't change the truth," he said. "I'd rather know what happened, even if it's painful, than not."

"I agree with you in theory, but in reality, you may find some truths you'd really rather not know."

His mocking smile returned. "See? Spoken like someone who knows all about secrets."

"I admit, I have some experience with the pain of deeply buried secrets," I said. "However, I also know that sometimes, those secrets can be used as a distraction from the truth. Perhaps even to hide the truth." I gave him a hard stare.

Again, my meaning wasn't missed. His eyes widened. "Are you trying to say you think *I* might have had something to do with George's death?"

"Did you?"

"You were here when I arrived. You think I found a quick moment to slip out back to the woodshed and off George without anyone noticing me gone?"

"I know when you came into the house," I corrected. "I have no idea when you actually arrived."

He stared at me for a moment, then burst out laughing. "See? I knew you were good."

I smiled slightly at him, aware of how alone we were. I wasn't sure how smart it was to reveal my suspicions, but I had been curious to see his reaction. There was something about him I didn't trust, but I couldn't figure out what it was exactly. Was he lying about some family secret causing George's death?

Or was he telling the truth, because he knew exactly why George had to die?

"Everything okay here?" Wyle was standing in the kitchen door, arms folded, his expression flat. I had no idea how he managed to sneak up on us. I would have expected to hear the creaking of the stairs if he had come down. At second glance, I realized Wyle was also wearing the same outfit he'd had on earlier.

Jeremy shot him a cocky grin. "Fine, officer," he said. "Just having a little nightcap. Care to join us?"

"Actually, Charlie, if you have any more of that tea, I would love a cup," he said.

"Sure," I said, turning back to the stove. I wasn't sure how I felt having Wyle there. A part of me was relieved, but another was almost as uncomfortable as I had been with Jeremy.

"Well," Jeremy said, backing away. "Three's a crowd, and it's getting late. I'll head up to bed. Nice talking to you, Charlie."

"Sleep well," I said lightly. There was something about his tone that sent shivers crawling up my spine. It sounded more intimate than our conversation had actually been … almost like he was trying to goad Wyle.

But why? Wyle was dating his sister, not me.

Wyle watched him saunter out of the room. A few minutes later, we heard the creak of the staircase as he climbed to his room.

I finished making the tea and handed it to him. "I didn't hear you come down the stairs."

"That's because I was in the den," Wyle said.

"Couldn't sleep?"

"Something like that." His eyes glinted in the moonlight as he studied me.

I leaned against the counter. "How much did you hear?"

"Enough."

Of course he did. "What do you think?"

"I think you should watch yourself."

"What, you jealous?" I smiled as I said it, teasing him, but his face didn't change.

"There's something about him I don't trust," he said. "It might not have anything to do with George, but I think you need to be careful."

"I can take care of myself."

"I didn't say you couldn't," Wyle said. "Consider this a friend- ly warning. Especially since it's clear he's interested in you."

I could feel my cheeks start to burn as I looked away. "Well, as I have no interest in dating anyone, there shouldn't be an issue."

"Why not?"

"Why don't I want to date Jeremy?"

"Why don't you want to date anyone?"

I picked up my mug. "Let's just say I haven't had the best of luck with men. It's better for all involved if I stay single."

"I'm a good listener."

"But I'm not a good talker," I said firmly, hoping that would be the end of it. "Back to what Jeremy was saying ... do you think he's right? That whoever killed George did it to keep him from revealing some sort of family secret?"

If Wyle was disappointed by the change of topic, he didn't let on. "That makes more sense than Hal being the culprit," he said. "Preventing the will from being read seems far more likely than anything else."

"What does Lucy think?"

"About a family secret?"

"About any of this," I spread my arms out. "Does she have a theory about who killed George?"

He paused to take a sip of tea, his eyes watching me closely. "You really want to know?"

"Of course."

"She thinks it was you."

"Me?" My jaw dropped. "Why on Earth would I kill George? I never even met the man."

He half-smiled. "Actually, what she really thinks is it was either Amelia or Claire, or maybe even both of them, and that they then brought you in to do the dirty work precisely because of what you said—that no one would suspect you, because you've never met George and have no ties to him."

"She seriously thinks that?"

His smile widened. "I don't know how serious she is. At least about you being the one to actually do the killing. But she really does think Amelia or Claire had something to do with it."

"Why? Because they were the ones who found him?"

"Partially," Wyle said. "She mentioned it would have been easy for them to off George and then come into the house saying they found him dead."

"That would have been some incredible timing on their part," I said. "They weren't out there very long, and George just happened to show up in that small window of time?"

"I pointed that out to her. Along with the fact that George was frozen stiff when I got there. I could tell he had been dead for at least a few hours."

"So what was Lucy's response?"

Wyle put his mug on the counter. "She said that Amelia was here the longest, and that maybe she had arranged for George to arrive earlier, before anyone else, and took care of him then."

I had to admit, that made a certain amount of sense. "I suppose that's possible."

"Lucy also mentioned that Amelia was the one who kept insisting that someone go get the wood. If it hadn't been for her, we still might not know George was out there."

"But why would Amelia want us to find George, if she did it?" I asked. "Wouldn't it be better if we didn't find the body?"

"Maybe, but Lucy thinks finding him makes perfect sense. After all, there's always the possibility someone else would have gone into the woodshed and found him. Because she was first, she could control it more. Plus, she would have the opportunity to set Hal up."

"So do you think she shocked herself with the toaster oven, too?"

"It's possible she didn't actually shock herself—that she just pretended to. But yes, she would have sabotaged the toaster oven to re-direct attention."

I mulled the possibility over. Amelia also appeared to be the most convinced of Hal's guilt, even if no one else agreed.

"But why?" I asked. "What motive would she have?"

"Lucy didn't really elaborate. And I admit, it does seem pretty clear she doesn't like Amelia very much."

My interest was piqued. "Why doesn't she like Amelia?"

He shook his head. "I'm not entirely sure. It seems to have something to do with Amelia's relationship with Iris. Apparently, Amelia and Iris are quite close … closer than Lucy is with her mother."

"So she's jealous of Amelia."

Wyle slightly inclined his head.

"Although," I mused. "Just because Lucy is jealous of Amelia doesn't mean her point is invalid."

Wyle raised an eyebrow. "Now you think Amelia killed George, too?"

"No. I doubt that, actually. Amelia was pretty hysterical after she and Claire found George. It's possible she was acting, but …" I shook my head. "No, what I was referring to was what Jeremy was talking about. Family secrets. According to Claire, Amelia wasn't close with their mother, but she is with her aunt. Iris treats Amelia more like her daughter than her actual daughter, while Claire is on the outside looking in. I realize family relationships are complicated, and it may just be as simple as Claire and her mother being connected because they share some sort of, I don't know what to call it … 'gift of seeing,' or something. And the rest of the family doesn't have it, so they don't understand … or maybe, they don't trust them. Maybe there's something else going on—something deeper than that."

"Back to the family-secret theory."

"Something like that. Claire did say that something had happened when Iris and Daisy were younger that drove a wedge between them, but she didn't know what. And what about this mysterious brother who disappeared? Billy. What's that about? And does his disappearance play any role in what's happening now? Not to mention we're staying in a house that literally kills people." I held my arms out wide.

Wyle half-smiled. "IF you believe the theory about what happened to the contractor."

"I don't think it's in dispute that the contractor died. But whether or not he was murdered by a ghost hasn't been proven."

"So now a ghost killed George?"

This house isn't safe.

"Maybe. Or maybe the house did." I eyed the kitchen.

"You do have to wonder how a haunted house ended up in this family," Wyle mused. "And for that matter, how it became haunted in the first place."

"Another family secret," I said.

Wyle was about to answer when a scream ripped through the house.

Chapter 14

"There's something here," Claire said. She was still in bed, huddled in a tight ball and pressed up against the headboard. Sweat glistened on her forehead, and clumps of hair were plastered against her face.

Amelia rolled her eyes. "Not this again."

Needless to say, everyone was now awake and crowded into our bedroom. I was sitting on the side of her bed, holding her hand while Wyle hovered behind me.

"I'm not doing this on purpose," Claire said.

"Yeah, you've said that," Amelia said.

"I'm not!"

"It's okay," Wyle said soothingly while giving Amelia the side-eye. "No one is accusing you of anything." Amelia glared at him.

"I'm just saying," Amelia said, her tone formal, "that over the years, we've all heard a lot of 'It's not my fault,' and 'I didn't mean to do it,' yet somehow, it still seems to keep happening."

"I can't help that the house is haunted," Claire said through gritted teeth.

"The house *isn't* haunted," Amelia began before Wyle interrupted.

"Enough," he said. "This isn't helping. Claire, can you tell us what happened?"

"She just had a bad dream," Iris said. "Which isn't surprising, after what we've all been through. I was having a doozy myself ..."

"I'd like to hear it from Claire, if you wouldn't mind," Wyle interrupted again, although his tone was a little gentler than it had been with Amelia. "Claire?"

Claire sniffed. "I'm sorry. I didn't mean to wake everyone up."

"We all know," Wyle said patiently. "Can you just try and tell us what happened?"

"I'm sure it was just a nightmare," Iris said again.

Claire shook her head. "It was more than a nightmare."

"I know it feels that way at this moment," Iris offered. "But it wasn't. Sometimes, dreams can feel so real. I know I had one once …"

"It was a warning." Claire interrupted.

There was an uncomfortable silence.

"What kind of warning?" Elliott asked.

"Don't encourage her," Amelia hissed. "Aunt Iris is right— she just had a bad dream."

"Did I dream that George is lying dead out in the wood-shed?" Claire asked.

"What does that have to do with anything?" Amelia snapped. "We all know what happened to George. It was trag-ic, and I'm sure it's what led to you having this nightmare."

"What happened to George is the symptom, not the prob-lem," Claire said. "There is something rotten here. In this house. With us."

The image of the stuck basement door popped into my head again, and I shivered, feeling as though I'd just plunged into an ice-cold bath.

"As usual, you're exaggerating," Amelia said.

"It's been rotten for a long time," Claire continued, ignoring her sister. "And for the most part, it's been quietly festering. But not any longer. It's growing, and sucking more and more people into its darkness …"

"Stop it, Claire," Amelia said, throwing her hands up. "What's wrong with you? Are you trying to scare the life out of everyone?"

"I'm trying to *warn* you," Claire said.

"*Warn* us? About what? We already know Hal killed George, so what else is there?" Amelia demanded.

"Hal didn't kill George," Claire said.

Amelia's eyes widened. "Of course he did," she said, her voice rising an octave. "Weren't you listening earlier?"

"Yes, and it's clear he had nothing to do with it," Claire insisted.

"You heard him say he knew George …"

"We *all* knew George," Claire said. "Well, except for maybe Charlie and Wyle. If simply knowing George is what makes Hal a suspect, we should all be suspect."

"Let's all take a breath," Wyle said, interrupting Amelia as she attempted to sputter a response. He held his hands up as if attempting to physically calm the room. "We're not here to debate Hal's guilt or innocence. Claire, is there anything else you want to share?"

"I know it's hard to believe someone we've known for years killed George," Iris interjected, before Claire could answer. "I don't want to believe it, either. Hopefully, it was all just a terrible accident, and Hal is very sorry about whatever he did. But it *has* to be him. Who else could it be? Certainly not one of us." Iris chuckled a little, as if the very notion of a murderer standing in the bedroom with us was a joke.

"Why couldn't it have been one of us?" Claire asked.

"What? How could you even say such a thing? Even in jest," Iris said.

"Are you confessing, Claire?" Amelia asked, her voice waspish.

"Hold on, girls," Martin offered. "I'm sure Claire just wants to think the best of Hal."

Iris turned to her husband. "What? Are you saying the rest of us don't? I feel sick at the thought of Hal doing such a thing."

"Of course not, dear," Martin said, patting her arm. "I'm just saying Claire is probably right in keeping all options open. What if someone was mad at George and followed him up here? It's possible whatever happened to George was truly just about George … that it doesn't have anything to do with us at all."

"Possible, but unlikely," Jeremy said.

"Jeremy, why do you have to be so negative?" Iris sighed. "Your father is right. We're probably blowing all of this out of proportion. Like I said, George's death was likely an accident, and if it wasn't, I'm sure it had nothing to do with us."

"I still think it was Hal," Amelia muttered.

"But what if it wasn't?" Claire asked again.

"Claire …" Amelia started, but Claire ignored her, continuing on.

"*This* is what I'm talking about. This is the meaning of my dream. We keep ignoring the elephant in the room, and it's not going away. In fact, it's getting worse."

"What elephant?" Iris asked, her voice exasperated. "What are you going on about?"

"The secrets," Claire said. Iris was shaking her head, but Claire continued. "Auntie, I know you know what I'm talking about. There is something going on here. I don't know what it is, but there is something, some secret, that was never shared with us kids. And you're the only one left who can tell us. Grandma is dead and mom is … well, she's not in any shape to share anything. What went on when you were younger? What aren't you telling us?"

"I don't know what you're talking about," Iris answered, her trembling voice betraying her attempt to sound firm. "Nothing happened."

"That's not true," Claire insisted, leaning forward and eyes wild. "Auntie, please. One person is already dead …"

"Are you blaming George's death on me?" Iris's voice was like ice.

"Of course not," Claire said quickly, trying to reach for Iris's hand, but Iris snatched it out of reach.

"Of all the nerve," Iris said, her voice growing colder by the word. "We tried to be good to you. We knew it wasn't your fault—not completely, at least. Unfortunately, Daisy infected you with her craziness when you were a child. Thank goodness Amelia at least saw through my sister's madness," Lucy's face tightened when Iris said Amelia's name, but Iris didn't seem to notice. "However, it was probably too much to hope that both of her children would be immune. Still, I tried with you. Lord knows I did. And for you to now blame me for what happened to poor George ... how dare you?"

"Auntie, I wasn't trying to hurt you," Claire said, her voice miserable, but Iris had already turned her back and was marching out of the room, followed closely by Martin.

"I'm sorry you had a nightmare," she said over her shoulder. "And I'm sorry for what my sister did to you, but pull yourself together. You're an adult now. You can make different choices. You don't have to follow Daisy down that dark path."

"See what you did?" Amelia asked, her voice venomous. "Why do you always do this?"

Claire snapped her head up at the sound of her sister's voice. "You know exactly what I'm talking about," she said, giving her sister a hard look. "All of you," she continued, glaring at both Jeremy and Lucy, who both seemed a little embarrassed. "You know they're hiding something. Why won't they tell us?"

"Even if they are, it doesn't necessarily have anything to do with George's death," Amelia argued.

"But we don't know," Claire said. 'That's the point."

"Why would our family secrets have anything to do with George?" Amelia asked. "George wasn't family."

"No, but he *was* about to reveal something," Claire said.

"About the will," Amelia corrected. "Not any deep, dark secret."

"Are you sure about that?" Claire asked.

"Claire has a point," Jeremy said.

"Not you too," Amelia groaned.

Jeremy shrugged. "You can fight it all you want, Amelia, but the truth is, it makes far more sense that George was killed to keep a secret buried than Hal suddenly deciding to whack him on the head."

"So, what are you saying?" Amelia asked, her hands on her hips. "One of us killed George?"

"Do you have a better explanation?" Jeremy asked.

"Yeah, I do," Amelia countered. "My sister is delusional ... as delusional as my mother."

"Amelia, you can't possibly be this naive," Jeremy said. "Why are you refusing to look at the facts?"

"The facts?" Amelia asked, an edge to her voice. "What facts? Claire here is accusing one of us of killing George based on a dream."

"That's NOT what I said," Claire said.

Amelia whirled around to face her sister. "Oh, isn't it? You just said you wanted to warn us, and then you practically accused Aunt Iris of murder to protect some silly secret."

"I didn't accuse ..." Claire began, but Amelia didn't let her finish.

"Don't you dare try and rewrite history," Amelia said. "We were all here, and we all heard it. You said that George was killed to protect some family secret—as if every other family doesn't have things they'd prefer the rest of the world not know about—and then you start berating Aunt Iris about it. Think about it, Claire. If George was killed because of a secret and, according to you, Aunt Iris is the only one who knows it, wouldn't that make her the most likely killer?"

"I wouldn't put it past her," Lucy muttered, but Amelia ignored her.

"Not necessarily," Claire argued. "There could be something else going on that's related to the secret."

"Oh, so who is the killer, then? Jeremy? Lucy? Me?"

Claire looked wildly between them. "I ... I don't know."

"No, you don't *think*," Amelia said. "You're accusing a member of your own family of murder. Murder! And why? So you can force Aunt Iris to share some dirty laundry? The same aunt who was always there for us when our own mother couldn't be? I always knew you were selfish, but I didn't realize how selfish you really are."

Claire's face turned white.

"Amelia," Elliott said, but Amelia waved him off.

"I think we need a break," Wyle said. "Amelia, why don't you make us some coffee? I don't think anyone is going back to sleep anymore."

Amelia threw Wyle a dark look. "I should have known you would take her side."

"I'm not taking anyone's side," Wyle said.

"Then why don't you just tell her it was Hal, so she stops this nonsense?" Amelia asked, pointing at Claire.

"Oh please," Lucy said. "Claire didn't say anything the rest of us weren't thinking. Including my sainted mother."

Amelia's mouth fell open. "How could you say that about her?"

"Because it's true," Lucy said. "And you would know it as well, if you didn't spend your life sucking up to her."

"I don't 'suck up' to her," Amelia said. "You have no idea what it's like to grow up without a mother."

"Actually, I do," Lucy said. "Because mine was too busy being yours."

"All right, that's it," Wyle said in frustration. "We're all going downstairs now. Claire, when you're feeling up to it, come down and join us."

Amelia tried to say something, but Wyle started physically herding everyone out of the room. "No. We're done. We're all going down to the kitchen for a cup of coffee. Charlie, do you want to join us or stay here?"

"I'll stay here," I said, answering the unspoken plea in Claire's eyes.

Wyle nodded as he, for all practical purposes, pushed the others out of the room, shutting the door firmly behind him.

"Are you okay?" I asked Claire in a low voice.

She was trembling, her hair hanging in greasy strands in her face. "I shouldn't have come," she said. "This was a mistake."

"You didn't come for yourself. You came for Daphne, remember?" I asked.

Claire shook her head. "It was still stupid. Daphne inheriting anything was a long shot. I should have known better. This whole thing is a waste." She looked up, her eyes glistening. "And to make matters worse, I dragged you into it."

"Don't worry about me," I said. "I'm a big girl and can take care of myself. And you're being too hard on yourself. You couldn't have known George would be killed, or that we'd all end up trapped here because of a snowstorm. It's true your sister has been horrid to you, but I suspect she's worse than usual because of all the added stress."

Claire gazed off into the distance. "She would have still been horrid. She's never forgiven me for being mom's favorite."

"Well, she sure seems to be your aunt's favorite," I said.

"Yeah, poor Lucy," Claire sighed.

"Yeah," I said, even though I wasn't really feeling all that sorry for her. "So what about this dream? What did you see? Why did you scream?"

Claire pressed her lips together. "Well, it's like I said ... there's something here. Something bad. I know Amelia doesn't want to think about one of us killing George, but ..." her voice trailed off.

This house isn't safe.

I folded my arms across my chest, trying to ward off the sudden chill. It felt like the temperature had dropped twenty degrees. The door in the basement danced before my eyes again.

Was Claire in danger? Was I?

"Who do you think killed George?" I asked.

"I don't know," she said. "I wish I did."

"But you do think it has to do with whatever your aunt isn't telling you."

Claire paused for a moment before slowly nodding.

I wondered if I should tell her that Jeremy had said the same thing—that their family secrets had killed George. Would it make things better, or drive an even deeper wedge between Claire and the rest of the family?

On the other hand, was it my place to keep secrets from my friend?

"For what it's worth, Jeremy said the same thing to me," I said.

Claire gave me a quick, sharp look. "He did? When?"

"Earlier tonight. Before you screamed."

She looked puzzled. "Like, after dinner?"

"No, like in the middle of the night." I filled her in on what had happened when I woke up.

Her face grew more troubled as I talked. "Be careful, Charlie."

"Of Jeremy?"

Claire looked down, biting her lip. "There's always been something about him. I could never put my finger on it, and I don't know exactly how to explain it. But please … just be careful."

I thought about how Jeremy had snuck up on me, and how aware I'd been of being completely alone with him in the kitchen.

Was it possible he was the killer? And if it was, why would he have blamed George's death on family secrets? Why wouldn't he insist it was Hal, like Amelia and Iris? Was he playing some sort of misdirection game, betting that the cops would assume him innocent because he *wasn't* blaming Hal?

Or were the family secrets themselves the distraction? In which case, Jeremy knew precisely why George was killed and was placing the blame on something that had nothing to do with it to keep everyone off the scent.

"You understand what you're saying," I said carefully.

Claire looked away, her expression miserable.

"I know you said you don't know who it was," I continued. "But it sort of sounds like you might."

Claire didn't respond for a moment, just continued to stare at the red and blue nine-patch star quilt that hung on the wall. I stayed quiet, letting her sort out the thoughts in her head.

Finally, she let out a long sigh. "Yes," she said, her voice resigned. "I do have my suspicions."

I waited, but it didn't seem like she was going to elaborate.

"Do you want to come down to the kitchen?" I asked instead. "Get some coffee and breakfast?"

She shook her head. "I think I want to stay up here for a while. I'm still pretty tired. Maybe I'll see if I can get a little more sleep."

I nodded, although I thought it more likely that she didn't want to face any of her family members at the moment.

"Do you want me to bring you anything?"

She shook her head again, giving me a wan smile. "Truly, all I want to do is sleep."

She wasn't the only one, but I seriously doubted I would be able to get any real sleep in that house.

I realized I hadn't told her about the stuck door in the basement and wondered if I should. But looking at her exhausted face, I decided to wait. Claire needed to sleep, and I had no idea if her knowing would make it easier or more difficult for her to get some.

"Okay, then," I said as I stood up and moved to the door. I had my hand on the doorknob before I turned back to her. "I think you need to lock yourself in."

She opened her mouth to protest, but almost immediately closed it. Her face was pale but resolved. "Okay."

"And maybe don't let anyone in other than me or Wyle."

Her eyes widened as her face became even paler, but she nodded slightly. I opened the door and stepped out into the hallway, but I didn't move away until I heard the unmistakable click of the lock and the faint scratching of the nightstand being dragged across the floor.

Chapter 15

The snowstorm appeared to be well and truly over. The clouds had cleared away, and the sun shone brightly, lighting up the pure-white blanket of snow. Clumps hung from the pine trees and completely covered the bushes. A bright-red cardinal perched on a dark branch of a tree that dripped with sparkling icicles.

The view from the front window of the cabin was stunning. In another time and under normal circumstances, I would have liked nothing better than to curl up on the couch with a cup of tea and book while enjoying the warmth of the fireplace.

However, staring out at the endless expanse of snow, with no sign of any sort of road, or for that matter, Claire's car, and knowing there was likely a murderer trapped in the house with me was a completely different story.

"Hopefully, Hal was able to convince his friend to come by with the snowmobile," Wyle murmured next to me. He didn't sound very hopeful.

"Still no phone?" I asked.

He pressed his lips together as he shook his head.

"Well, even if Hal doesn't show up, the snow has at least stopped," I said. "Shouldn't they have the plows up here at some point today?"

"Maybe," he said. "Although I'd feel better if we could send a message with someone by snowmobile."

He had a point. I would, too, especially since I was growing more and more uncomfortable the longer I remained stuck in the house. I was also becoming increasingly worried about Claire. Was she a target now, being the only one who decided to say out loud what everyone else was surely thinking? It was impossible to know.

Breakfast was a quiet affair. I wasn't entirely sure what to expect when I came down to the kitchen, but I had assumed there would be at least some discussion of what had happened. Instead, it seemed that all the anger had sucked the last bit of energy out of everyone, leaving them shells of their former selves. They sat around the large kitchen table gulping down scalding-hot coffee and picking at the scrambled eggs, bacon, and toast Amelia had prepared.

With all the furtive looks on everyone's face as they eyed one another around the table, I realized it was also possible that everyone was feeling as untrusting as I was. Before Claire's outburst, it was easier for everyone to pretend everything was all right. The culprit was either Hal or some nameless, faceless stranger, and we could all pretend we were relatively safe in our own company.

But now, it was all out in the open, and gone was any illusion that they were all just one, big happy family.

"What's going on?" Lucy asked, appearing next to Wyle's elbow. She was wearing pink again, although today's ensemble was more casual—a sweatshirt over a white turtleneck. Her full makeup still couldn't cover up the black, puffy circles under her eyes.

"Nothing," Wyle answered, staring out the window.

"Well, why are you two standing here by yourself?" She was trying too hard to sound like she was teasing, and it fell flat. I had seen a desperate look in her eyes as she tried to get Wyle's attention at breakfast, but he was too busy gazing into his coffee cup to notice. It had to be tough on him, wondering if a member of his girlfriend's family was guilty of murder. How would he possibly explain this to the rest of Redemption's finest? Lucy had to know that, as well. I was almost feeling sorry for her.

Almost.

"We're just hoping Hal's friend with the snowmobile shows up," I said.

Lucy edged closer to Wyle. "You think we might be able to leave today?"

"Doubtful," he said. "But there's always hope."

Just then, a low buzzing noise sounded in the distance.

Wyle cocked his head. "Am I hearing what I think I'm hearing? Or is it just wishful thinking?"

"If it's wishful thinking, I'm hearing it, too," I said.

"What?" Lucy asked. "I don't hear anything."

"Quiet," Wyle said. "Let's listen."

We obeyed. The buzzing sound was definitely getting louder, like whatever was making it was coming closer.

Wyle turned to me, a sparkle in his eyes. "The calvary has arrived."

"Is it a plow?" Lucy asked, craning her neck to see.

"No," I said, feeling a mixture of relief and euphoria. *Soon, this nightmare will be over.* "It's a snowmobile."

In that moment, the machine burst into view, carrying two passengers.

"Hal must have come with him," Wyle said as we watched the snowmobile slow and then come to a stop. The person on the back, presumably Hal, got off first. His movements were clumsy, though, and he ended up falling into the snow. The driver then dismounted to help pull him up from off the ground.

"I don't think that's Hal," I said slowly, watching the two carefully make their way to the door, the driver half-dragging, half-carrying the other person through the heavy snow. There was something so familiar about the second person, but I couldn't put my finger on it.

It wasn't until both of them tromped up the porch and I saw a glimpse of the face behind the scarf that I realized who it was. "It's Pat!" I said in surprise.

"Pat?" Wyle asked. "As in Pat Barron?"

I was already at the front door, yanking it open and letting in a burst of frigid air.

"Oh, thank goodness," Pat said, her voice muffled from behind a bright-green scarf. "I was worried this wasn't the right house."

"Again, you mean," grumbled the other voice, who I recognized as Pat's husband Richard. "That's happened twice already, actually."

"Oh, hush," Pat said, stomping her feet and coming inside. "I've never been up here with this much snow on the ground. Everything looks so different."

"Pat?" Amelia came into the living room, wiping her hands on a towel. "Is that you?"

"In the flesh," Pat said, unwinding her scarf. Snow had stuck to her eyelashes and eyebrows, and her face was bright red.

"What are you doing here?" Amelia asked as Elliott and Jeremy wandered in behind her.

"What do you think? I've been worried! We just had the worst snowstorm in decades, and your phones are still out. I had to come out here to make sure you were okay."

"But how did you even know we were here?" Amelia asked.

"I told her," I said. "She's watching my cat."

Amelia blinked. "Cat?"

"How is Midnight?" I asked.

"Still fat and happy," Pat said, removing her jacket and rubbing her hands briskly together.

"Midnight isn't fat," I said. "He's big-boned."

"Not only is he fat, but he's also spoiled rotten," Pat said.

"Oh, now I get it," I said. "How many treats has he conned out of you?"

Pat huffed. "I don't know what you're talking about. Although you might want to ask Claire to stop at the store on the way home to pick up another bag."

"Enough about the cat," Amelia interjected. "You surely didn't come all this way to give Charlie an update on her cat."

"Of course not," Pat said. "The cat is fine. I wasn't so sure about Charlie."

"Are the roads open?" Elliott asked.

"No, we used the snowmobile," Pat said, blowing on her hands as she glanced around the room, greeting everyone. "Where's Claire?"

"She's resting in her room," I said.

Pat gave me a startled look. "Is she okay?"

"Long story. But first, let's get you something hot to drink," I said. "Why don't you come into the kitchen? I'll get you some tea or coffee."

"Your blend?" Pat asked.

"Of course," I said, heading into the kitchen.

"I'll take coffee," Richard called out.

Amelia watched us file into the kitchen, an expression of disbelief on her face, as though she couldn't quite comprehend what was happening.

I began making the tea while everyone else gathered around the table. Wyle asked Richard about the condition of the roads.

"In town, they aren't too bad," Richard said. "Not so good when you get outside the city limits. They still have a lot of catch-up to do."

"Did you ride the snowmobile all the way from your house?" Elliott asked.

"Heavens no," Pat said.

"We have a pick-up truck," Richard explained. "We used that to haul the snowmobile as close as we could get and used it for the rest."

"I still can't get over you going through all that trouble," Amelia repeated. Her voice was almost envious, making me wonder if anyone had ever gone out of their way for her.

"Ah, it was no trouble," Pat said as I handed her a mug of tea.

Richard shot her a quick look. "Speak for yourself."

Pat shook her head as she took a sip. "Don't let him fool you. He loves a challenge."

Richard grunted as I deposited a cup of coffee in front of him, but his expression was fond as he gazed at his wife. I sat down across from Pat, cupping my refilled mug.

"So," Pat said, putting down her tea and surveying the kitchen. "It doesn't look like you're too worse for wear. You still have heat and power."

"We did lose power, but luckily, there's a generator," Elliott said.

Pat's eyebrows went up. "Yes, that is lucky."

Wyle leaned forward across the table. "Actually, I'm really glad you came. We do need your help."

Pat's face lit up as she nudged her husband. "See? I told you we needed to come. What can we do?"

"This is ... a little unorthodox," Wyle said carefully.

"Hey, I'm friends with Charlie ... I'm used to things being unorthodox," Pat said.

I stuck my tongue out at her.

"The situation is a little delicate, as well," Wyle said.

"I can handle it," Pat said. "Lay it on me."

"You'll also need to be discreet," Wyle continued.

"Of course! 'Discretion' is my middle name." Next to her, Richard rolled his eyes. "What's going on?" Pat asked. "I'm dying to know."

There was a pause as the rest of us glanced at one another. I could see Wyle trying to figure out the best way to word it.

"Our lawyer is dead," Amelia blurted out.

Pat blinked. "What? Oh my goodness, that's awful. What happened? Was it a heart attack? Stroke? Could you not get help because of the storm? Oh, you must feel terrible."

No one said anything. Pat looked around the table. "*Was* it a heart attack?"

"We don't actually know how he died," Wyle said.

"What do you mean, you 'don't know'?" Pat asked, knitting her brows together in confusion. "I mean, I know you're not a doctor, but surely you have some idea of what happened."

"It's a little more complicated than that," I said. "Hence, why Wyle here said it was a 'delicate' situation."

Pat blinked. "I don't understand."

"I need you to ask the cops to come up here to investigate," Wyle said.

Pat's mouth dropped open. "Investigate? Why would the cops need to investigate?"

Wyle was looking more and more uncomfortable. "They have to investigate when there's a suspicious death."

"'*Suspicious*' death?" Pat's eyes were as round as her mouth as she stared at each of us. "Are you saying your lawyer was murdered?"

"By our neighbor," Amelia said firmly.

"Your *neighbor* murdered your lawyer?"

"We don't know that," I said quickly. "We don't know who did it."

"You don't know who killed your lawyer?" Pat's expression was a strange mix of shock and the creeping realization that she could now be next on the list. She threw a quick glance over her shoulder, as if to make sure no one was sneaking up on her.

"Yes, we do know who it was," Amelia said, glaring at me.

"No, we don't. Which is why we need the cops," I said. "They have to investigate what happened, just like Wyle said."

"But what DID happen?" Pat asked. "Why was your lawyer killed?"

"Other than the obvious? Because he was a lawyer," Richard said.

"We don't know. That's why we need the cops to investigate," I said.

"I still don't understand," Pat said. "What actually happened to him?"

"We're not sure," Wyle said. "We found him in the woodshed."

Pat raised her eyebrows. "The woodshed? What was he doing out there?"

"Again, we're not sure," Wyle said.

"Is that where he is now?" Pat asked.

"Yes," Wyle answered.

"And this isn't a joke?"

"I can take you out to the woodshed and show you," I offered.

Wyle shot me a look. "There will be no more disturbance of the body. It's already been contaminated enough."

"This is insane," Pat muttered, clutching at her tea mug as if trying to suck the warmth out of it.

Wyle nodded his head in acknowledgement. "Do you understand why we need to get the cops involved as quickly as possible, while being as discreet as possible?"

"Of course," Richard started to say, but the telltale creak of someone coming down the stairs made him jerk his head around. The rest of us looked toward the kitchen doorway, as well.

Iris's head popped in. "I thought I heard voices ... oh, hello."

"Hello," Pat said.

Martin's head appeared next to Iris. "We have visitors? Are the roads clear?"

"Not quite," Wyle said. "They came by snowmobile."

Martin looked surprised. "A snowmobile. Really?"

"I'm afraid I haven't had the pleasure," Iris started.

"This is Pat Barron," Amelia said. "You remember Pat."

Iris's eyes widened in recognition. "Oh. Of course. Yes, I do remember you now. Sorry, it's been a stressful weekend."

"There's nothing to be sorry about," Pat said. "You're Iris, right? I think we've met once or twice."

"Yes, I think you're right," Iris said, coming into the kitchen. "Did you come all the way out here on a snowmobile to pay your respects?"

"She's watching Charlie's cat," Amelia said. "And apparently, she got worried when she couldn't get in touch with Charlie."

"Oh. Well, what a stroke of good luck," Iris said. "You probably heard about poor George, then." Iris shook her head. "So sad."

"If George was your attorney, then yes. I'm sorry to hear about your losses," Pat said.

Iris sighed, bending her head.

"Speaking of George," Richard said, swallowing the last of his coffee. "We should probably get a move on."

Pat started to nod, then took another look around the table. "Is Claire still in her room?"

"Yes," I said.

"I want to see her."

"Oh please," Amelia said, rolling her eyes. "My sister is fine. She woke us all up in the middle of the night because she had some sort of nightmare, but she's the one who gets to stay in bed all day."

"You just told me you have a dead attorney here," Pat said, her expression determined. "I'd like to see Claire before I go." She stared directly into my eyes.

Immediately, I understood. Pat wanted to talk to Claire and me alone. I immediately stood up. "I'll take you to her."

"You're making a mountain of a molehill," Amelia grumbled, but she didn't protest any further. Pat's comment about the dead lawyer probably hit a little too close to home.

I led Pat out of the kitchen and up the creaky stairs, glancing furtively behind me to make sure no one was following us. It didn't appear anyone was, but I did catch Iris's face turning toward us, watching as we disappeared down the hall.

"You really got yourself into it this time," Pat hissed into my ear. "I told you not to come. Didn't I tell you not to come?"

"And you were absolutely right," I said, my voice low.

Pat shook her head. "Man, if whatever was haunting this house wasn't bad enough before, now there's going to be a lawyer joining the mix? Bad, bad, bad." She shivered.

I reached the bedroom door and knocked softly on it. "Claire, it's me," I said. "Can you open up?"

There was a pause followed by the sound of the nightstand being dragged away from the door. Pat's eyebrows went up, but she didn't say anything. There was a soft click, and the door opened a crack, revealing Claire's pale face.

"Pat?" She looked stunned. "What are you doing here?"

"Apparently rescuing you and Charlie," Pat said, pushing the door open to give Claire a hug. I slid in behind them, closing the door behind us and reengaging the lock.

"What did you two get yourselves into?" Pat asked, keeping her voice down as we settled ourselves on Claire's bed. "A dead lawyer? How did this even happen?"

I reached out to hold one of Claire's hands, which was ice cold. I hoped she wasn't going into some sort of shock. "We don't know," I said. "Claire found his body."

Pat's eyes widened. "*You* found his body?"

She nodded. "Amelia and I were going out to the woodshed for wood, and there he was."

"What, just lying there?"

"He was under a tarp."

"Someone covered him *with a tarp*?"

"It looks bad," I acknowledged.

"*'It looks bad'*?" Pat's gaze went back and forth between us. "Charlie, Claire, you do understand what this means, right?"

"That someone in my family is likely a murderer ... yes," Claire said. "We all had that discussion earlier. It didn't go well."

Pat gave Claire a sympathetic look. "I'm not surprised. But you get that it also means you're trapped in this house with that person," Pat said.

"Yeah, we know," I said. "Which is why it's so great you're here."

"I should have come yesterday," Pat said. "I wanted to, but the roads were still too bad, and Richard didn't want to chance it."

"You really did all of this because our phones weren't working?" I asked.

Pat hesitated. "Well, it was a little more than that."

"What do you mean?"

Pat didn't say anything for a moment as she seemed to struggle for words, which was not like her. "I guess ... I was just having a bad feeling."

"You and me both," Claire said.

I eyed Pat. There was definitely something she wasn't telling us. "What kind of bad feeling?"

Pat gave me a look. "Are there different types?"

I half-smiled. That sounded more like Pat. "I don't know. You're being awfully cagey."

"It's just ...." She paused again, her expression torn.

"Out with it," I said. "You can't possibly say anything we haven't already considered."

"Alright, fine," she huffed. "I had a bad feeling ever since you told me you and Claire were coming up here. I really felt like the whole thing was a mistake, and then, when I couldn't get ahold of you on the phone ..." She raised her hands helplessly.

"Well, you were absolutely right," Claire said.

I still didn't feel like that was everything. "Was there something that triggered this bad feeling, or did it come out of nowhere?"

Pat sighed. "Look, it's not really my place," she said to Claire.

Claire shook her head quickly. "Don't censor yourself on my part. Is there something you know? Did my grandma tell you something?"

"Not in so many words," Pat said. "You know how much I liked Flo. But there was something about the rest of your family. Not you, of course, but ..." she sighed again. "Flo never came out and said anything to me, you understand, but there was just something. It's hard to explain. I just always felt like she was never telling me the full truth when it came to her children or grandchildren. That there was something there that she didn't want to talk—or even think—about. At the time, when she was alive, I thought it was just family stuff. Tensions and whatnot. Like your aunt ... no offense, but I never really got a good vibe from her."

"None taken."

"I can't put my finger on it. She was always perfectly pleasant when I met her. But like today, she acts like she doesn't recognize me. I mean, what's that about?"

"My aunt is a strange bird," Claire said. I thought about what Claire had said about Jeremy earlier and wondered if Claire blamed her aunt for how Jeremy turned out.

"Anyway, it's not like I have anything concrete. Just a lot of bad feelings about it all. And then, to find out your family lawyer ended up dead? It's really just ..." Pat paused and shivered.

"Creepy," Claire finished.

"Exactly," Pat said.

"And I'm not surprised you think that," Claire continued. "I agree there's something off with my family. There are a lot of secrets that no one has ever talked about, and it does make me wonder if that's why George died."

"So, neither of you honestly have any idea why George was killed?" Pat gave us a hard look, especially me. We both shook our heads.

Pat bit her lip. "I really don't like this."

There was a gentle knock on the door. "Pat?" Richard's voice called out. "You in there? We really ought to get going."

"He's right," I said. "You should go. The sooner you go, the sooner you can send help back."

Pat groaned. "I don't want to leave you two."

"We'll be fine," I said, hoping it true. "Honestly, it's better that you guys get out of here and send in the calvary."

Pat's eyebrows were furrowed and her eyes full of worry, but she gave us a faint nod before leaning over to hug us both. "I know you're right," she whispered. "It still doesn't make me feel any better."

"Honestly, it will be fine," I said.

Pat still didn't look convinced, but she stood up and headed for the door. I glanced back at Claire to remind her to the lock the door behind me, but she was moving toward the closet. "I'll be down shortly," she said, pulling a blue snowflake sweater and a pair of jeans out of the closet.

I nodded and followed Pat out of the room. Richard was waiting on the other side, talking with Wyle in a low voice. "Ready?" he asked Pat as she emerged from the room.

"As ready as I can be," Pat said with a sigh.

Richard nodded at Wyle as we trooped down the steps to the front door. Amelia poked her head out of the kitchen. "You going?"

"Yep," Richard answered as he put on his coat. Pat was winding her scarf around her neck.

"You're getting us plowed out, right?" Lucy asked from behind Amelia. Jeremy was there, as well.

"That's the plan," Richard said, pulling on his gloves. "With any luck, you'll be out of here before dark." He glanced up at Wyle and gave him a quick nod as he opened the front door. Wyle nodded back.

We stood by the window watching as Pat and Richard tromped through the snow toward the snowmobile. Lucy shivered. "I'm cold just watching them."

Richard got on first as Pat waited. He fiddled with the engine, and we heard the faint noise of the engine trying to start.

Wyle cocked his head. "Something isn't right," he said.

Jeremy's head was tilted, as well. "It's not catching."

"What does that mean?" Amelia asked.

The noise stopped, and Richard got off the snowmobile and opened up the engine.

"I suspect it means they aren't going anywhere," Jeremy said.

Pat joined him as they both studied under the hood. Richard fiddled with the engine for a few minutes before closing it and turning to head to the house.

"This doesn't look good," Lucy said as we watched them stumble through the snow once more. Wyle went to the door to open it for them.

"What happened?" Amelia demanded as they entered the house in a flurry of ice crystals and frosty air.

"Snowmobile won't start," Pat said.

"What?" Wyle asked. "Why?"

"Not sure," Richard said. "We're going to need to get someone to take a look at it. Does anyone here know anything about engines?"

"Uncle Martin could look it," Amelia said. "I don't know how much he knows about snowmobiles, though. Could it just be cold?"

"Maybe," Richard said, but his voice was doubtful.

"Have you had any problems before?" Lucy asked.

"Not to my knowledge," Pat said. "Right, Richard?"

"Yeah, but that doesn't mean there couldn't be a problem now," Richard said.

I met Pat's eyes, and I could see the question in my mind mirrored back. It seemed awfully suspicious that the snowmobile would suddenly have a problem just as Pat and Richard were about to go get help.

Instantly, the house seemed even more isolated than before.

Chapter 16

"It probably needs a new fuel filter," Martin said, rubbing his hands together to warm them up. His nose and cheeks were red from cold as he tried (unsuccessfully) to get the snowmobile started.

"Impossible," Richard said. "I just had it serviced a couple of months ago."

Martin shrugged. "Well, something isn't right. You have plenty of fuel, yet it sounds like it's not getting to the engine. You may have bought some bad gas, which could have clogged up the fuel filter. I would start by changing that."

"We've never had a problem with it before," Pat said.

"Sometimes, these things happen," Martin offered.

"Where could we get a new fuel filter?" Amelia asked.

"The store," Martin answered.

"There's none in the garage?" Amelia asked.

"Why would there be a fuel filter for a snowmobile in the garage?" Jeremy interrupted. "Especially considering there's no snowmobile."

"How should I know? There seems to be at least one of everything else out there," Amelia countered.

"I doubt it," Martin said.

"Wasn't there a snowmobile here at one point?" Claire asked.

"There was," Lucy said, giving her brother a hard look. "Until Jeremy totaled it. Grandma wouldn't allow them after that."

"So, we're stuck here, too?" Pat asked.

"Appears so," Martin said.

Wyle muttered something under his breath as he glanced outside. Even though the sun was still shining, the shadows were already lengthening as the winter darkness fast approached.

There was no sign of Hal or Hal's friend, or of the phones getting fixed.

How was it possible we were still so isolated after two full days?

"Well, we do have plenty of food," Amelia said. "But not enough beds."

"There are couches," Claire reminded us. She had come down while Martin was outside with the snowmobile. Amelia had given her a wide berth.

"We'll be fine," Pat said.

"What about this Hal person?" Richard asked Wyle. "Did you say he has a snowmobile?"

"He does, but it's not working," Wyle said. "It's his friend who supposedly has one that actually runs."

"I was thinking maybe Hal would have a spare fuel filter," Richard said.

"He did say he was keeping his for parts," I added.

"It's possible, but there is really no easy way to his house," Wyle said. "I haven't been able to find any snowshoes, nor do I have the right boots for such deep snow. But I'm about ready to try muddling through regardless."

"I wouldn't advise doing anything now," Martin said. "It's getting dark. Tomorrow will be soon enough. And who knows? Maybe the phones will be back by then, or Hal will be over."

Wyle squinted at the sun. He seemed to still be mentally debating whether or not to try to make it to Hal's regardless of how ill-equipped he was. Lucy put a hand on his arm.

"One more day won't hurt," she said. "There's no guarantee Hal is even there right now. And even if he is, it will probably be too dark and cold to come back safely tonight."

The idea of leaving us alone overnight seemed to seal the deal, and he grudgingly decided to stay.

"Well, I guess I better get dinner started, or we'll never eat," Amelia said. "I hope you're okay with chili," she said to Pat.

"You don't need to cook," I said quickly. "Pat and Richard are here for me, so please, let me. I can make the chili, and I think we have all the ingredients for homemade cornbread, as well."

"I'll help," Claire said.

"And I'll take care of the drinks," Jeremy piped in. "Richard, what can I get you? Wine, beer, whisky?"

Amelia ignored her sister and stalked off, clearly still upset from the morning's events. I headed into the kitchen, followed by Pat, Claire, and the sound of Jeremy's voice as he took drink orders from the rest of the family.

I had an ulterior motive for wanting to cook—at that point, with how weird everything was getting, I wasn't sure I trusted anyone else other than myself, Claire, and Pat with food preparation.

"At least now I can keep an eye on you," Pat hissed in my ear.

"Someone needs to," I said, keeping my voice equally low. I quickly glanced around, but it appeared we were alone in the kitchen. I went to the fridge and started pulling out ingredients.

"We should keep an eye on one another," Claire said quietly. "None of this feels right."

"No kidding," Pat snorted as I placed onions and peppers on the counter and pressed a knife into Claire's hand. "What clued you in? The dead attorney in your woodshed? Or perhaps it was our snowmobile suddenly not starting?"

"It's possible that was just bad luck," Claire said, although her tone was doubtful.

Pat's eyes widened. "Seriously? With how much Richard babies his toys?"

Claire frowned as she selected an onion and started automatically chopping. "Still doesn't mean it was sabotaged."

"Oh, come on," Pat said as I handed her the ground beef and a frying pan. "I can't be the only one who thinks it's awfully convenient that it just wouldn't start today."

"But it doesn't make sense. Why would someone mess with your snowmobile? It's not like you have anything to do with any of this," Claire said.

"How does any of this make any sense?" Pat asked. "I realize this was supposed to be a family get-together, and people often wish a family member would drop dead at those. But in your case, it actually happened."

"George wasn't a family member," Claire said. "He was our lawyer."

"Oh yes, because no one ever wants anything bad to happen to a lawyer," Pat countered.

"Fair enough," Claire said. "But you weren't even here when we found George. So why the sabotage?"

"Probably to keep Pat and Richard from leaving," I said.

"I get it, but why?"

"Claire, you can't possibly be this obtuse," I said gently as I started measuring flour for the cornbread.

"I'm not being 'obtuse,'" she replied as her onion-chopping became more aggressive. I was beginning to regret handing her a knife.

"Okay, you're not being obtuse," I said. "Now, will you stop taking it out on that poor onion?"

Claire paused, knife poised in the air, and loudly sniffed. "The onion is making me cry," she said as she reached for a paper towel.

My eyes flickered toward Pat, who appeared to be similarly concerned. "Yeah, onions can do that."

Claire mopped her eyes. "I still don't understand why anyone would want to keep Pat and Richard here," she said, her voice muffled by the paper towel.

"Probably because they were going to get help," I said.

Claire eyed me. "But what would that do? It's just delaying the inevitable."

"Well, as Pat keeps pointing out, there's a dead body here," I said. "My guess is, whoever killed George doesn't want cops poking around."

"But again, that's inevitable," Claire said. "Eventually, the roads will be plowed, and we'll be able to leave. Or the phones will work. Or someone will come by, like Pat and Richard did."

"Well, it could be a delay tactic," I said. "Maybe they're trying to figure out how to cover up what they did. Or maybe they're looking for a way to escape before the cops get here."

"Or maybe they want to make sure they've covered their tracks enough to get away with it," Pat said.

Claire crumpled the paper towel. "This is nuts," she muttered, furtively looking around as if expecting the rest of her family to suddenly appear.

"I don't understand," I said. "You were the one who practically accused the rest of your family of killing George. Why is it such a stretch to think whoever killed him is also buying time by preventing the cops from arriving to investigate?"

Claire selected a green pepper and went back to chopping. "It's hard to explain," she said finally. "It's silly. Because you're right—why would sabotaging a snowmobile be that much of a stretch if someone could actually kill George? I guess it just feels a lot more ..." her voice trailed off.

"Creepy?" I asked.

Claire grimaced. "Something like that. The idea that someone doesn't want us to bring the cops in is kind of ... well, scary."

"It is that," Pat said grimly, adding the onions to the beef.

"We definitely need to watch our backs," I said. "But it's also possible this isn't as bad as it seems. Maybe it's just a crazy coincidence."

Claire gave me a faint smile. "And George was just an accident."

I shrugged. "It's possible."

"Speaking of coincidences," Pat said, "does anyone else think it's super weird that the phones still don't work?"

"Well, yes," Claire said. "But the weather ..."

"They're working in town," Pat interrupted.

"Town is different."

"Regardless, it usually doesn't take this long for the phone company to repair whatever's wrong," Pat said. "It's been almost 48 hours."

Claire eyed us both. "So, whoever killed George and sabotaged the snowmobile has taken out the phones, as well?"

"Like I said … we need to watch our backs," I answered.

Claire went back to her chopping. "This is crazy," she muttered.

"What I want to know," Pat said while vigorously stirring the ground beef, "is who do you think sabotaged our snowmobile?"

"Do we know who was upstairs with us and who wasn't?" I asked.

Pat gave me a look. "You mean when we were in the bedroom with the door closed so we wouldn't be able to see anything?"

"Ha, ha," I said. "Did you ask Richard if he saw anything?"

"I did," Pat said. "It turns out he wasn't paying attention."

"Why not?"

"Because he was busy talking to Wyle."

I sighed as I started mixing the batter. "Perfect. The two other people who we were already fairly certain had nothing to do with this were together. So, we have no idea who might have snuck outside."

"Pretty much," Pat agreed.

"Of course," Claire said. "That's been the theme of this weekend. Somehow, nine people can live in one house over a couple days without anyone noticing a murder taking place and … ouch." She dropped her knife and clutched her hand.

"What?" Pat asked.

"I cut myself …"

I left the batter and hurried over to Claire to look at her hand. "It's not too bad," I said, leading her to the sink to wash it.

"Can this weekend get any worse?" Claire asked.

"Sure it could," Pat said cheerfully. "You could bleed to death."

Claire glared at her. "You're not helping."

I wrapped a towel around Claire's hand. "Press down," I ordered. "I'll go find some bandages."

"I think they're in the downstairs bathroom," Claire's voice followed me as I hurried out of the kitchen.

The bathroom was empty. I went in, closing the door behind me, and started pawing through the cupboards looking for a Band-Aid.

There was a quiet knock on the door, causing my heart to jump in my chest. "Anyone in there?" Martin's voice called out.

I took a breath, pressing a hand against my chest. Martin was probably safe. Probably. Truth be told, I didn't trust anyone new to me as of that weekend. However, in this case, Pat and Claire both knew where I was and would likely come looking for me if I delayed too long. "Just me," I answered, opening the door. "I'll be out in a sec. Just looking for a Band-Aid."

Martin drew his eyebrows together. "Did you hurt yourself?"

"It's for Claire," I said, going back to my digging. "She cut herself."

"Ohhhh," Martin said.

There was something about his voice that made me eye him. "What?"

His expression was concerned ... more so than the situation warranted. "I'm sure it's nothing."

"What do you mean?"

He gave his head a quick shake. "I probably shouldn't have said anything."

At that, he had my full attention. I stopped my searching and faced him. "What are you talking about?"

He gave me an ashamed look. "I don't mean to make a big deal out of it."

"Out of what?"

He let out a deep sigh. "Claire."

The hairs on the back of my neck stood up. "Claire? What about her?"

"It's just ... I'm a little worried about her."

"Why?"

He cocked his head and studied me. "What do you know about her mother?"

"Her mother?" The change of subject momentarily took me aback. "Not much, other than she has dementia."

"Yes, early-onset dementia. Do you know how it started?"

"Ah, not really. I mean, I assumed it started with the deterioration of her mind, as she began forgetting things. Is that not what happened?"

"No … I mean, yes. Daisy did start forgetting things, that's true. But there was more to it. She also became extremely paranoid. She was convinced her life was in danger. She would call the cops constantly, saying there was someone in her yard or trying to break in. The cops investigated, and at first, they couldn't find any evidence that anyone was there. But then things started escalating. There were cigarette butts outside and footprints in the mud … that sort of thing. Then, the garage was broken into, and someone threw a brick though the window. Eventually …" Martin hesitated, almost like he couldn't bear to continue.

Inexplicably, I found myself thinking about how cold Claire's hands had been upstairs. "Eventually what?"

Martin sighed again. "Apparently, Daisy had been doing it all to herself."

I stared at him. "Wait, what? You're saying she was making it look like someone was after her?"

Martin nodded sadly. "That's exactly what was going on. And because it was escalating so quickly, everyone was concerned she might start hurting herself. The doctors wanted Daisy in a hospital, but Daisy didn't want to go. It was a messy, horrible time, especially for Claire."

"Just Claire?" I asked. "What about Amelia?"

"Well, of course it was hard on Amelia, too," Martin said. "But Claire is so similar to her mother. She has the same … 'weakness,' shall we say? Mental illness runs in the family. Flo's mother apparently had a similar condition."

"Really?" I wondered if that was part of the issue between Flo and Daisy. If Flo saw the same mental disease in her daughter that had also plagued her mother, it was no wonder she struggled with her.

"Yeah. It was really rough. Luckily, Iris was spared, along with Amelia and Lucy. But it's still a tragedy."

I was starting to get a bad feeling about this. "I agree, but I don't understand why you're telling me all of this. What does it have to do with Claire?"

Martin looked even more sad. "I was there when Daisy started to lose her mind. I saw the signs. And I'm seeing them now in Claire," he finished quietly.

"Charlie? Everything okay?" Pat's voice floated down the hallway.

"Yeah, I'll be there in a second," I hollered back. I had nearly forgotten about the Band-Aids. I thought again about Claire's cold hands and the wild look in her eyes after her nightmare.

No. It couldn't be. I arrived with Claire. I was with her the whole time.

Well, maybe not the *whole* time. It was true she had disappeared for a little bit—a very little bit. There was no way she was gone long enough to sneak out and kill George.

Or sabotage the snowmobile.

Although she *was* upstairs in her room while we were in the kitchen. Was it possible she could have snuck outside, sabotaged the snowmobile, and gotten back to her room before Pat and I went to see her?

Surely there was not enough time for that.

Yet I couldn't be sure.

My mouth was dry, so dry I wasn't sure if I could push the words out even if I wanted to ask the question burning on my tongue … but I had no choice. "What exactly are you seeing with Claire that you saw with her mother?"

Martin gave me a small, sympathetic smile. "Before it escalated with Daisy, she had a lot of delusions. Someone was after her … something was in the attic or the basement …"

"Basement?" I interrupted, my voice a bit higher than normal.

Martin slowly nodded. "Yes. She kept saying something had rotted in the basement, and whatever it was, it was destroying everything else."

I couldn't move. I felt like the blood was draining from my body.

"Charlie?" Pat yelled again. "You sure you're okay?"

"Yes, yes, sorry," I called back. "I'll be right there." I looked at Martin. "I need to go."

"Wait," Martin said, opening a drawer I hadn't gotten to yet and pulling out a box. "Band-Aids, right? That's what you came in here for."

"Yes. Thanks," I said, my fingers numb as I reached for the box and started to ease past him. "I better get this to Claire."

"Hang on," Martin said, rummaging through the cupboard. "You might want this, as well." He handed me a bottle of hydrogen peroxide.

"Thanks," I said, hurrying away before he could stop me again. My head was spinning, and I wasn't sure what to think. All I knew was that I wanted to get back to Claire as quickly as possible.

It felt even more imperative I not let her out of my sight. But whether that was to protect her or the rest of the family from her, I wasn't sure.

Chapter 17

"What? You think Claire is involved? Seriously?" Pat hissed in my ear.

"I don't know what to think," I whispered back.

After we bandaged Claire up and finished dinner preparations, we joined the rest of the family in the living room. Once everyone was settled, I was able to pull Pat aside and gave her a quick summary of what Martin had confided in me.

"What is the deal with Claire's mother?" I asked. "Is it true about the paranoia? And that she did all of that stuff to herself?"

Pat sighed. "That was the talk at the time. Although Flo never said anything to me about it."

"What was Daisy like?"

Pat frowned, thinking back. "I didn't know her very well. Even when she was 'healthy,' she wasn't very … social. She pretty much kept to herself. Although now that I think about it, I don't know if that was by choice or by circumstance."

"What do you mean?"

Pat pressed her lips together. "People can be cruel. Especially when things happen they don't understand. Daisy had a … well, I guess you could call it a 'knack' for knowing things. Things she really had no business knowing. Some people called her 'psychic.'"

"Was she?"

Pat shrugged. "Who knows? But she definitely had some scary-accurate premonitions. Especially around finding missing people. And some found that intimidating."

"Was she harassed?"

"Some. Some people even thought she had something to do with the disappearances. It was difficult for her, which is why

I think she decided it was easier for everyone if she just kept to herself." Pat cocked her head. "For that matter, Claire did, too. It was only when Daisy was committed that Claire got hired at Aunt May's, and then she really opened up. She made a bunch of friends and was always up for a smile and a chat."

I thought about how warm and welcoming Claire had been when I had first moved to Redemption. "Why do you think she changed so much?"

"I always assumed she grew up. Teenagers can be moody and difficult, but then they hit their twenties and turn into different people. Especially with what Claire had gone through with her mother ... that would change anyone."

I glanced over at Claire. She was sitting on the couch, resting the glass of wine Jeremy had pushed on her in her lap. As far as I could tell, she hadn't touched it. "Do you think Claire takes after her mother?"

"That's what everyone certainly thinks," Pat said. "Even Flo said it a few times. My guess is, it's true."

"So, it's possible that whatever happened to Daisy could happen to Claire."

Pat's eyebrows furrowed. "It's possible, sure. But Claire is at least fifteen years younger than Daisy was when she had her breakdown. If it's going to happen, I would assume it wouldn't be now."

"Unless it's being triggered by Flo's death," I said.

Pat stared at me. "You think this could be happening because of Flo? Claire wasn't that close to her."

"Not until recently," I corrected. "Think about it. You and I both know Claire hasn't been herself since Daphne was born. Her mother is, for all intents and purposes, gone. She's then able to start rebuilding her relationship with her grandmother, who then suddenly dies."

Pat chewed on her lip as she glanced over at Claire, who was now playing with her glass. "I didn't consider that."

"Do you know if there was any sort of trigger event with Daisy?" I asked.

"What do you mean?"

"Like, did something bad happen to trigger Daisy's breakdown? Did someone maybe die or get sick? Or some other sort of bad life event happen?"

Pat screwed up her face. "I'm trying to remember, but I don't think so. In fact, I think it was the opposite."

"The opposite?"

"Yeah, it seems to me that Flo was talking about opening this house back up again. Getting the family back together like she used to."

"Oh wow. So Daisy's breakdown must have been especially devastating to Flo, then."

"Yeah, it really was. If I'm recalling correctly, Flo and Daisy had started mending their relationship. I think it was Daisy who had reached out to Flo. And that's why Flo was thinking about starting the family get-togethers again. I believe Flo had even reached out to some contractors about finishing the house. She was hoping enough time had gone by for all the haunted talk to have died down. But then Daisy had her breakdown and was committed, and that was that."

"That's really sad," I said.

"Yeah, it is. It's also why I wasn't completely surprised Flo had this weekend get-together requirement in her will. Family was so important to her, and this house was like a physical symbol of that importance. But after losing Billy and Daisy, she couldn't handle it anymore. The pain was just too great."

I studied the scene in the living room, how the rest of the family smiled and laughed as they sipped their drinks. The candles were lit again, and the scene was warm and cozy ... nothing to reveal the tragedy and grief buried beneath the surface.

"What about Claire's dad?" I asked. "I haven't heard anything about him."

"He left years ago, when Amelia and Claire were little," Pat said. "I'm not sure why, although it was rumored that he couldn't deal with Daisy's abilities, either. I don't really know, though. No one talks about him much."

I studied Claire, noting how pale she was, the dark-purple circles under her eyes and clear signs of exhaustion. My mind flashed back to the first night, when she stood holding a candle, her face in shadow, and I had the very clear sense that she wasn't Claire at all … that there was something else watching me.

This house isn't safe.

"Pat, I want you to be really honest with me," I said. "You've known Claire longer than me. You knew her mother and grandmother. What do you really think is going on?"

Pat paused, her eyes on Claire. "I don't know," she finally said, her face troubled. "On one hand, I can't believe Claire would kill anyone, no matter the circumstance. But on the other hand, if she is heading down the same path as her mother …" Her voice trailed off before giving herself a quick shake. "No," she said more firmly. "I can't believe Claire could have done anything like that. Even if she was experiencing some sort of mental breakdown. First of all, it doesn't even make sense. Why would she kill the attorney, anyway?"

"Well, to play devil's advocate, if her mind is going, she might have killed George because she was confused and thought he was someone else," I said.

Pat sighed. "I suppose that's possible. Anything is possible. And it is true she hasn't been herself for a while now. I was hoping it was just her getting used to being home with a new baby. It can be a big transition for some women. But it's going on two years now, so maybe there is something deeper going on." She shook her head sadly. "I'm still having trouble believing she could ever hurt, let alone kill, anyone."

I pictured Claire huddled in bed after waking from her nightmare, her eyes wide with fear. Yet despite all of that, she still stood up to her family and told them what none of them wanted to hear—that whoever killed George was a member of the family.

If she was the killer, wouldn't it have made more sense to let everyone think Hal was to blame?

"Okay, so let's look at it the other way. If it wasn't Claire, then who?"

Pat chewed on her lip as she studied the family members. "I've never trusted Jeremy," she said at last. "Which doesn't mean I think he's a killer. But there is something shifty about him. It's in his eyes."

"Claire told me to be careful with Jeremy, as well," I mused, watching him refill his sister's wineglass.

"But then I go back to questioning Jeremy's motive to kill the attorney," Pat said.

"The inheritance?"

Pat snorted. "What inheritance? Don't get me wrong, Flo had enough to be comfortable. And she did have the two houses, this one and the one in town, which I guess is something … but I don't see it being enough to kill an attorney over."

"People have been killed for far less," I said. "Do you know who is going to inherit the houses?"

"I would imagine Iris," Pat said. "It probably would have been split between Daisy and Iris if Daisy was well, but if I had to guess, Iris would get the bulk of it, with all the grandkids and Daphne getting a small piece each. Again, nothing worth killing someone over. And of all the grandkids, Jeremy is probably doing the best financially. Plus, it's his mom who will benefit most."

"Doesn't seem fair to Claire and Amelia."

"No," Pat agreed. "But what do you do? I suppose it's possible Flo split the inheritance, so half will go to Iris and the other half into some sort of trust in Daisy's name that will eventually pass to Claire and Amelia. But again, how much are we really talking about here? Enough to kill?" She sighed again. "As much as it pains me to admit it, Claire killing the attorney while temporarily insane or in the middle of some sort of delusion makes far more sense to me than Jeremy killing him to somehow manipulate the inheritance."

As if sensing we were talking about him, Jeremy glanced up and caught my gaze. He raised the wine bottle and winked at me. "Want to join us?" he called out, as everyone turned to look at us.

"What are you talking about?" I responded. "We're here."

"Barely," he said.

"See what I mean?" Pat muttered, as we entered the living room further. "There's just something about him that doesn't feel right."

With everyone's eyes on us, I couldn't respond, so I instead made my way over to Claire. Martin especially seemed to be watching me carefully, no doubt wondering if I had shared our earlier conversation with her.

Pat noticed, as well. She glanced at me, the message clear in her eyes, before veering toward Martin. "It's so great seeing you two again," she said. "Although I'm sorry it has to be under these circumstances."

"Yes, it hasn't been easy," Iris answered. I noted how Pat positioned herself so Martin wouldn't be able to watch me as I talked to Claire. I mentally sent her a "thank you" as I settled myself next to my friend.

Before I could say anything, Jeremy appeared at my elbow, as if by magic. "Where's your glass?"

"Oh, I'm good for now."

"Nonsense," Jeremy said. "You need some wine. Brandon, want to grab a glass for me?"

"Charlie, would you like some wine?" Wyle asked.

"Of course she does," Jeremy answered on my behalf.

"I'd rather hear it from her," Wyle said.

"Sure," I said, thinking the sooner Jeremy poured me a glass, the faster he would drift away. But after doing so, he stayed where he was. "How do you know Pat?" he asked me.

"She's a client."

"A client?"

"I make custom tea for her."

He raised an eyebrow. "Maybe I ought to try this tea. It must be something special, for Pat to track you down in the middle of a snowstorm."

"We're friends, too," I said. "And she didn't come out here just for me. As you know, she's a friend of the family, so she of course wanted to make sure everything was okay."

"Yes, I'm sure that's the reason," Jeremy said drily as he sipped his wine.

"Oh, come on," Claire said impatiently. "What are you insinuating, Jeremy?"

"Just that it's … a little strange, for a friend of the friend to just show up to rescue us," Jeremy said. "Don't you agree, Amelia?" He turned to Amelia, who was doing a terrible job pretending not to listen to our conversation. She flushed red.

"There's nothing strange about it," Claire said. "You know Pat as well as I do. It's the sort of thing she does."

"But she probably wouldn't have, if you hadn't brought Charlie up here in the first place," Amelia said.

"How do you know?" Claire asked.

"Well, because she said it, for one," Amelia said. "She said she was calling for Charlie and couldn't get through because the phone lines were down."

"It wasn't just for me," I said. "Amelia, you know how long she knew your grandmother."

"That's true," Amelia said, but she continued to direct her words at Claire. "But would Pat have even known about this weekend family get-together if you hadn't brought Charlie in the first place?"

"What are you saying?" Claire asked. "That Pat showing up is somehow my fault?"

"I'm saying," Amelia said, "that it's awfully convenient for Pat to miraculously appear at a time when we really needed someone to miraculously appear."

Claire stared at her. "Are you saying what I think you're saying?" she asked, her voice low and a hint of danger in its tone.

"I'm not saying anything," Amelia said.

"It sure sounds like you are," Claire said. "In fact, it almost sounds like you're accusing me of something."

"Now you're being paranoid," Amelia said. "What would I be accusing you of?"

"I don't know, Amelia," Claire said, her voice rising. "What *are* you accusing me of?"

"Hey," Wyle said, stepping between them. "This isn't the time or the place. Right now, we need to focus on figuring out a way out of here."

"Maybe Amelia thinks that's my fault, too," Claire said bitterly. "That I caused the storm that snowed us in."

"Of course I don't think that," Amelia said stiffly. "That was just luck. You've always been the lucky one, haven't you?"

"What are you talking about?" Claire demanded, getting to her feet and facing her sister.

"Just that only someone very lucky would have the weather's full cooperation in her murder plan," Amelia said.

Claire's jaw dropped. "So you really are accusing me of killing George."

"If I recall, *you* are the one accusing one of us of being the killer, not me," Amelia said.

"But now you think it's me," Claire countered. "That doesn't even make sense. What on Earth would be my motive?"

"What on Earth would be any of ours?" Amelia asked. "That didn't stop you from blaming one of us."

"So, what? Is this payback for earlier?"

"It doesn't feel good to be accused, does it?" Amelia asked.

"What is wrong with you?" Claire was incredulous as Elliott attempted to guide his wife away.

But Amelia shook him off. "What is wrong with *me*? I'm not the one with the obvious motive making wild accusations here."

"Enough," Wyle said as Elliott again tried to intervene and Claire gasped. "This is the last thing we need right now."

Amelia turned on Wyle. "Oh? And how is it that you know what we need?"

The entire living room erupted in chaos as Wyle and Elliott tried to calm a fuming Amelia. Claire started to jump in as well, but I nudged her away. Amelia had crystalized a feeling that had been brewing inside me—that there was a subtle-but-clear closing of the ranks occurring that was leaving Claire squarely on the outside looking in. I wasn't sure who was leading the charge, but my money was on Amelia. She made the most sense, as she also could have been the one to put a bug in Martin's ear to come talk to me about Claire.

Claire gave me an exasperated look as I leaned closer to whisper in her ear. "We have to talk," I hissed. "You're in trouble."

"What are you talking about?" Claire asked in her normal voice. I gave her a hard look, touching my finger to my lips, but with the commotion, I suspected no one was paying any attention to us.

"Keep your voice down," I whispered. "And control your expression. I don't know who is watching us."

"I don't understand," Claire said, but her voice was much lower.

I glanced quickly around, but everyone seemed to be focused on The Amelia, Wyle, and Elliott Show than us. I leaned closer. "I can't get into all the details, and remember to control your reaction, but more people in your family than Amelia think you're the one who killed George."

Claire's eyes went wide as the blood drained from her face. It also looked like she was literally biting her tongue to keep from screaming. "Are you kidding me? Why? Why would I kill George?"

"Because you have early dementia, like your mother. Your uncle told me you're acting just like her right before she was hospitalized."

Claire's skin turned greenish, and I was a little afraid she might faint. "But that's not true. None of it is. Charlie, you have to help me."

"How?" I hissed, stealing a peek behind me. Amelia was starting to calm down, so I knew I didn't have much time. "Where do I even start?"

"I don't know! But you have to do something. If they're actually planning to pin this on me, what will happen to Daphne?" The pain in her voice was unmistakable, raw, and honest.

Was this entire thing a set-up? A way to frame Claire, the black sheep of the family, for murder?

Or was she truly just like her mother, so innocent-sounding simply because she wasn't even aware of what she was capable of?

"Before your mother was committed, was she doing things to herself? Like throwing a rock through her own window?"

Claire pressed her lips together. "Why are you asking me that?"

"Because that's what Martin told me. Is it true?"

"Are you saying you don't believe me?" Her voice had an edge of hysteria.

"I'm saying I have questions," I said. "And if I have questions, others have them, too. If you want me to help, we need to be able to answer those questions satisfactorily."

She stared at me, her eyes full of betrayal. For a moment, I thought she was going to walk away, maybe even refuse to talk to me, but something I said must have sunk in. "Yes," she said quietly. "Although she kept denying it, there was proof."

"What kind of proof?"

"An eyewitness. One of her neighbors."

I nodded. "Okay, so while we came here together, I wasn't with you the whole time before George was discovered. You disappeared while I was in the kitchen with Amelia."

"I told you, I wanted to call home and talk to Daphne. Good thing I did, seeing as I haven't been able to since."

I paused, wondering how to put my thoughts delicately. "You were gone a long time," I said. "Longer than needed for a simple phone call."

She glanced away. "Doug and I got into a fight," she said quietly. "And after Amelia, I didn't think I could face her, so I went upstairs to lay down for a few minutes and collect myself."

I studied her face. She seemed to be telling the truth. And it was certainly plausible. She and Doug didn't have a good marriage even when things were going well, which they certainly weren't now. With all the people moving around the house, I personally wouldn't have noticed any extra creaking had she moved up and down the stairs.

But it also meant no one could vouch for her, during the period of time George could have been killed.

"When Pat and I came up to your room, your hands were cold … *really* cold," I said. "Do you have any idea why?"

She tilted her head and gave me a puzzled look. "My hands? I don't understand. What are you asking?"

"It's just that the room was warm. I can't understand why your hands were so cold."

"They get that way sometimes," she said. "My feet, too. Especially since Daphne was born. My circulation isn't what it used to be. Plus, with the lack of sleep and feelings like I keep getting, my body tends to do a lot of whacky things. But I still don't understand. Do you think I snuck out of the room and went outside or something? Why would I do that?"

I didn't answer, but I didn't have to. A moment after she asked the question, her eyes widened. "You think I sabotaged the snowmobile."

"I'm asking the question."

"Charlie, you know I'm hopeless with mechanical things! I can't believe you would think this about me."

That was true, and I probably should have remembered it sooner. "I'm sorry," I said. "I'm not trying to upset you. But Martin is making a case that you aren't in your right mind, by claiming you're doing things without even being aware you're doing them. So, I have to ask the questions, because you know other people are going to."

She was silent. "I'm in trouble," she said softly. "Aren't I?"

I wanted to tell her no, we would figure out a way out of all of it. But glancing around the room, Claire's family kept shooting her looks that ranged from pity to contempt. I couldn't bring myself to even pretend.

"I think so," I said. Martin and Iris still seemed to be in deep conversation with Pat, which was good, but I knew I was running out of time. "Unless you can give me some idea of what I can do to help."

Claire bit her lip as her eyes darted around the room. "My dream," she said.

I glanced sideways at her. "What?"

"How you can help. There's something in this house. My dream made that clear. You need to find it."

"Okay. What am I looking for?"

She frowned. "I'm not sure."

"Do you know where I should start looking?"

She shot me a helpless look.

I wanted to swear in frustration, but right then, the image of the stuck door tucked away in the basement suddenly and magically appeared before my eyes again. "Hang on," I said. "I might know exactly where to start."

Chapter 18

My hands were sweaty as I yanked on the string to turn on the first naked lightbulb in the basement. I surveyed the scene as I nervously wiped one off on my jeans, transferred the flashlight to that hand, and wiped off the other. It was as messy as it was when I had first ventured down to the laundry room with Lucy.

I really hoped I wasn't making a big mistake.

Claire knew I was there, but I told her to cover for me as I slipped out of the living room and into the kitchen under the pretense of checking on the food. Everything was done, of course. The homemade cornbread was on the counter, the salad was in the fridge along with the homemade salsa for the chips, and the chili was simmering on the stove. I gave the latter a halfhearted stir before digging around for a flashlight.

Suitably armed, I headed for the basement.

I would have preferred telling Pat, as well, or even Richard, but both were busy chatting and mingling with the rest of the family members, albeit guardedly. With any luck, Pat would be able to keep them entertained, and no one would realize I was missing.

The last thing I wanted was for the real killer among us to realize I was alone in the basement and come looking for me.

There was no time to waste. The sooner I checked out the stuck door, the quicker I could get back upstairs and into the relative safety of the main group.

I took another deep breath, wiped my hands again on my jeans, and ignoring the deep sense of wrongness in the pit of my stomach, started to wind my way around the piles of debris.

I have to help Claire, I kept repeating to myself, as my steps grew slower and slower seemingly on their own accord. A darkness seemed to descend upon me, like I was sinking into some sort of pit of quicksand, unable to move, unable to breathe. I kept forcing myself to take one step after the other, despite each becoming more and more difficult. The door loomed in front of me, growing even larger … becoming so huge, it could very well open to a monster lurking in the shadows, just waiting to burst through.

A monster with sharp, pointed teeth.

This house isn't safe.

I froze, unable to push myself any further. A drop of sweat trickled down my forehead, leaving an icy trail in its wake. All I wanted to do was run back up the stairs into the warmth and safety of the living room. Even knowing there might be a killer mingling in that room, sipping on a drink, engaging in small talk, wasn't enough to keep me from desperately wanting to flee.

It's not real.

I blinked. The words sliced through the black fog in my brain like a beacon of white light, and in that moment, I found I could focus again.

I was alone in the basement. There was no one else there, and if anyone tried to sneak down after me, the old, creaky stairs would give them away.

Claire was the one in trouble, not me. I had a job to do, and I needed to do it.

I took a deep breath, squared my shoulders, and marched over to the door. It was time to get to the bottom of whatever dark secret was rotting Claire's family's house from the inside out.

With my mind cleared, I couldn't help but wonder if what I'd just experienced was what Claire had meant about the house being 'haunted,' when she'd said it wasn't by ghosts. If it was, no wonder the contractor fell off the ladder. Consumed with that feeling that he was about to be devoured combined with an irrational urge to flee could easily have pushed him to take a wrong step, resulting in his fall.

I was sure the same could have easily happened to me. I was just lucky to not be on a ladder.

I took another deep breath and grasped the doorknob. No luck. It still wasn't budging.

I felt something inside me deflate, like a balloon. All of this build up for nothing?

No. I wasn't going to accept that. There was something there. I knew it. I could feel it. And it had to do with that door. I just wasn't seeing it yet.

I clicked on the flashlight and shone it around the edges, searching for swollen wood or some other sort of blockage I might be able to work around. Nothing.

To be fair, I wasn't sure if I would even know what wood-swelling would look like. I examined the entire door regardless, but as far as I could tell, there was nothing.

Now what? Frustrated, I stepped back. Should I try and force it open? I wondered how the rest of the family would feel if I ended up damaging it. I shone the light around the basement, looking for some sort of tool … maybe a crowbar would be less destructive than say, a sledgehammer.

Of course, there was nothing obviously helpful close by. I would have to search through all the debris, which would likely take hours, and even then, there were no guarantees.

But the toolshed would surely have something.

Getting to it would obviously complicate matters.

Argh. I swung the flashlight back to the door again, hoping against hope to find something. Anything.

And then I saw it.

A flash at the bottom of the door.

What on Earth …?

I aimed the flashlight and saw it again. Yes, there was definitely something down there. The bright sparkle inexplicably reminded me of the words that had cut through the terror in my head, and suddenly, I knew that whatever it was, I was meant to find it. And just as there was something rotten in the basement, there was also something else.

Something that might even be considered good.

I got down on my hands and knees, the cold of the cement floor seeping through my jeans. There it was—a piece of metal … maybe a necklace of sorts.

Even though it gave me the willies to do it, I was able to slide my finger under the door far enough to touch it. I held my breath the entire time, sure that I was about to touch something slimy or gross … or that my finger was about to be bitten off.

Ugh.

"Claire, you definitely owe me," I muttered as I pressed myself closer to the door and slowly pulled the cold, hard object that certainly felt like metal out from under the door.

It was a necklace. The links were thick and heavy, like something a man would wear, and the silver was tarnished. There was also a medal attached, the etching well-worn. I picked it up, rubbing it against my sweater so I could get a better look. It was a St. Christopher medal.

Alarm bells started ringing in my head as I knelt on the floor, the cold from the floor leaching into my veins, freezing me like a statue.

I had seen a St. Christopher's medal somewhere else in the house … in a picture of a happy little boy, grinning from ear to ear as he held up a fish he had just caught. It was around his neck.

My fingers went numb. I stared at the door, reminding myself that I didn't actually know if the little boy in that picture was Billy. No one had told me, and I hadn't thought to ask. It could be someone else. Jeremy, even.

And even if that little boy in the photo was Billy, it didn't necessarily mean the St. Christopher's medal in my hand was his. They were common, after all. And even if it was his, there could very well be some other reasonable explanation for it being where I'd just found it.

It didn't necessarily mean anything at all.

A particularly loud creak from upstairs burst through my thoughts, causing me to scream and topple over, falling against the door. It held, of course. It might have made things easier on my body if it had opened, although if it had, I might have started screaming and never stopped. I frantically scrambled to my feet, the flashlight jittering madly as I fought to get up.

That was when I saw it—the little round mark on the wood. What the ...?

I bent to get a closer look, trying to figure out what it could possibly be. I ran my finger across it. It too felt like metal and had a tarnished look to it. If I didn't know better, I would have said it looked like a nail, pounded in until it was flat against the wood.

Of course, that was silly. There was no good reason to hammer a nail in the middle of the door like that.

I swept the flashlight to the right and saw a couple more of the same. Why would there be nails in the door like that? It didn't look like it was falling apart, so why would someone hammer a line of nails into it?

Unless ...

I gasped, almost dropping the necklace and the flashlight as I jumped back as though the wood itself had scalded me.

The pieces clicked together in my brain.

Unless someone purposefully nailed the door shut.

Chapter 19

I burst into the living room, my breathing ragged and throat raw. I had been so loud, so abrupt, that everyone paused mid-sentence to stare at me.

"Charlie?" Claire asked tentatively as Pat and Wyle both took a step toward me.

My gaze fell on each of them. Martin. Iris. Amelia. Elliott. Jeremy. Lucy.

One of them was a killer.

I knew it.

"I found Billy," I said.

The silence was so complete, I was sure I could hear a mound of snow falling off a tree and hitting the ground outside.

Amelia spoke first. "That's not funny." Her voice was cold. "Haven't we suffered enough this weekend? Now you want to play some sort of joke on us? I always knew something was off with you. Louise said you had something to do with her brother going missing, and I should have listened to her ..."

I ignored her, instead holding up the necklace. The St. Christopher's medal glinted in the light. Amelia's voice died away.

Iris gasped. "Where did you find that?"

"By the cistern."

"That's impossible," Iris said as the blood leached from her face. "The cistern was walled off. No one can get back there.'

"There's still a door," Lucy said.

"Well, yes, I know that, but it doesn't even open, does it?" Iris shot me a hard look. "You're lying. Tell us the truth. Where did you find that necklace?"

"I told you. By the cistern."

Iris started shaking her head frantically. "No, no, no. That's not possible. There's no way you could have found that necklace there." At that, she looked directly into my eyes. "My brother was wearing a necklace like that when he disappeared. So, I ask you again. *Where* did you find it?"

"By the cistern," I said, keeping my voice calm. Iris was looking more and more hysterical, and I was starting to worry she might be going into shock.

"I thought the door was stuck," Lucy said. "How did you manage to open it?"

"I didn't. I fished it out from under the door."

Iris's eyes flashed. "*Under* the door? You were snooping? Or are you making all of this up?"

"It's the truth," I said quietly.

"What I want to know is how you even know that Billy had a necklace like that?" Amelia interrupted. "You weren't here when he was around. Who told you he had a necklace like that?" She glared at Claire. "You two are in on this together, aren't you? Trying to trick us into thinking that our uncle … you should be ashamed of yourselves. How low will you go?"

"No one told me," I said. "There's a picture of Billy wearing this necklace on the fireplace mantle."

Amelia glanced behind her at the massive fireplace and opened and shut her mouth.

"She's lying," Iris said again. "Billy can't be here. He left years ago. That can't be his necklace. It just can't."

"Maybe it's not," Jeremy said. "It's also possible Billy left his necklace here before he disappeared. Just because Charlie found it in the basement doesn't mean Billy is actually in the basement."

"I think it's more likely that Charlie planted it," Amelia said.

"'Planted it'?" I asked, raising my eyebrows. "What, do you think I brought with me a spare St. Christopher medal in case of such an emergency? Or are you suggesting I found a way to hike into town, in the middle of a snowstorm, in order to find this exact necklace, so I could pretend to find it here?"

"St. Christopher's medals are pretty common," Amelia said. "Maybe you found one somewhere else in the house and are just pretending you found it in the basement."

"Yeah, maybe I actually found it in your room, tucked away in your clothes," I fired back.

Amelia's eyes widened. "You went through my things? How dare you?"

Pat looked at Amelia in surprise. "You have a St. Christopher's medal in your room?"

"No, that's not what I'm saying. But Charlie's talking about going through my things," Amelia said.

"There is a way to find out for sure if Charlie is telling the truth or not," Jeremy said.

"How?" Iris asked.

Jeremy flashed a sardonic grin. "Easy. Let's check the cistern."

"The cistern? What will that do?" Iris asked.

"Well, if Billy is in there, then we know that Charlie is telling the truth," Jeremy said.

Iris pressed a hand against her heart. "Jeremy! How can you say such a thing? Billy's not in the cistern. Don't be ridiculous."

Jeremy shrugged. "Well, then, what's the problem? We should check just to be sure."

"No, we absolutely should NOT," Iris said, her voice shaking. "We absolutely should NOT give this terrible lie any more credence by even pretending to take it seriously."

"I agree with Jeremy," I said. "I think we should check it out. There's only one problem."

"What?" Wyle asked.

"The door to it is nailed shut."

"It is not," Lucy scoffed. "The wood just swelled up."

"How do you know?" Iris asked.

"Because Charlie was trying to get in there earlier, and the door wouldn't open," Lucy said.

"So, you *were* snooping," Iris said. "Was that when you got the idea to pretend you found the necklace there?"

I took a breath. "Someone has nailed the door that leads to the cistern shut," I said slowly, keeping my tone calm. "It was under that very door that I found your missing brother's necklace. I have no reason to pretend anything."

Silence. This one longer than the last.

Wyle was the first to break it. "You said someone nailed the door to the cistern shut?"

"Yes."

Iris gave a little shriek as her knees buckled and she fell onto the couch. "It can't be, it can't be," she moaned, burying her face in her hands.

"I don't believe her," Amelia said indignantly. "Why would anyone nail the door shut? It doesn't even make sense."

Wyle ignored Amelia. "Charlie, how do you know the door was nailed shut, as opposed to being stuck, or some other perfectly rational explanation?"

"Because of the nails," I said.

"You can see the nails?"

"Yes."

"Isn't it normal to have nails in doors?" Amelia asked suspiciously.

I took another deep breath, fighting the urge to snap at her. Amelia was probably in shock, as well, and I needed to be compassionate. "Maybe we should all go into the basement together, and I can show you what I found," I said.

"Splendid idea," Jeremy said. "I'm in. I just need a refill. Anyone care to join me?"

"This isn't a joke," Amelia snapped. "You do understand Charlie is now accusing us of murder, too, don't you?"

"I'm not accusing anyone of anything," I said. "I simply said Billy is in the cistern."

"If he is, he certainly didn't put himself there," Amelia said. "And he absolutely didn't nail the door shut."

"This all must be a big mistake," Iris attempted weakly.

"Well, there's one way to find out," Jeremy said. "Let's all go down into the basement."

"Actually," Martin said, taking a step forward. "That won't be necessary."

Everyone stared at him. "Martin?" Iris asked cautiously. "What are you talking about?"

"It won't be necessary, because she *is* telling the truth," Martin answered.

Nobody said a word. Iris's face was chalk white, and her hands shook.

"Martin," she squeaked, her voice barely a whisper. "Are you saying that …"

"Yes," Martin said with a sigh, rubbing his bald head. "It's true. All of it is true. I'm so sorry Iris, but yes … your brother is in the cistern."

Iris let out a little scream before fainting dead away.

* * *

By the time Iris came to, we had rearranged ourselves in the living room. Claire, Pat, and I clustered around Iris, loosening her clothes and pressing a cold washcloth to her face. Jeremy, Lucy, Elliott, and Amelia were huddled in another corner, Amelia looking like she was next in line to faint. Richard and Wyle had positioned themselves on either side of Martin, carefully watching him.

Martin, for his part, didn't look like a killer. He was hunched over, his expression tired, as if he had been carrying a heavy burden for a long time and had just finally set it down.

"So, Martin," Wyle said in a formal tone, once we had helped Iris to a sitting position and she had taken a few sips of water. "Why don't you tell us all exactly what happened."

Martin hung his head even lower. "I didn't want it come out like this. But I was trying to protect Daisy."

"Daisy?" Iris asked, her voice still too high-pitched. I shifted position, so I could catch her if she fainted again. "My sister? What does she have to do with this?"

Martin looked even more miserable. "Because she's responsible."

"Responsible?" Claire asked, a dangerous edge to her voice, as Iris pressed her fingers against her temples and shook her head, moaning to herself. "How precisely is she responsible?"

Martin's expression was sad as he regarded her. "Oh, honey. You know the truth."

Claire straightened her shoulders. "I most certainly do not. What are you saying?"

Martin looked around the room as though searching for help, but everyone, even Jeremy, seemed shocked into silence. "I'm saying that Daisy was responsible for Billy's ... death."

Iris jerked her head up. "My sister killed my brother?" Her voice was very close to a scream. "And you knew this? And you're just telling me now, after all these years?"

"It wasn't my idea to keep it from you," Martin said.

"*Then whose was it?*"

Martin paused. "Well, I guess it's all going to come out now anyway," he said sadly. "It was Flo's idea."

Iris gasped, clutching at her throat, and I started to worry she might keel over from a heart attack right then and there. "My mother?" she rasped, like her throat had closed, and she could no longer get any air through. "You're saying my mother knew that Daisy killed Billy, and she didn't tell anyone but you?"

"Martin, I think you need to start from the beginning," Pat said, her expression as concerned as mine as she started rubbing Iris's back.

Martin sighed again and nodded. "I didn't know until after Daisy was committed," he said. "One afternoon, Flo called and asked if I could stop by the next morning. She asked me to come alone and keep it to myself. I thought maybe she wanted to plan a surprise birthday party for Iris, since her birthday was coming up. But that wasn't it. She told me she suspected Daisy had killed Billy.

"Of course, I was shocked. I said we should call the police, but she refused. Daisy wasn't herself anymore, so what would be the point? It's not like she was in any position to hurt anyone again, so putting her in jail or some prison hospital would be useless. Plus, Flo was convinced that when Daisy killed Billy, she wasn't in her right mind and didn't even remember doing it, so it wasn't even like punishing her would help her repent. It would just confuse and upset her, which would likely exacerbate her mental condition."

"Why *did* she think Daisy killed Billy, then?" Wyle asked.

"She wouldn't tell me specifics. Only that she first started to suspect Daisy when Daisy told her Billy was dead."

Out of the corner of my eye, I saw Claire start, like she had been poked with a hot iron.

Martin looked around at everyone. "I mean, how would she know Billy was dead unless, well, she was the one who did it?"

"But why did she tell you this?" Wyle asked. His expression was what I had come to think of as his "cop face"—smooth and devoid of emotion.

"Because she wanted me to look into it. See if Daisy really did kill Billy, or if it was just part of her delusion."

"And so you came up here?" Wyle asked, the tiniest bit of skepticism creeping into his tone.

"Well, I didn't start here," Martin said defensively. "I started with her home, of course. Looking for clues. I didn't find anything. When I reported that back to Flo, I thought she would be relieved, but she asked me to check this house. Again, she didn't give me any specifics. So that's what I did.

"You can imagine my horror when I checked the cistern and found Billy. Again, I wanted to call the cops, but again, Flo refused. She asked if I would take care of it. So ... I did."

"You were the one who nailed the door shut?" Wyle asked.

Martin nodded. "I couldn't think of anything else to do. I didn't want anyone else stumbling onto the body, and it wasn't like I could easily move it somewhere else. It seemed the best thing would be to nail the door shut to keep anyone else from stumbling in and, well, finding Billy."

"You didn't tell me," Iris said again, her voice numb with grief. "How could you not tell me?" There was no sign of tears yet, and I wondered if she was still in too much shock to even cry.

"Flo didn't want me telling anyone," Martin said. "And quite honestly, I agreed with her. I didn't want to put you in the position of knowing and not being able to tell anyone, either."

"But now Flo's dead," Wyle said. "Why didn't you call the police? Or tell your family?"

"She's only been dead a week," Martin said. "I had planned to, once we were able to have a funeral and properly mourn her."

"You really think the family would have said anything to anyone?" Iris asked. "No one would have said a word. You didn't give us a chance to mourn my brother properly. I know my mother would have known that, too. I can't believe she did this. I can't believe *you* did this."

Martin hesitated, eyeing Claire. "There was another reason Flo didn't want me telling anyone."

"What?" Iris asked tentatively.

Again, he paused. "She was afraid."

"Afraid of what?"

Martin looked more and more uncomfortable as he kept his eyes on Claire. Iris glanced between them. "What? Is this about Claire?"

"Yes, what about me?" Claire asked.

"It's just … Flo thought she saw the same, shall we say 'weaknesses,' in Claire that were in Daisy, and she didn't want to upset anyone."

Claire's mouth fell open. "What? Are you trying to say my grandmother thought I might be a murderer?"

"She didn't say it like that," Martin said quickly. "And to be clear, she didn't think your mother is a murderer, either."

"You just said my mother is the one who killed Billy!"

"Yes, but she wasn't in her right mind," Martin said. "Flo was sure it only happened because she was in some sort of delusion and had no idea what she was doing. I didn't see it, of course, and I told her that." He paused. "I thought you were fine, Claire. But after this weekend and George …" his voice trailed off.

Claire's face was white, and she took a step back. "You think I killed George," she said in a strangled voice.

"Not because you meant to," Martin said quickly. "I don't think it was your fault."

"Then whose fault was it?"

"Bad genes and bad luck. We'll get you the very best help, Claire. We're your family," Martin said.

Claire took another step back as her eyes darted around the room. "What help are you talking about?"

"Wait," Iris said. "You think Claire is responsible for killing George?"

"Not responsible," Martin corrected. "It's not her fault."

"I did NOT kill George," Claire said firmly.

"We're going with Claire?" Jeremy asked, attempting to capture his normal sarcastic tone, but his face was too pale for it to completely believable. "That's a plot twist I didn't expect."

"This isn't a joke, Jeremy," Martin said, his tone disapproving. "Claire needs our help and support. Not snarky comments."

"I did NOT kill George," Claire repeated, her voice louder.

"You were so quick to blame the rest of us," Amelia said. "How do we know that wasn't just to hide a guilty conscience?"

Claire whirled on her sister. "You really think I'm capable of killing someone?"

"I think you're capable of all sorts of things," Amelia said. "Especially if it furthers your goal."

"And what goal would killing George further?" Claire asked.

"In this case, to make the point about the house being haunted," Amelia said.

"*What?*" Claire looked flabbergasted.

"I think you set this whole thing up to prove Mom isn't crazy," Amelia said.

"Are you out of your mind?" Claire seemed barely able to comprehend what she was hearing.

"I'm not the one constantly apologizing for Mom," Amelia said. "Or pretending to believe her nonsense. Look, I get why you did it. I wanted a real mother, too. But we didn't get one. And for you to keep pretending she had some sort of 'gift' when it actually drove her mad ... it's just not true."

"You honestly think I would kill George to prove Mom isn't crazy?" Claire asked. "That I would be capable of killing another human being, because of Mom?" Her voice was truly bewildered. "Forget the convoluted logic around how that might somehow prove Mom isn't crazy. You honestly think I'm capable of killing another human being?"

"You tried to kill me," Amelia said.

"What are you talking about now?" Claire asked.

"Yesterday, with the toaster over," Amelia said.

Claire's eyes went wide. "Seriously? We're back on the toaster oven …"

"We don't know what happened with that," Wyle interjected.

"Well, someone tried to kill me," Amelia said. The color had come back into her face, as if blaming her sister somehow allowed her to push aside the horror that was just revealed. "And you're clearly the most obvious suspect."

"Amelia, listen to me," Claire said, her voice urgent. "I did NOT try to kill you with the toaster oven. Nor did I kill George. I could never kill anyone."

"I really don't think anyone was trying to kill you with the toaster oven," Wyle said yet again.

"Fine," Amelia said, her voice huffy. "Obviously, no one cares if I live or die, so let's talk about George, because you do all seem to care about him. Maybe you didn't kill George on purpose. Maybe it was an accident."

Claire's voice rose an octave higher. "An accident?"

"I'm just saying," Amelia said. "You could have been trying to set something up this weekend to make it look like the house was haunted. Maybe you just wanted to do something to scare George. Let's face it, if you could convince boring old George the house is haunted, you could convince anyone. And if we were all convinced that it was, then Mom isn't crazy after all. She was actually right—the house was haunted. But something happened, and George died, so you panicked. And now, here you are trying to blame the rest of us."

"The rest of you? Amelia, this is insane. I'm not trying to blame anyone," Claire said. "I have no idea what happened to George."

"Amelia, you don't truly believe your sister could have done this," Iris broke in, her voice hollow and exhausted. "I know you two girls haven't always seen eye to eye, but come on. What your uncle is saying makes far more sense … that Claire wasn't in her right mind."

"Listen to me. I did not kill George!" Claire said forcefully. "And furthermore, there is nothing wrong with my mind."

"But, honey, how would you know?" Iris asked. "If your mind is going, would you have any idea what's happening?"

Claire looked wildly around the room before turning to me, a desperate look in her eyes.

I had been frozen, unable to believe what was unfolding in front of me. I never for a second believed that finding Billy's necklace would somehow descend into Claire being accused of George's death. On the other hand, if the real killer was trying to deflect blame onto someone else, Daisy and Claire were ideal candidates—Daisy couldn't even defend herself, and Claire already had credibility issues with the family. I had to hand it to Martin … there was no one alive and in their right mind to collaborate his story.

Which left only one question: was Martin the killer, or was he protecting someone else? His wife or one of his children, maybe? Or Amelia? She had been pretty quick to jump in to support Martin's explanation. Could they be in it together?

"There's no way Claire could have killed George," I said. "I was with her the entire time."

"Not the *entire* time," Martin said. "I know I saw you in the kitchen with Amelia, and Claire wasn't there."

How did he remember that? "Okay, I was with her the entire time except for ten minutes here and there when she was in the bathroom," I said. "She was not alone long enough to kill George. It's not possible."

"Why should we believe you?" Amelia asked. "Maybe this is exactly why Claire brought you … so you could lie about her whereabouts."

"That's absolute nonsense," I said. "Besides, if Claire's mental facilities were deteriorating the way you're all claiming, we would have seen evidence of it. But we haven't."

"Yes, waking us up in the middle of the night to go on about something rotten in the house is perfectly normal behavior," Amelia said.

"Well, it's certainly not comparable to killing someone in a delusional state, and you know it," I shot back.

"Enough," Wyle said. "This isn't helping. I think we all need to take a breath and calm down."

"And then what?" Amelia asked. "I, for one, do not feel safe in this house unless she," she pointed at Claire, "is restrained."

Claire's expression was horrified. "You want to tie me up? Is that what you're saying?"

"I'm saying we need to treat you like the danger you are," Amelia said.

"I hardly think that's necessary," Wyle said.

"I cannot believe you …" Claire began, but a loud knock on the door interrupted her.

Chapter 20

Everyone stared at one another. "Who could that be?" Iris asked in a hushed voice.

"We could answer the door and find out," Jeremy said.

Wyle was already striding across the floor to do the honors. A bundled-up figure stepped inside. "Hello," said Hal. "I can't stay long, as it's going to be dark here pretty quick, but I thought I'd better check on your phones."

Wyle gave him a puzzled look. "Our phones?"

Hal unwound his scarf from his face. "Yeah, I'm thinking someone knocked a phone off the hook or unplugged something without realizing it when the phones were out. Figured you might not know they're back."

Wyle stared at him, his expression uncomprehending. "Wait. You're saying the phones are working again?"

Hal nodded. "Yep. Since sometime this morning. That's why I didn't come by with the snowmobile … I figured you were able to get your message out. And I thought I heard a snowmobile come by, but I didn't hear anyone leave, and I … well, it probably sounds a bit silly, but I decided to call and make sure everything was fine. But your line was still dead. That's when I realized you might not know, so I headed on over to get it straightened out."

Hal paused, and only then did he seem to have some sense of the growing tension in the room. "Uh, is everything okay? Do you need help with the phones?"

"You know, I think we're okay," Wyle said, keeping his voice pleasant. "You're right, one of us must have accidentally knocked a phone off the hook, and we'll just need to run around and find it. There's no need for you to mess around with that, especially since you're right—it's getting dark. I'm sure you're needed at home."

"Okay, if you're sure," Hal said, seeming a little uncertain. He looked around the room, clearly sensing the energy was off, but not sure what was going on.

"I am," Wyle said, clapping him on the back. "But can you do me a favor? When you get back to your house, would you mind calling the Redemption police and letting them know that Officer Brandon Wyle is here and might not be in tomorrow as scheduled?"

Hal took a step back. "Well, uh, sure. But won't you be able to do that once you get the phone working?"

"Yes," Wyle said firmly. "I will most definitely call as soon as we've figured out why the phones aren't working, but in case there's a bigger problem, it would be good to know you're my backup." He let out a little chuckle that sounded perfectly normal. "They're short-staffed and counting on me, you see, so the sooner they know I won't be able to make it in, the faster they'll be able to find my replacement."

Hal's face cleared. "Oh. Of course. I'd be happy to." He started wrapping the scarf around his face. "I'll get that call in right away."

"I appreciate that," Wyle said, clapping him on the back again, his eyes flickering past everyone in the room as if warning us to keep calm and not make any sudden moves. He waited until Hal was safely out of the house and the door was shut firmly behind him before turning to everyone, arms folded across his chest.

"What is going on with the phones?" he asked. His voice was quiet, but there was a dangerous edge to it.

"What do you mean?" Iris asked. I got the distinct feeling that she was trying—and failing—to convince herself that her entire life wasn't imploding … aware that one wrong move might cause the veneer of normalness to fall away, revealing the violence that was bubbling under the surface. "It's probably just an accident, just like what Hal said."

"An 'accident,'" Wyle repeated.

"Of course it is," Lucy said, her voice nervous. "What else would it be?" Her eyes were just as nervous, shifting around the room as if she was unsure which side she should be on.

"I think your boyfriend is asking us if someone did something to the phones on purpose," Jeremy said.

"Oh hush," Iris intervened. "That's not funny."

"I'm not trying to be funny," Jeremy said.

"Are you accusing us of something now, too?" Amelia asked.

"You heard Hal," Wyle interrupted. "His phones are working, and ours aren't. So, I'm asking again, what's going on with our phones?"

"Maybe ask Claire," Amelia said, nodding her head. "She's the one who killed George."

"How many times do I have to say it? I had nothing to do with George's death," Claire said in exasperation. "And I certainly didn't have anything to do with the phones being sabotaged. I wouldn't even know where to start."

"Anyone can take a phone off the hook," Amelia said.

"Let's not get ahead of ourselves," Wyle said. "We should start with finding the problem. I suggest we check every phone." He paused and gave us each a hard look. "All of us."

"You want us all to come with you?" Iris asked.

"I think that would be best, don't you?" Wyle said. His tone was polite, but his meaning was clear. No one was leaving his sight until this was either resolved or he had backup.

No one said a word as we all shuffled forward in a large, unruly mass into each room to examine the phones—first, the two downstairs before moving upstairs.

All appeared to in working order, plugged into the wall, and on their respective cradles.

And still, no dial tone.

"Are there any other phones anywhere?" Wyle asked as everyone filed back into the kitchen.

"That's it," Martin said.

"I guess we better check the outside wiring then," Wyle said.

"We're not all going out there," Iris said, alarmed. "It's cold and dark outside."

"We should all go," Wyle said, but his eyes flickered to the outside window, where the shadows were already lengthening.

"I'll go check it," Martin said.

"Not alone," Wyle said.

"Nonsense," Martin replied, moving to get his coat and boots. "I'll be fine."

"I'll go with him," Richard offered, joining him.

"That's not necessary," Martin said.

"It *is* necessary," Wyle said. "No one goes anywhere alone."

"What does it matter?" Amelia asked, her voice waspish. "We know who did it, and she's right here."

Claire balled her hands into fists, but managed to keep from saying anything.

"Maybe someone else should also go," Wyle said, looking around. "Charlie, what about you?"

Richard shook his head. "It's fine. We can handle it." He and Wyle locked eyes for a second as some unspoken communication passed between them. I suddenly wondered if Richard had a weapon—maybe his pocketknife? I also had to wonder whether it would be enough, if Martin suddenly turned on him. On the other hand, Richard was a solid decade younger than Martin and in pretty good shape, so he could likely handle himself.

"Okay, then," Wyle said. "You two check it out, and we'll all have a seat here while you're gone."

Richard nodded again at Wyle as he and Martin marched out the door. Wyle gestured for the rest of us to sit down, although he remained standing.

"This is ridiculous," Amelia muttered. "We all know what happened."

"Amelia, just stop," Elliott said, his voice sounding tired. "You're not helping."

Amelia glared at him, but she kept quiet.

No one else said anything either, not even Jeremy, who usually had some sort of sarcastic remark ready to fire at any given moment. It seemed to take hours for Martin and Richard to return, but in reality, it was more like ten to fifteen minutes.

"What did you find?" Wyle asked as the two men tromped into the kitchen.

"Wires are cut," Richard said briefly.

Wyle's eyebrows went up. "Cut?"

Richard nodded. Martin was making a point of not looking at anyone as he focused instead on removing his scarf and hat.

I found myself glancing outside again, watching the darkness start to fall. *Another night trapped in this house.*

With no phone.

And one of us a killer.

I turned and met Pat's gaze, seeing those same thoughts reflected in her eyes, along with a question:

What are we going to do about it?

"That can't be," Iris said, but her voice was hollow as reality sank in.

"Alas, it is," Richard said.

"But who would cut the phone lines?" she asked.

Jeremy snorted. "The same person who sabotaged Pat and Richard's snowmobile, I would imagine," he said.

"That was just bad luck," Iris said. "That's what your father said."

"I don't know why we're beating around the bush," Amelia jumped in again. "We all know it was Claire."

"It wasn't," Claire insisted again.

"Then prove it," Amelia said. "Let us search your room."

"Search my room? Why?"

"To see what you're hiding," Amelia said.

"Amelia," Elliott began, but Claire interrupted.

"Fine," she said. "Go ahead. I keep telling you I had nothing to do with any of this. If that's what it's going to take to prove it, then fine."

"Alright then," Amelia said, getting up from the table so fast, her chair tipped over. Wyle grabbed her arm as she rushed by him.

"If we're doing this, we're going to do it right," he said. "Let's all go up together."

Silently, we all stood up and trailed after Wyle and Amelia, who was leading the charge. She marched down the hall and flung open our bedroom door. "You're on the left, correct?" she called over her shoulder.

"Yes," Claire said, her arms folded across her chest and her lips pressed together in a thin, white line.

Amelia immediately turned and started pawing through the closet. Claire didn't say a word, simply watched.

"Amelia, is this really necessary?" Elliott asked.

"We have to know the truth," Amelia answered, crouching down to go through Claire's bags.

"You don't really think your sister had anything to do with this," Elliott said.

Amelia gave her husband a murderous look. "How are we going to know for sure unless we check?" she asked. "Besides, you heard Martin. Claire is starting to show signs of mental instability, just like Mom."

"Right here," Claire said, her voice flat.

Amelia flickered her eyes at her. "No offense. I'm just stating facts."

"Of course you are," Claire said.

Amelia moved to the chest of drawers, opening each one and rustling through the contents. I eased my way through the crowd to move closer to Amelia, who gave me the side-eye as she continued digging through the drawers.

"Can I help you with something?" Amelia asked, her voice like acid.

"I'm just here in case you need a hand," I said. "The faster you realize your sister didn't have anything to do with George's death, the better it will be for everyone."

"You're hardly objective," Amelia said.

"Well," I said, flashing a crooked smile at her. "Neither are you."

She paused, the drawer half-open, and stared at me. Her eyes narrowed. "What is that supposed to mean?"

"You tell me," I said. "You're the one who has already decided Claire is guilty."

"Because she *is* guilty," Amelia said.

"So you keep saying," I said. "Do you have any proof?"

"What do you think I'm looking for?"

"What do you expect to find? A copy of the will? Maybe whatever was used to whack George on the head?"

"We won't know unless we look," Amelia said. She tilted her head, her expression becoming more suspicious. "Why are you so interested in stopping me?"

I crouched down to face her. "Do you understand that the more you push this, the less likely you are to ever heal your relationship with your sister?"

"If she's a murderer, why would I want to have a relationship with her?" Although her voice was harsh, her fingers tensed on the drawer.

"Let's just play this game, for a moment. Let's say she did it. What if it wasn't her fault?" I asked. "What if it's exactly what your uncle is saying, and what's happening to her is the exactly what happened to your mother? Is this really how you want your relationship to go?"

Amelia didn't respond, but her fingers continued to flex and tighten. I found myself holding my breath. Would she finally give up this ridiculous crusade against her sister? There was no question someone was behind everything that was happening, but the longer they focused on Claire, the less likely we were to figure out who the real culprit was.

"Charlie is right," Martin said. "Your relationship with Claire is more important than whatever you find or don't find. We can deal with the truth later. Right now, it's more important to come together as a family."

Something shifted in Amelia's face at her uncle's words. "No," she said. "We'll deal with the truth now." She yanked the drawer open, so hard it came out of the bureau. She tumbled backwards with a yelp, dumping the contents on the floor with a clatter.

No one said a word. We all stared at what was lying on the floor.

Amelia was the first to recover. She turned to Claire, her eyes bright with vindication. "Why is a wire cutter in your drawer?"

Claire was frozen, her eyes like saucers. "I have no idea how that got there," she said. "Someone else must have put it there."

"Who would put a wire cutter in your drawer?" Amelia asked.

"I have no idea, but I didn't even use that drawer. I never opened it." Claire lifted her gaze, her eyes wild. "It could have been there for months. Years, even."

"You expect us to believe that? *Somebody* used a wire cutter to cut the phone lines this weekend, and we just happen to find one in your bedroom drawer, but you know nothing about it?" Amelia whirled on me. "And you! You're clearly in on it, too."

"What are you talking about? I had no idea that was in there," I said.

"Of course you did! You tried to stop me from opening that drawer."

"I tried to stop you from putting a wedge between you and your sister," I said through gritted teeth. "Clearly, this was planted."

"Why was it 'clearly' planted?" Amelia asked.

"Because I don't know the first thing about cutting phone lines," Claire said. "I don't even know where they are."

"Let's all take a breath," Wyle started to say, but Amelia turned on him.

"Are you going to finally do something about her?" she asked, pointing at Claire. "Is this enough proof that she's dangerous? Or are you going to wait until she murders us all in our beds?"

"Claire isn't dangerous," Pat said. "Don't be so melodramatic."

"How do you explain this?" Amelia asked, waving wildly at the wire cutter.

"Exactly what Charlie said. It was planted," Pat said.

"Honey, we're going to get you the best help possible," Iris said, sidling up to Claire. "Don't you worry. Everything is going to be fine."

"Auntie, I didn't do this," Claire said, sounding like she was close to tears. "You have to believe me"

Iris patted her shoulder. "I know it's confusing, dear. Try not to let it upset you."

"We'll do whatever it takes to help you," Martin said.

Claire wrenched herself away. "I'm not crazy," she said. "And I'm not a killer."

"You shouldn't upset yourself," Iris said. "It's all going to be fine."

Claire backed up against the wall, her hands pressed against her temples. "I can't believe this is happening." Iris stepped forward, trying to put her arms around Claire, but Claire kept pushing her away.

"So," Jeremy said, pushing his hands in his pockets and catching my eye. "I guess I was right after all."

"Oh, yeah, right. You thought it was Claire, too?" Lucy asked, her tone dripping with disbelief.

"No, I didn't think it was Claire," he said. "But it *was* apparently all related to one of our, let us say, 'inconvenient family stories.'"

"Jeremy, what are you talking about?" Iris asked. "We don't have any 'inconvenient stories.' Everyone knows we've just had more than our share of family tragedies."

I studied Iris as she kept trying to put her arms around Claire. She looked like she had aged ten years since Friday, but no wonder. She had found out her brother's body was in the basement cistern, put there by her sister, and her niece was apparently suffering from the same mental ailment as her sister.

I also thought about what Jeremy said. To me, it seemed clear he was substituting "inconvenient stories" for "family secrets," and in a way, he was right. There was a history of mental illness, and no one wanted to talk about it, but it hardly seemed a secret. It was also hardly a secret that Billy had disappeared, although obviously it was a secret that Daisy had killed him.

But, if we were to believe what Martin said, Billy's death didn't have anything to do with George's. The only thing they had in common was that they were in the wrong place at the wrong time with the wrong person.

Which suddenly seemed very ... convenient, to me.

"Martin," I said. "Why did Daisy kill her brother?"

Martin looked at me in surprise. "Well, clearly I don't know for sure, but I always figured she had snapped some way and didn't even know what she had done."

"So, you think she was delusional, or in some sort of deluded state, and that's when she killed Billy?"

"Yes, that's it exactly," Martin said.

"Okay, but you also said when you came here, you found Billy's body in the cistern," I said. "Are you trying to say that even though Daisy was so delusional that she killed her own brother without understanding what she was doing, she had the wherewithal to hide the body afterward?"

Martin's pleasant expression faded. "Well, I wasn't there," he said. "So I couldn't say. I do know when people are in that sort of state, they can have a great deal of strength. Or maybe she had help."

"Help?" Claire asked. Amelia and Iris were looking at Martin with strange expressions, as well. I wasn't sure if they had seen what I had seen ... the flicker in his eyes.

It was Martin.

"It's possible she found someone to help," Martin continued as my mind whirled, the pieces falling together so quickly, I could barely keep up. "I realize it's a long shot. It's probably more likely she figured something out herself. But it's still possible there was someone else involved."

"Would this other person be the same person who just killed George?" I asked.

Martin paused, blinking at me. "I thought it was clear who killed George."

"Yes, I think it is clear," I said. "You think it's Claire, and that she's showing signs of having the same mental issues as her mother."

"That's right," Martin said.

"But here's what I don't understand," I said. "If you suspected Claire was heading in this direction, then why would you allow her to come to this house knowing Billy was in the cistern?"

Martin stared at me, still blinking rapidly from behind his glasses. With his neat brown and white sweater vest and bald head, he resembled a befuddled-but-kind grandfather. No wonder no one suspected him for so long.

"Well, first off," he said. "I didn't know for sure. I hadn't spent that much time with Claire recently, which I'm sure you know. But even if I had known, there was no reason for me to think the truth would come out now. So why would it affect her?"

"You knew Daisy was uncomfortable in this house," I pressed. "In fact, she was so uncomfortable, apparently her first major breakdown, during which she killed her own brother, happened here. Wouldn't you be worried about Claire having the same type of reaction?"

Something unpleasant flashed in Martin's eyes. "Um, well, now that you say it like that, I suppose I should have been. But you have to understand, it was a really difficult week. My beloved mother-in-law just passed."

"What are you getting at, Charlie?" Iris asked. "You know how difficult of a time this has been for all of us."

"Of course, and I'm not trying to make things more difficult," I said. "I just have some questions that I'm sure others have, as well," I spread my arms wide to indicate the rest of the room. "So, you said you didn't know about Claire's state of mind because you hadn't spent much time with her. Fair enough. But when did you first start to suspect there was a problem this weekend?"

He stared at me. "I … um … I'm not sure. What does that matter now?"

"Well, it matters because maybe we could have prevented some of this from happening," I said. "We could have kept an eye on Claire, or the snowmobile, and if we had, Pat and Richard would likely have already sent help back for us."

"I had no idea Claire was capable of sabotaging the snow-mobile, or I would have said something," he said.

"And that's exactly my point," I said. "You're trying to say that both Claire and Daisy experienced a mental breakdown, killed someone during that breakdown, and never consciously realized they were killers, yet each managed to take steps to hide what they did. For Daisy, she hid Billy's body in the cistern. For Claire, she cut the phone wires and sabotaged the snowmo-bile."

"Don't forget she also tried to kill me with the toaster oven," Amelia said.

I ignored Amelia. "Don't you see?" I asked. "What you're saying doesn't make sense."

Martin took a step back, his eyes shifting from side to side. "Well, maybe it wasn't a mental breakdown after all," he said. "Maybe it was an accident. In both cases."

"Or, maybe it was you," I said pointedly.

There was an audible gasp around the room. Martin's eyes widened. "What are you talking about? Why would you blame me?"

"Martin didn't kill anyone," Iris said, her lips white with strain. "How dare you accuse him!"

"He was the only one who knew about Billy being in the cistern," I said. "He would also have the skills to sabotage the snowmobile and cut the phone wires."

"But that doesn't mean he's a killer," Iris said.

"Here's what I think," I said. "I think that you, Martin, killed Billy years ago and hid his body in the cistern. I think you as-sumed, as you did, Iris, that you two would be inheriting this house. I don't know if you were planning on selling it, which would mean having to get rid of the body first, or if you were planning on hanging onto it, in which case, the body wouldn't matter as much. But, regardless, you would be in control and could keep your secret safe. I suspect once we find a copy of the will, the real will, we'll discover Iris wasn't the sole beneficiary of this house. If I had to guess, I would say it was split—half going to Iris and half to Claire, with the intention of it eventually going to Daphne and any other grandkids. Or, maybe that was too messy for Flo. Maybe Flo gave Iris the house in Redemption and Claire and Daphne this house.

"Either way, if you and Iris didn't inherit this house outright, that would be a problem for you, and you couldn't let that happen. So, you did the only thing you could think of—make the will disappear. If not permanently, at least temporarily, in order to give you some time to figure out how to get rid of Billy's body. And the easiest way to do that would be to get rid of George, along with any paperwork he brought with him. In the confusion of his death, it would likely take weeks, if not months, to sort out Flo's estate … more than enough time to find another spot for Billy's body." I cocked my head and studied him. "Was it your idea to have Amelia invite George up here on Friday? Did you put a bug in her ear about it, or did you mention something to Iris, and have her do it?"

Martin straightened his shoulders. "Inviting George up here early was Iris's idea, and it was a good one. He was a good friend to Flo over the years. It's insulting, what you're accusing me of. I shouldn't have to listen to this. Iris, say something." He turned to his wife, seemingly expecting her to jump in and defend him, but Iris was staring at him like she had never seen him before.

I shrugged. "Well, we'll see. Once we locate the actual will, we should definitely know more."

"This is preposterous," Martin sputtered. From the corner of my eye, I saw Wyle and Richard slowly shift their positions, moving closer to Martin as everyone else began to edge away—except for Iris, who looked shellshocked and utterly unable to move without collapsing. "I suppose I should be glad Claire inspired such loyalty, for you to make up such stories to defend her, but this needs to stop. Now. Before you say something that gets you in legal trouble."

"It makes sense, Martin killing George," Pat said conversationally, as if Martin wasn't in the room, while Wyle and Richard positioned themselves on either side of Martin. "But what I don't understand is why he would sabotage our snowmobile and cut the phone wires?"

"Well, only Martin can answer that for certain, but if I were to guess, none of this went according to plan," I said. "Let's say Martin coordinated with George, so he knew approximately when George was going to be here and could meet him outside as George was coming in. Martin pretends to be fetching wood and asks George to help him by grabbing a few pieces. George agrees, and in the woodshed, Martin hits him over the head and covers him with a tarp. My guess is, Martin never imagined the body would be discovered. Even if people went in there to get wood for a fire, no one would look under the tarp. I'm thinking because Martin got away with killing Billy for so many years, it made him confident … like he could easily get away with a second murder. Once we all left, Martin could get rid of the body, and no one would be the wiser. But Claire found the body, so Martin panicked. He didn't want the cops investigating, because then, Billy would be found, too. The weather cooperated, which helped, as it gave him time to figure out a plan. Maybe he was going to burn the woodshed down in the middle of the night tonight, and then take off with the snowmobile." I smiled pleasantly at Martin, who was looking more and more aggravated. "I bet whatever you did to the snowmobile can be easily reversed, allowing you to escape."

"You have quite the imagination," Martin sneered. He glared at me, eyes full of hate. The affable grandfather image was gone, and in its place was something probably a lot closer to the real Martin. "And I'm done listening to this. Iris, let's go." He tried to turn on his heel to leave the room, but both Wyle and Richard each grabbed an arm.

"That's an excellent idea," Wyle said, wrestling a struggling Martin out through the door . "Let's all go downstairs together."

"Let go of me," Martin said loudly. "I insist. I had nothing to do with any of this. It was Claire."

"And we'll definitely investigate that angle," Wyle answered. "As soon as the cops get here."

"Don't tell me you believe the garbage that just came out of Charlie's mouth?"

"I'm keeping an open mind," Wyle said neutrally. "Let's all head downstairs. We haven't eaten yet. Charlie, is dinner ready?"

I had completely forgotten about dinner. I wasn't the slightest bit hungry and I didn't think anyone else was either, but clearly Wyle still wanted to keep an eye on all of us, and having everyone sitting around the dinner table would be one way to do it.

"Yes, it should be," I said. "Just as long as nothing burned."

"Hopefully not," Wyle said. "Let's go, everyone. I'm starving."

Chapter 21

"I'm still having trouble believing Martin killed Billy," Pat said as she reached for another chocolate chip cookie.

We were in my kitchen, nearly a week after Flo's memorial weekend fiasco.

Luckily, it had ended with a whimper, rather than a bang, although there were a couple of dicey moments when it seemed it could have gone either way. Eventually, Wyle and Richard had managed to tie Martin to a chair, and that seemed to settle everyone down.

We were all still poking at our food when the cavalry arrived. Hal had called the cops as promised. He had also made it clear that there was something not at all right at Flo's old house, and the city should get the area plowed and out there ASAP.

Luckily, they listened.

We had to stick around longer than I would have liked while they did their initial questioning of witnesses, but eventually, they allowed Claire and I to go, with our assurance that we wouldn't be leaving Redemption any time soon. We dropped Pat and Richard off at their truck (as it turned out, the snowmobile was fine—the fuel line had been pinched off with a clip—remove the clip and ta-da, it started without problem). It was too late for them to drive it home, though, so they planned to pick it up in the morning.

Martin was eventually arrested for the murder of both Billy, who was indeed found in the cistern, and George. As far as I knew, he had lawyered up and hadn't said one word.

"I know," I said, topping off both of our mugs with fresh, hot tea.

"But not just that he killed Billy, but how he kept it quiet," Pat continued, taking a bite of cookie. Since our ordeal, Pat had been eating even more sugar than normal. She said it was because sugar was good for shock. I decided not to point out there was no way she was still suffering from shock a week later. "How can that be? He killed Billy over twenty years ago. How is it possible to not say anything all those years? How was he able to face Flo and Iris, watching them grieve and knowing he was the reason Billy was gone, and still not say anything?"

"I don't know," I admitted.

"He must be a sociopath," Pat decided. "That's the only explanation."

"Maybe," I said. "I wish I knew why he killed Billy, though. That might shed a lot of light on his silence all these years."

"You and the rest of the town," Pat said glumly, popping the last bite into her mouth.

"Not to mention the rest of the family," I said, thinking specifically about Lucy and Wyle. According to the word on the street, the two had decided to put their relationship on pause. I couldn't blame Wyle—he was investigating her father, after all—but I still almost felt bad for Lucy. First, she lost her father, and then, her boyfriend.

Almost.

The phone rang. I went to answer it, leaving Pat to gaze at the plate of cookies, contemplating a third. It was Claire.

"Are you free tomorrow at two?"

"I think so," I said, reaching for my calendar. "What's up?"

"Aunt Iris wants to see us."

I paused, hand hovering in midair. "Iris wants to see *us*? Why?" Pat's head snapped up at the mention of Iris's name.

"I have no idea, but she asked specifically if you could join us."

"Well ... sure," I said. Pat started frantically pointing toward herself. "Pat's here. Can she come?"

"Aunt Iris didn't say anything about Pat." Claire's voice was doubtful.

I frowned and shook my head at Pat. She shot me a disgusted expression.

"Never mind," I said. "Pat can stay home."

Pat stuck her tongue out at me.

* * *

"Thanks for seeing me on such short notice," Iris said as she ushered us into her living room. The decor was muted and formal, all glass and leather, with a lot of white, cream, and accent colors.

I perched on the sofa, wondering if the room was ever lived in or just used for entertaining. I suspected the latter. There was a coldness to it … a feeling of neglect.

In contrast, Iris looked like she had been ridden hard and put away wet. It appeared she hadn't showered in a few days, and her outfit, a cream shirt with a black cardigan and beige slacks, was wrinkled and stained. She had chosen an unfortunate shade of pink lipstick, too, which was smeared across her teeth.

"Tea?" she asked, gesturing to the china teapot on the glass coffee table.

"Sure," I said, mostly to be polite. She poured three cups and handed me one.

I took a sip, trying to hide my expression. Store bought. Exactly what I thought. Bleh.

"You're probably wondering why I asked you both here," Iris said, stirring her tea. "Especially you, Charlie, as you're not family."

"The thought did cross my mind," I said.

A faint smile appeared on her face. "After the weekend we went through, you certainly could be considered family. But the truth is, I figured after everything you did, you deserved to hear the truth."

"I didn't do anything," I said.

"Don't dismiss yourself," Iris said. "You helped me realize the truth."

I glanced at Claire, who looked as surprised as I felt.

"Truth?" I asked. I had hoped Iris would finally come clean about whatever family secret she was still hiding, but Claire had told me not to get my hopes up. "Our family isn't known for being all that forthcoming," she had said on the drive over.

"About everything." Iris wrapped her hands around her mug before glancing at Claire. "And I realized it was time to share it. You deserve to know. Both of you." Her gaze flickered at me.

Neither of us said anything as Iris paused to take a long drink of tea, as if fortifying herself. "My marriage is a fraud," she quietly began.

Claire and I glanced at each other again, but neither of us said anything.

"Martin is …" she paused to rub her forehead. "Well, at this point, it probably doesn't matter. Suffice it to say he's been lying and cheating on me our entire marriage. For many years, I ignored it … told myself it was more important to keep the marriage together for the sake of our family. I told myself Martin did love me, in his own way, and he had always been a good father. If he cheated every now and then, well, men do that. It didn't mean he didn't love me.

"But, until this past week, I had no idea how deep his lies went or the lengths he would go to keep his secrets safe."

She paused to take another sip of tea. I barely dared to breathe, afraid that any movement might cause Iris to rethink her confession.

"Daisy knew from the beginning that Martin was bad news," Iris continued. "She didn't know why, though, nor did she have any proof. It was just one of her 'feelings.'" Iris rolled her eyes. "You have no idea how much I hated hearing about her 'feelings.' Mostly because of how upset it would make our mother. Daisy wasn't the first in our family to get them. We never met our grandma, my mom's mom, but it was clear she had something similar going on. I don't know the details, as Mom was famously tightlipped about such things. But whatever was going on with Daisy clearly reminded her of her own dealings with her mother.

"Anyway, Daisy told me right away that Martin wasn't right for me, and I should break it off. I didn't listen to her, of course. But what's worse is that I told Martin what she said." She paused to rub her forehead again. "In retrospect, I think that was the biggest mistake I could have made."

"But why?" Claire asked.

Iris sighed. "Because I think that's ultimately what led to Billy and George being killed."

She looked at both of us, and seeing the confusion on our faces, smiled faintly again. "Martin won't talk to me, so I don't know if it's true or not, but this is what I think happened …

"Around the time that I started dating Martin, both Daisy and I were working at the same dress shop. The owner was a good friend of Mom's, and she ended up hiring both of us. During one of my shifts, some dresses went missing. The owner, of course, held me responsible, if not for the actual theft, for not preventing it. It was horribly embarrassing for everyone—myself, Mom. So, you can imagine how shocking it was when about a week later, I discovered the dresses hidden in Daisy's closet.

"I couldn't believe it. Clearly, she had set me up. I was furious; Mom was furious. Daisy kept saying she had no idea how they got in her closet, but of course, no one believed her. Mom marched her down to the shop to return the dresses and apologize. It was a horrible, horrible time. There had always been tension between Daisy and the rest of the family, but this event severed everything. Nothing was ever the same.

"In retrospect, it was precisely what Martin wanted."

"You think Martin set my mother up?" Claire asked.

Iris nodded. "Yes. It was the perfect way to discredit Daisy to us."

Claire looked puzzled. "I don't understand. Did he work at the dress shop? How was he able to do it?"

Iris rubbed her forehead again, as if trying to massage away a headache that would never disappear. "He came into the store to talk to me the day the dresses went missing. I know there was at least one other customer there, because I kept telling him I had to go help her, and he kept making a point of keeping my attention on him. He could be very charming when he wanted." She shook her head.

"Plus, the reason I was looking in Daisy's closet was because of Martin. He mentioned something about seeing Daisy wearing my shoes, which weren't in my closet. So, I went to go find them and instead found the dresses. I mean, thinking back now, it seems so obvious. I can't believe I was so easily fooled, but … well, what can I say? Clearly, I didn't want to believe what was right in front of my eyes.

"Anyway, this rift never healed. I never felt like I could trust Daisy, no matter how much time passed. After Amelia was born and I had Jeremy, my mother forced us to reconcile … to at least spend some time together as a family. She didn't want her grandchildren to not get to know each other. Family was very important to my mother. Not only was she an only child, but she also didn't have any cousins, aunts, or uncles. She insisted the cousins know each other." Iris paused and looked away, swallowing heavily. "She also begged me to forgive Daisy. Told me that Daisy was young and my only sister, and that I should give her another chance. In my arrogance, I refused, and that is something else I'm going to have to learn to live with."

"Mom loved you," Claire said. "And she forgave you."

Iris snapped her head around. "How can you know she forgave me?"

"Because she told me," Claire said. "It was when she was starting to get sick, but she was still lucid. She didn't tell me the details, but what she did say was that you had been misled, and it wasn't your fault … and that someday, you would know the truth. I asked if that made her angry, and she said 'No, not anymore.' You were her sister, and she loved you. She understood."

Iris swallowed hard again, picking up her napkin to dab at her eyes.

Claire didn't say anything more, simply waited until she had more or less composed herself. "But what does all of this have to do with Billy?" she asked, after Iris had picked up her teacup.

Iris made a face. "Daisy was Billy's favorite. She used to play with him all the time and was happy to babysit when Mom needed her to. He was devastated when the dress-stealing happened. He was still pretty young, ten or eleven I think, but old enough to understand right and wrong. He was so upset that she had done that to me, and he didn't want anything to do with her, either. Daisy was heartbroken, as you can imagine. Their relationship was never the same.

"I think that a few months before Billy disappeared, he discovered one of Martin's lies. If I had to guess, he likely caught Martin cheating on me, and somehow put the pieces together that Martin was behind the whole dress-stealing incident. Once he figured that out, he probably confronted Martin and demanded he come clean and repair the relationship between Daisy and the rest of the family. Of course, if Martin were to come clean, that would likely lead to the whole house of cards coming down. We would have to address the elephant in the room—Martin's lying and cheating—and if that happened …" she held up her hands helplessly. "We're talking divorce, losing his home, his income, his reputation … and that's what he would never risk. If there was one thing Martin puts above everything else, it's his standing in the community. Admitting what he'd done would ruin everything, and there was no way he could let that happen."

"But wait a second," Claire said. "Didn't Billy say he was leaving to join that commune? Martin didn't make that up, did he?"

"No, Billy did say that. But you might not remember the rest. Earlier that year, Mom had begged him to stay home for a bit, and he'd agreed. Then, suddenly, he changed his mind and was going to be gone for a year or two. No one really understood his change of heart, and he refused to explain it.

"In retrospect, I think what happened is that when he discovered Martin's lies and gave Martin an ultimatum, Martin agreed, but wanted time. For whatever reason, Billy gave it to him and decided it would be easier for everyone if he just left town until Martin told the truth. Or maybe it was Martin's idea he leave. It would have been impossible for Billy to have bit his tongue for months on end waiting for Martin to come clean. Of course, Martin clearly had no plans to do any of that. Heaven knows how he got Billy to the cottage … probably told him he wanted to talk through a confession strategy without having to worry about being overheard. We all now know what really happened."

Iris stopped talking, staring off into space again, as if lost in a sea of regret and what-ifs. The silence stretched out longer, as neither Claire nor I had anything to add. How does one respond to what we'd just heard?

Finally, Iris gave herself a quick shake and focused back on us. "There's one more thing we need to discuss," she said, her voice crisp and business-like. "It's about the will."

Claire looked surprised. "Did you find it?"

"The cops did. It was shoved in an unused pocket of Martin's suitcase. I'm not sure what his plan was for it—whether he was going to destroy it or try and modify it somehow. But that's neither here nor there. The reason I brought it up is because, as it turns out, you did inherit the house."

Claire nearly spilled her tea. "Me?"

"Well, not precisely you. The house is in a trust for any and all grandkids. However many there are, they'll split it evenly. And you're the executor."

"Wow. I … I had no idea," Claire managed.

Iris made a face. "Neither did I. I have no idea how Martin found out, but now, looking back, it was clear something had shifted. Over the years, Martin had been the main liaison for the cottage. He would always go up once or twice a year to check on things and talk to Hal, and if there was ever a problem, Mom asked him to deal with it. I was always so grateful he was taking care of it, as I wanted nothing to do with it. Of course, now I know better. But I wonder if Mom was starting to suspect Martin as well, which is why she asked Hal to work with George instead of Martin. My guess is putting George in charge tipped Martin off that something had changed with the will. Whether he knew for certain before he hit George on the head or if it was just a lucky guess …" She shrugged.

"Well, um," Claire said. "I don't know what to say. I know you thought you were inheriting all of it …"

"It's fine," Iris cut her off. "Now that I know the truth, I want nothing to do with that cottage anyhow. It's yours with my blessings. Maybe this is what needs to happen to change the luck around that place. It's always been cursed. I don't know how it ended up in my dad's family, but I do know that no one wanted it. That's how Mom ended up with it. For some reason, she loved that house. I don't know if it was what it represented—being financially well off enough to have a second home—or what. But whatever it was, Mom truly did love it. It was her most cherished possession, and she gave it to you."

Claire looked down at her lap. I caught a glimpse of tears in her eyes. "Thank you."

Iris reached over to grasp Claire's hand. "I can't tell you how sorry I am," she said. "The way we treated you over the years. You and your mother. I hope one day, you can find it in your heart to forgive me, even though I don't deserve it."

"Of course I forgive you," Claire said immediately. "You didn't know. No one knew."

Iris seemed to struggle, her expression contorting. "But I was the one who brought that monster into the family."

"We've all made mistakes," Claire said. "You shouldn't blame yourself. The important thing is we can move on now. As a family."

Iris took a deep breath and smiled through her tears. "I'd like that."

Chapter 22

"It was kind of worse than what we even thought," Claire said. She was sitting in my kitchen, sipping a cup of tea. Next to her, Daphne was in her stroller eating a cookie. Well, either eating it or just smearing it all over her face. It was hard to tell.

It had been a week since Iris had talked to us. Since then, Claire's health seemed to have rebounded. She looked rested and relaxed, her face had filled out, and the color had returned to her cheeks.

Maybe the truth really does set you free. In Claire's case, it definitely seemed so. She had finally turned a corner on her health.

"What was worse?"

"What Martin did," Claire said, tucking her hair behind her ear. "So, first off, it looks like he really did do something to that toaster oven after all. Amelia was right."

I looked at her in surprise. "Martin wanted to kill Amelia?"

"No. I think he just wanted something to self-destruct, so he would have a reason to pull out the toolkit. I guess he had also messed around with the VCR."

"So, he was the one who hid the knife in the toolkit."

Claire nodded. "Yup. The cops found traces of Billy's blood on the handle."

I stared at her. "That's what he killed Billy with?"

"It seems so. And it makes sense, when you think about it. It's not like he would have been able to get Billy into the basement easily. I mean, there's nothing down there. And if he had told Billy he wanted to talk, well, no one is having a chat in that basement. But sitting in the kitchen? Of course. And if Martin was making a pot of coffee, and Billy was standing next to him, it would have been easy to pull a chef's knife out and stab him."

"Why didn't Martin just clean it up and put it back in the knife block?" I wondered. "Although," I blanched, thinking of all the food preparation we had done. "That would have been super gross."

"Maybe it grossed him out, too," Claire said. "He probably didn't want it used for food preparation any more than the rest of us would. And after George was killed, he apparently got the bright idea of pinning it all on Hal, so hiding the murder weapon in Hal's toolkit made a lot of sense."

"But the cops would have eventually figured out that Hal didn't do it," I said.

"Yes, but it would have taken some time," Claire said. "Martin could have easily planned a disappearance, if he thought the cops were zeroing in on him."

"Makes sense," I said. "And he always had the theory about your mother in his back pocket, if Hal didn't work out as a suspect. Or maybe he could have tried to pin it on both of them—your mother killed your brother in a fog of delusion, and Hal felt sorry for her and cleaned up the mess."

Claire made a face. "Actually, that's probably exactly where he was going. Which leads me to the rest of how horrible Martin is. He also apparently drove my mother mad."

I raised my eyebrows. "Really?"

She nodded. "It turns out she might not have been sabotaging herself after all, but it was Martin making her crazy. Wyle went back and interviewed some of Daisy's old neighbors, and one in particular remembers Martin hanging around quite a bit back then."

"Wow," I said. "Why didn't the cops find this out back then?"

"I guess they didn't ask," Claire said. "They only asked about strangers hanging around, not family members."

"I guess that makes sense," I said. Then, a particularly dreadful thought hit me. "Do you think he also ... well, caused her mental breakdown?"

Claire sighed. "I don't know. I don't think so. I did ask my mom's doctors that question, and they said 'no.' But ..." she sighed again. "It's possible, I suppose. It's also possible that getting her committed sooner than she should have hastened her decline. So, even if he didn't directly cause it, he might have indirectly."

"I'm sorry, Claire," I said. "That's really rough."

Claire pressed her lips together. "Well, it is what it is. One thing that's clear is he really hated my mother. So, I shouldn't be surprised by any of this."

"Well, at least you know the truth now," I said.

Claire gave me a sideways smile. "Yeah. At least there's that."

* * *

Shortly after Claire left, the doorbell rang. Assuming it was Claire, I headed to the door.

It wasn't. It was Amelia.

"Amelia," I said, not sure what to do. "This is a surprise."

Amelia pressed her mouth into a flat line. "May I come in?"

Wordlessly, I held the door open wider. She entered, stomping her feet on the mat.

"Can I get you some tea?" I asked.

She shook her head. "Actually, I'm here to buy some."

"Buy some tea?"

"Yes." She gave me a hard look. "That is what you sell, right?"

"Well, yes," I said, feeling completely off-balance. "But I just never thought you'd be a customer."

"It's not for me," she said. "It's for Claire."

"Claire?"

"A gift." She gave me another hard look. "Are you sure you're feeling okay?"

"Yes, I'm fine. I just … this isn't what I was expecting."

She sighed as she unzipped her winter jacket and unwrapped her scarf. Now that I got a better look at her, I realized she looked a little worse for wear. At the cottage, she had always been well put-together and perfectly made up. Now, her face was pale, and her eyes haunted. Her hair was in a crooked ponytail with strands falling out, and she wore no jewelry over her plain, black sweater.

"It's a peace offering," she said. "I ... I'm planning on stopping by to talk to her, and I thought it would be nice to bring her a gift, except I'm not really sure what she likes or what her tastes are. But I know she likes your tea, so I thought ..." she shrugged, a faint blush creeping up her neck.

"Tea is a wonderful gift," I said. "In fact, I have her favorite. Give me a moment, and I'll go get it."

"Thank you," she said, her expression relieved.

I hurried upstairs to grab a couple bags of my lemon lavender tea, one of my most popular blends. I quickly wrapped in some purple tissue paper and tied it with a bow before bringing it back downstairs.

"Oh. You didn't have to bother," she said, but she was clearly touched.

"No bother," I said, handing it to her.

"How much do I owe you?"

"Nothing," I waved my hand. "On the house."

"No, I insist." She opened her purse and pulled out a wallet. "It's my gift to Claire. I want to pay for it."

Seeing the set expression on her face, I gave in, giving her a price. She handed me a fifty-dollar bill. "Keep the change."

"It's too much," I protested, but she shook her head.

"After everything you did, I should be giving you more."

"Amelia, that's not true ..." I tried to say, but she silenced me with a look.

"I know I was horrible," she said. "I have a lot to atone for. The least I can do is overpay you for tea as a gift to try and start building a bridge with my sister."

"Well, when you put it like that," I said. "Thank you."

She nodded stiffly. "Thanks again for your help. Maybe I'll see you again?"

Her voice was gruff, and if I hadn't seen the longing in her eyes, I would have assumed it more of an "old Amelia" insult.

Instead, I smiled. "I'd like that. And I think Claire would, too."

Her face softened with relief. I wondered how much she had thought about one of the last things I'd said to her, when I'd warned her about damaging her reputation with her sister beyond repair.

But that was before the cost of all those buried secrets was revealed.

Now, it was time to forgive.

Author's Note

Hi there!

I hope you enjoyed *Ice Cold Murder* as much as I enjoyed writing it. If you did, I would really appreciate it if you'd leave me a review and rating on Amazon or Goodreads.

If you want more Charlie, I've got you covered.

First off, you can access exclusive bonus scenes from *Ice Cold Murder* for free right here:

MPWnovels.com/r/q/ice-cold-murder-bonus

In addition, if you keep reading, you can check out an excerpt from book 2, *Murder Next Door* which is available here.

The *Charlie Kingsley Mysteries* series is actually a spin-off from my award-winning *Secrets of Redemption* series. *Secrets of Redemption* is a little different from the *Charlie Kingsley Mysteries,* as it's more psychological suspense, but it's still clean like a cozy.

You can learn more about both series, including how they fit together, at MPWNovels.com, along with lots of other fun things such as short stories, deleted scenes, giveaways, recipes, puzzles and more.

For now, turn the page for a sneak peek at *Murder Next Door.*

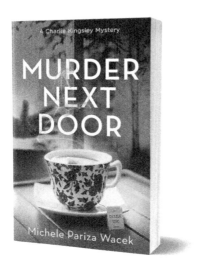

Murder Next Door - Chapter 1

"Charlie!" Mildred, my tea customer, opened her door and ushered me inside, straight into a cloud of floral perfume so strong, I could feel my eyes watering. Her blue pantsuit was clean and pressed, and her grey, permed hair looked freshly styled, like she had just returned from the hairdresser. "Oh, you didn't have to make a special trip for me. But since you're here, come in, come in."

"It's no trouble," I said, trying to unobtrusively dab the tears from my eyes still stinging from the overbearing fragrance. Hopefully, they would quickly adjust. "I was running errands anyway, and your house was on my way."

"Oh, you could probably use a break then. I'll make you a nice cup of tea, and you can have a seat and just relax."

Before I could answer, she was already bustling off toward the kitchen. I wiped my eyes for the second time and hung up my spring jacket. Then, I tucked my brownish-blondish-reddish hair (which was particularly wild and curly that day) behind my ears and made my way after her.

To be fair, I had expected this. Mildred was a sweet, albeit slightly overbearing, elderly woman. A retired school teacher who had never married and had no kids of her own, she had devoted her life to keeping a very close eye on all the happenings in her neighborhood, and then making sure whoever would listen was kept up to date.

I knew far more than was healthy about the marital life of the Thompsons ("He drinks too much, but I don't know if I can blame him, as she's always coming home late from work … I can't remember the last time she cooked a nice dinner for him"), the family life of the Swanns ("Jamie is running for student council president, and little Teddy was on the JV basketball team … can you believe it?"), and Mrs. Miller's pregnancy ("She is so huge … I'm sure she's having twins").

Yes, Mildred was a bit of a busybody, but she was harmless and lonely, so I didn't mind spending a little time with her when I dropped off her orders.

I ran a tea and tincture business out of my home, so I was typically out and about delivering orders at least a couple of times a week. I had a handful of clients who always asked me to stay and visit, so I made a point of spreading their deliveries out over different days, allowing me the time and space to chat with them. This was Mildred's day.

"Oh my goodness, I have so much to tell you," she said excitedly as she placed a pot of tea and platter of shortbread cookies in the middle of the table. The teapot and matching cups were made of a delicate white china and sported a pink rosebud pattern. Rimmed with gold, they were quite lovely. "You would not believe what just happened with the Thompsons."

I listened to her prattle as I nibbled on the cookies and sipped my special blend of chamomile and rose petal tea that she always saved for my visits. As always, her kitchen was bright and cheery as the sunlight slanted through the sparkling windows. The scent of lemon and bleach was barely detectable under her perfume. Even her orange tabby sleeping in his basket in the sun matched the yellow and white decor.

"But that's not even the most important news," Mildred continued after recounting her very pregnant neighbor's emergency hospital trip. Apparently, Terri had thought she was in labor, and Mildred kindly offered to drive her to the hospital, but it ended up being a false alarm. Mildred took a deep breath and a quick sip of tea, making a slight face in reaction to it having grown cold. "Jonas seems to have hired a housesitter."

"Really?" Jonas lived in the house right next door to Mildred. He was a middle-aged single man who worked in the Redemption post office. I rarely heard about him, as it seemed all he did was go to work, come home, heat up a microwave dinner, and eat it in front of the television while enjoying a couple of beers before going to bed and repeating it all the next day. Needless to say, Jonas didn't garner Mildred's attention the way the rest of her far more interesting neighbors did.

Mildred bobbed her head up and down as she reached for the teapot to top off her cup. "I know. I can hardly believe it myself. I was sure he would have mentioned something if he was planning a trip, but he didn't breathe a word to anyone. I can't even remember the last time he took a vacation."

"Maybe he was saving up his vacation days," I suggested.

Mildred frowned. "Well, that still doesn't explain why he didn't tell anyone. I mean, I have no idea when he left or when he's coming home! It's very upsetting."

"If you didn't see him leave, how do you know he's gone?" I asked.

"His car is gone," Mildred said.

"He parks his car outside?"

"No, in the garage. It's not in there."

I tried hard to keep my expression neutral. "You … looked in his garage?"

"Of course! I hadn't seen him leave for work or come home for a few days, which made me worry he was sick or hurt and needed help. So, I went over to check, but no one answered the door. Well, I was beside myself. Did he have a heart attack?

Stroke? Or maybe he slipped in the shower and was lying there in the tub, wet and cold and starving for days on end! I mean, how could I do nothing, knowing he might be suffering? I debated calling the police, and I would have, but I also didn't want to bother them with such a matter when I was sure they had better things to do. I certainly didn't want to waste taxpayers' money, especially when there was an easier solution."

"Of course," I murmured, hiding my smile against the cup.

"So, before I called anyone, I decided to check the doors, on the off chance one was unlocked. I started with the garage. It was locked, of course, but when I peered into the glass, I saw his car was gone, and there was a different one in its place."

"Maybe he got a new car?"

Mildred pursed her lips. "That thought crossed my mind, too, but the one in there now is old. Much older than Jonas's. I can't imagine why he would trade his in for that. Remember, Jonas bought his car just a few years ago, so it's still nearly brand new. Plus, it has an Illinois license plate, and that doesn't seem right at all."

"You were able to see the license plate from outside?"

"Oh, heaven's no. It was way too dark for that."

I blinked. "I thought you said the garage door was locked."

"I meant the door to the house," Mildred said. "That was locked."

She stared at me, sipping her tea, an innocent expression on her face. Briefly, I wondered if the side door that led to the garage was unlocked, as she seemed to be implying, or if her busybody skills included lockpicking.

I decided I didn't really want to know.

"So, is that when you realized Jonas was gone?"

"Well, that's what I thought, but I decided I'd better call his employer just to make sure everything was on the up and up."

"Very smart," I said.

"They said Jonas was on vacation for a month. A month! Can you believe it?" She shook her head. "He hasn't had a vacation in years, and now he decides to leave for a month? And not tell anyone?"

"Well, clearly, it was overdue," I said.

"I suppose. But he still should have let the neighborhood know. I could have kept an eye on his house for him, instead of him inviting a weird housesitter to stay."

"You met his housesitter?"

She shook her head. "Not yet. I've gone over there twice to introduce myself, but there was no answer when I knocked. And I know he was there, because his car was in the garage. Talk about not being very neighborly."

"No, that doesn't sound very neighborly," I said. *Of course, Mildred skulking around in the garage wouldn't have anything to do with him not answering the door*, I thought, but refrained from verbalizing it.

"But I did see him," Mildred continued. "Once. He was walking around the yard in the middle of the night. I couldn't imagine what he was doing out there. How could he see anything?"

"Maybe he heard something in the yard, like an animal or something."

"I didn't hear anything," Mildred said. "I'm sure there was nothing there. But that's not even the strangest thing about him. Come." She heaved herself out of the chair and beckoned me to follow her to the window.

"See that?" She pointed to the nondescript ranch house next door. As far as I could tell, it looked as it always did.

"See what?"

She sighed. "The windows! See how the shades are pulled down?"

Indeed, all the shades were tightly closed.

"Why would he pull all the shades on such a nice day?" she asked.

Maybe to keep out noisy neighbors who had no qualms poking around in other people's garages, I thought. Instead, I said, "Maybe he works nights and sleeps during the day."

"But I don't see him leave," she countered. "I don't see him at all, except when he's walking around the backyard in the middle of the night."

I had to admit, it was a little peculiar. "Maybe he's an artist or writer and has strange hours."

"Maybe. But still, it's not normal." She put her hands on her hips as she shook her head. "I just don't know what this neighborhood is coming to."

"I haven't a clue, Mildred."

Murder Next Door - Chapter 2

"Did you see Redemption's new psychic yet?" Pat asked, helping herself to a brownie. We were in my sunny, warm kitchen enjoying a cup of tea and afternoon snack. Midnight, my black cat, had joined us, and was curled up in one of the chairs closest to the window, which overlooked my very-brown-and-dead garden. Spring had barely sprung, and it was still freezing at night, so it was a little too early to get to planting all the flowers and herbs I customarily used in my teas. But soon, that would change.

"You mean it isn't a joke?" I asked. I had heard the talk about a psychic setting up shop on Main street, just in time for the summer tourist season, but I thought it was just that … talk.

"Well if it is, it appears they've taken it so far as to pay rent," Pat said. She was a good decade or so older than me, and the best way to describe her was "round." She was plump, with a round face, round black-rimmed glasses, and short, no-nonsense brown hair that was turning grey. She was one of my first tea customers and had since become a good friend. "'Psychic Readings by Madame Rowena.' At least, that's what the sign says."

I raised an eyebrow. "Rowena? Seriously?"

"Her full name is Rowena Tanveer."

"Like that isn't a totally made-up name."

Pat shook her head. "You mock at your own peril."

"I'll take my chances." Considering I not only lived in a "haunted house," but that half the town thought I was some sort of witch who was actually selling potions under the guise of "herbal teas and tinctures," I thought I had some expertise on subjects like spells and psychics. "Is she actually open for business?"

"Not yet. She's supposed to have some sort of grand opening next week."

"A grand opening for a psychic. That should be interesting."

"We should go," Pat said as she picked up her mug. "Maybe you can talk to her about reselling your teas in her store."

"Oh, that sounds like a great idea," I said drily. "With my luck, she'll rename my lavender rose tea 'Cupid's Arrow by Rowena,' or some nonsense, and then I'll have even more people asking me to make them love potions."

"'Cupid's Arrow' ... that's actually kind of catchy," Pat mused with a grin.

"Well, psychics and love potions aside, any new gossip? Or," she waggled her eyebrows. "Any new cases you're busy solving?"

Despite my best efforts, I was starting to develop a reputation for being an amateur sleuth. It wasn't something I had sought out. I was very content keeping a low profile and not calling too much attention to myself as I baked, made teas, and gardened. But over the past few months, I had discovered two things that had changed all of that. One, I had a knack for solving crimes. Two, my customers had a knack for attracting the kind of trouble that required assistance from someone with my particular knack.

"I'm still between cases," I said as Pat's face fell. Unlike myself, she had no mixed feelings around amateur sleuthing. "Unless you count the case of the missing neighbor," I added. Sure enough, her face lit up.

"Missing neighbor? That sounds promising. Do tell."

"There's not much to tell, as I think the case was pretty much solved by the time I was brought into it," I said. "It's one of Mildred's neighbors."

"Oh, well, of course she would know if one of her neighbors went missing. But I don't understand. Is the neighbor actually missing? Or not?"

"Well, I guess he's sort of 'missing.' It's Jonas, the one who works at the post office. Apparently, he's on a month-long vacation, and Mildred is miffed because he didn't bother to share his plans with her. She's even more miffed at his apparent housesitter."

Pat gave me a surprised look. "A housesitter? Jonas doesn't strike me as someone who would need a housesitter, even if he is gone for a month. Especially with Mildred next door. She would have been happy to do whatever was needed while he's away, I'm sure."

"Mildred would definitely have been thrilled with the job," I agreed. "Although maybe he didn't want the neighborhood's number-one gossip going through his medicine cabinet and underwear drawer. Anyway, she apparently didn't see Jonas leave or the new housesitter move in, which is bothering her."

Pat pursed her lips. "Well, actually, I would find that odd, as well. Not to mention a little creepy. I mean, you know how Mildred watches the neighborhood like a hawk. For her to miss something like that, they would practically have had to plan it at a time when they knew she wouldn't be watching. And why would they go through all that trouble? What are they hiding?"

"You've got a point," I said. "Although I would assume Jonas just wanted his privacy. Same for the housesitter."

"But why would Jonas care about his 'privacy' when leaving on vacation?"

"Well, I suppose it's possible he thought Mildred might not notice anything at all, if he snuck out," I said.

Pat snorted. "Fat chance. What's worse is, if he WAS looking for privacy, he just guaranteed getting an earful when he returns."

"Yeah, I wouldn't want to be in his shoes."

Pat finished her brownie and wiped her hands with a napkin. "Now, this housesitter ... I guess I can see why he would want his privacy. I'm assuming it's a 'he'?"

"Mildred saw him, so yes. And I agree—he definitely seems to want his privacy." I then filled her in about the shades being drawn and only coming out at night.

"That's weird," Pat said.

"Yeah, it is, but as I told Mildred, maybe he works at night."

"Even so, most people who work that kind of schedule are still seen in daylight," Pat said.

"Maybe he's some sort of artist and only likes the dark."

Pat widened her eyes dramatically. "Or, maybe he's a vampire."

I rolled my eyes. "That's probably it."

Pat slapped the table. "I'm serious. If he were, it would make so much sense. Keeping the shades pulled, only going outside in the dark ..."

"With a flashlight," I interrupted. "Wouldn't a vampire be able to see in the dark?"

Pat waved her hand airily. "I'm sure he had a good reason for the flashlight."

"Yeah, because he's NOT a vampire and can't see in the dark."

"Or, he was trying to scare some animal away without drawing attention to himself," Pat said. "But forget about the flashlight. If he's a vampire, it also explains why he wouldn't want to draw attention to himself. The last thing he would want is to have someone like Mildred checking in on him. So, he tried to be sneaky, not realizing that doing so is probably the one thing that would draw Mildred's attention to him like bees to honey."

"When you say it like that, you're absolutely right," I said matter-of-factly. "Jonas's housesitter is a vampire. I don't know why I didn't think of that sooner. Case solved."

Pat preened. "Not everyone is blessed with my special combination of smarts *and* good looks."

"No question there," I said. "And of course boring, stable Jonas, whose most exciting activity appears to be mowing the lawn on the weekend, would not only seek out, but know where to find, a vampire."

"Maybe the vampire found him," Pat said, wagging her eyebrows again. "Maybe the vampire put him under a spell and told him to take a month-long vacation, so he could housesit."

"Because Jonas's house is the perfect lair for a vampire?"

"Maybe. How do you know what a vampire likes or doesn't like?"

"Fair point. I've never met one."

"That you know of," Pat said mischievously. "But we are talking about Redemption, after all. Is it so surprising to think we might have a vampire or two roaming around?"

Redemption, Wisconsin, had quite a history. In 1888, all the adults suddenly disappeared during a terrible blizzard, leaving only the children. They swore they had no idea what happened to their parents, and the mystery of what happened to them continues to this day.

But that was only the beginning of all the strange events that plagued Redemption. It has had more than its fair share of disappearances, murder, and madness, not to mention ghosts and hauntings. Take my house, for example. Back in the early 1900s, Martha Blackwell, the lady of the house, killed her maid Nellie and then herself. The locals are sure Martha continues to haunt my house to this day, although I have my doubts. However, I can't say I haven't experienced some ... well, *odd* occurrences.

"A few ghosts floating around isn't the same as vampires," I said.

"No, but if there was going to be a vampire anywhere, Redemption would be the place."

"That is true," I agreed. "If vampires exist, you'd likely find them here."

"We really should investigate," Pat said. "Maybe we can visit Mildred ..."

I was already shaking my head. "We are absolutely NOT telling Mildred about this. The last thing we need to do is give her more ideas about her neighbor's housesitter."

Pat pouted. "You're no fun." She leaned back in her chair, considering. "Maybe we should ask Madame Rowena about the vampire. Maybe she's seen something ... you know, like in her crystal ball, or whatever."

"Yes, that sounds like a plan. We can ask a make-believe psychic about a make-believe vampire."

"You don't know if either are make-believe. At least not until we've actually investigated."

I rolled my eyes. "Fine. We'll ask Madame for her take on the situation. But unfortunately, we'll have to wait until next week's grand opening."

"Actually, we could go tomorrow," Pat said. "She IS open … it's just low-key until the grand opening."

"WE have a party to go to tomorrow, remember?" I asked.

Pat hit her forehead. "Of course. How could I forget?"

Claire, my first friend in Redemption, was having a party for her two-year-old daughter Daphne in the back room at Aunt May's Diner, which is where I met Claire. She was a waitress, and I had stopped by for a bite to eat while I figured out where I'd gone wrong with my driving. I had always been directionally challenged. One thing led to another, and I ended up staying in Redemption.

"So, I guess Madame Rowena will have to wait for another time," I said.

"I suppose," Pat sighed. "Hopefully, the vampire won't need a a snack, or worse yet, a meal, before then."

Want to keep reading? Grab your copy of **Murder Next Door** _here_.
https://www.amazon.com/gp/product/B09QZ476FW

More *Charlie Kingsley Mysteries:*
A Grave Error (a free prequel novella)
Murder Before Christmas (Book 1)
Murder Next Door (Book 3)
Murder Among Friends (Book 4)
The Murder of Sleepy Hollow (Book 5)
Red Hot Murder (Book 6)
A Wedding to Murder For (novella)
Loch Ness Murder (novella)

Secrets of Redemption *series:*
It Began With a Lie (Book 1)
This Happened to Jessica (Book 2)
The Evil That Was Done (Book 3)
The Summoning (Book 4)
The Reckoning (Book 5)
The Girl Who Wasn't There (Book 6)
The Room at the Top of the Stairs (Book 7 coming soon)
The Secret Diary of Helen Blackstone (free novella)

Standalone books:
Today I'll See Her (free novella or purchase with bonus content)
The Taking
The Third Nanny
Mirror Image
The Stolen Twin

Access your free exclusive bonus scenes from *Ice Cold Murder* right here:
MPWnovels.com/r/q/-ice-cold-murder-ebonus-content/

Acknowledgements

It's a team effort to birth a book, and I'd like to take a moment to thank everyone who helped, especially my wonderful editor, Megan Yakovich, who is always so patient with me, Rea Carr for her expert proofing support, and my husband Paul, for his love and support during this sometimes-painful birthing process.

Any mistakes are mine and mine alone.

About Michele

A USA Today Bestselling, award-winning author, Michele taught herself to read at 3 years old because she wanted to write stories so badly. It took some time (and some detours) but she does spend much of her time writing stories now. Mystery stories, to be exact. They're clean and twisty, and range from psychological thrillers to cozies, with a dash of romance and supernatural thrown into the mix. If that wasn't enough, she posts lots of fun things on her blog, including short stories, puzzles, recipes and more, at MPWNovels.com.

Michele grew up in Wisconsin, (hence why all her books take place there), and still visits regularly, but she herself escaped the cold and now lives in the mountains of Prescott, Arizona with her husband and southern squirrel hunter Cassie.

When she's not writing, she's usually reading, hanging out with her dog, or watching the Food Network and imagining she's an awesome cook. (Spoiler alert, she's not. Luckily for the whole family, Mr. PW is in charge of the cooking.)

Printed in Great Britain
by Amazon

13933405R00149